D1616983

Books by Nicholas Sansbury Smith

The Hell Divers Trilogy (Offered by Blackstone Publishing)
Hell Divers
Hell Divers II: Ghosts
Hell Divers III: Deliverance (Coming Summer 2018)

The Extinction Cycle Series (Offered by Orbit)
Extinction Horizon
Extinction Edge
Extinction Age
Extinction Evolution
Extinction End
Extinction Aftermath
Extinction Lost (A Team Ghost short story)
Extinction War (Coming Fall 2017)

The Trackers Series
Trackers
Trackers 2: The Hunted
Trackers 3: The Storm (Coming Winter 2017)

The Orbs Series (Offered by Simon451/Simon & Schuster)
Solar Storms (An Orbs Prequel)
White Sands (An Orbs Prequel)
Red Sands (An Orbs Prequel)
Orbs
Orbs II: Stranded
Orbs III: Redemption

HELL DIVERS II
GHOSTS

HELL DIVERS II
GHOSTS

NICHOLAS SANSBURY SMITH

BLACKSTONE
PUBLISHING

Published in 2017 by Blackstone Publishing
Cover and book design by Kathryn Galloway English

Printed in the United States of America

First edition: 2017
ISBN: 978-1-5047-2601-6

1 3 5 7 9 10 8 6 4 2

CIP data for this book is available from the Library of Congress

Blackstone Publishing
31 Mistletoe Rd.
Ashland, OR 97520
www.BlackstonePublishing.com

For Maria ... You're the best thing that ever happened to me.

The greater the difficulty, the more glory in surmounting it.
Skillful pilots gain their reputation from storms and tempests.
—Epictetus

PROLOGUE

The last man on Earth knew that monsters were hunting him. It didn't matter that he was already dead and condemned to hell; the beasts would never quit.

Lightning guided him and the dog through the ruins of the city. They moved through the darkness with calculated precision, his radiation suit snug around his lean muscles and scarred flesh. His Siberian husky, Miles, wore a similar suit to protect him.

The dog turned to check out a noise coming from a heap of rubble. A bottle rolled down the side, bounced, and shattered at the bottom. The wind whipped over the crest of the mound, picking up a tin can and whirling it away in the draft.

The man swept his assault rifle back and forth for contacts. He couldn't see the creatures, but he could sense them out there.

Miles trotted on, uninterested.

The ground ahead was clear for now, but the path ahead was treacherous. Taking cautious strides over the debris field, the man melted into a passage through the crumbled ruins of a city block. Blackened metal bruised with rust littered his path. The jagged ends could rip his suit open with ease.

He stopped and signaled Miles to halt. The dog sat on his hind legs, and they waited for a flash of lightning to illuminate the path forward. The man knew this route well and had memorized where the main hazards lay, but even so, every step was fraught with danger.

A sinkhole fifteen steps ahead had nearly swallowed him and Miles a few months back. Twenty more steps beyond the pit was a wall of sharp rebar that had ripped his suit twice before. But the biggest danger aside from the monsters were the clusters of poisonous weeds growing here. No matter how many times he cut them down with his machete, they would grow back even thicker. Their sting would maim him, but it could kill a dog.

A flash of lightning spread its blue glow over the flayed iron ribs of an old building. The man didn't waste the light. He never wasted the light. He made a quick sweep for hostiles with his rifle muzzle, checked for the lethal weeds, then plodded forward into the belly of the building.

Thunder boomed overhead, like a war drum urging him forward. He listened for other sounds: the skittering of clawed feet, or, worst of all, the otherworldly wailing of the Sirens.

But tonight, he did not hear them. Whatever hunted them was a different kind of monster.

He and Miles moved silently through the gutted corpse of an old-world building. Steel girders rose above them like the bones of a gigantic beast. When he first discovered this place, it had reminded him of the fossils of dinosaurs he had seen in books, growing up.

Another flash of lightning lit up a pair of real fossils. The remains of two souls rested in the dirt ahead, curled up in the fetal position. The larger skeleton hugged the smaller one—a mother protecting her child from the blast that had leveled the city hundreds of years ago.

The man tried to feel something at the sight. Memories flooded his mind, but he pushed them away as he always did. Damned men had no right to feel.

His old life seemed far away now, and he wasn't sure what he had done to deserve such a horrible punishment. Part of him wished he had just died in the sky two years ago, fried by lightning or snatched by the winged hunters. But he had Miles. A dog and a dream—that was all he had.

They pushed on through the waste, toward the one thing that kept him venturing out into the darkness. Today was the last time he would check the radio transmissions. If there was no response to his SOS, he would finally leave Hades.

For two years he had waited to hear something from the people in the sky. For two years he had scavenged the wastes with Miles, in search of food and supplies to keep them going until help arrived. They had evaded the monsters and fought them when they couldn't run anymore.

Time was hard to measure, especially when he had no idea whether it was night or day. He lived his life in the darkness, and he had given up marking the wall of his shelter over a year ago. As the days turned into months, and the months into years, he had realized that in hell there was no salvation—and no escape. If he tried to leave now, he would have to abandon their supplies, food, and only source of water. Trekking to the wastes beyond Hades would likely mean death for them both.

Time was everything, and time was nothing. And as it slowly passed, details of his earlier life eroded away like bones turning to dust. The faces and voices of people he had lost became harder to remember.

That was how he knew he was dead. His body might still be alive, but the loneliness and isolation had killed whatever remained of his soul.

And yet, there was still a seed of something human inside the man. Perhaps it was his affection for Miles. He wanted to protect the dog, as he had once protected people.

Something else pushed him on through the merciless world that humans had once called home. The man had a strong desire to fight. It was something deep in the marrow of his bones, like a cancer that he couldn't kill.

Miles stopped before a pocket of glowing bushes. Tentacles with needle-lined suction cups reached out for the dog, and the man motioned him back.

The wind swayed the stems dangerously close, and he took another step back. A year ago, he had almost died when one stung his leg. He still had the suction-cup scar—yet another badge on his tormented flesh.

Raising the rifle, he checked his surroundings again. Awareness was the key to survival. Miles provided keener ears and eyes, but his sense of smell was handicapped by the mask he wore.

The man listened, scanned, listened again, then directed the dog onward. The Industrial Tech Corporation bunker wasn't far now, but it was buried deep in the guts of the city.

The lightning continued to guide him through the skeletal remains of the building. He pulled out his machete and hacked through a bush in their path. The limbs plopped to the ground, wriggling like decapitated snakes.

He wiped the gooey sap off carefully on the ground and resheathed the blade. They took a slight detour around the next clump of weeds. The stems, activated by their presence, blinked alive with a dull pink glow. Like most life-forms on the surface, this one was carnivorous.

The sky boomed and he glanced up at the swirling soup of clouds and static electricity. The storm was growing.

A single raindrop splashed across his visor. One beat later, the clouds erupted, pouring sheets of radioactive acid rain over the city. Miles, scared by the sound of thunder, brushed up against his leg.

The man considered turning back to his shelter but decided to brave the storm. He was almost to the place where he had discovered Miles a year ago. They pressed on, the dog trotting closely alongside as they navigated the final stretch of flashing bushes. The glow pulsing over the path was eerie yet beautiful. The sign of life offered a slim hope that maybe, someday, the surface would thrive again.

Perhaps hell wasn't for eternity.

A shotgun blast of lightning snapped him back from his thoughts. It arced into a debris pile three stories high on the western edge of the open tunnel. Sparks rained down over hunks of brick and spikes of rebar.

He took a step forward but halted when he saw movement. Miles saw it at the same time and took a few crouching steps forward, then let out a low growl.

The man's eyes weren't as good as the dog's, and he had to squint. Rain slammed into him as he waited for light. Three beats passed before lightning arced overhead and backlit the city blocks. This time, he didn't need to squint.

His finger moved instinctively to the trigger, and his dead heart flinched when he saw the creatures hunting them. He had been wrong earlier. The Sirens were stalking him all along—hundreds of them, skittering across the mounds of rubble.

Never in his life had he seen so many.

He tried to move, but his aching muscles were frozen. Maybe if they stood perfectly still, the monsters wouldn't find them. After all, he didn't have a battery pack or any other energy source that would draw the beasts to him.

Swallowing, he watched them stampede right for his position. He couldn't outrun them, and he couldn't fight them all. Hades had finally won. Surprisingly, the only sadness he felt about his impending death was for Miles. His dog's death would be on him.

All at once, the glow of the bushes brightened, flashing from pink to a fiery red. The Sirens shrieked louder and hurried onward. The beasts were coming for the plants, not him.

Their high-pitched wails rose over the loud crack of thunder.

The sound, no matter how many times he heard it, still turned his blood to ice.

Miles backpedaled, and the man snapped into motion. He ran, boots slogging through the mud. The dog lunged through a gap in the concrete, but the man had to stop and flatten his body. He lowered his rifle to squeeze through the narrow space. Rebar jutted out, but he ducked under it. He made it through without any more tears and kept running. He leaped over a grove of the glowing weeds. His boots hit the earth with a splash and sank into the toxic muck. He pulled free and continued onward.

Miles was waiting for him, sitting on his haunches.

Breathing heavily now, the man looked past the dog and focused on the tunnel exit. It opened onto a city street framed on both sides by sagging structures. This was one of many ITC campuses, and the buildings had been constructed to survive the apocalypse. Humans, however, were not.

The screeching rose into the familiar wail, like an emergency siren. He twisted to see the monsters entering the open tunnel. The bushes growing throughout swayed back and forth, tentacles groping for the eyeless beasts. He stopped for a moment to watch as the Sirens fed, ripping the stems off and jamming the tentacles into mouths rimmed with jagged teeth.

Heart pounding, he moved back as one of the monsters, still chewing on a glowing stick, turned its head toward him. The leathery, eyeless face locked onto him, and it spat out the stem it was munching on to release a high-pitched call.

Two dozen conical heads all seemed to home in on him at once. Thunder boomed overhead as if answering their wails.

"Run!" he yelled at the dog.

The man felt the trickle of fear but pushed it away. Planting his boots firmly, he squared his shoulders and fired off a volley into the beast that had first made his position. His aim was true, and the rounds punched through the thick skull. Blood darkened the mud as the Siren crashed to the ground. He fired another burst that took down two more of the beasts to his left. The rest fanned out, some taking to the sky, others darting for cover in the toxic rubble.

He wiped his visor clean and turned to run down the street after the dog. He could see the bunker's domed entrance in the distance, but clusters of the poisonous bushes had grown along the path since he was here last. As Miles approached, their stems activated, blinking like warning lights.

"Watch out!" he shouted after the dog.

Miles navigated the minefield of plants with ease and galloped down the final block, then sat in front of the double doors leading to safety.

The man slung the rifle over his shoulder as he ran. He reached for the key in his vest pocket. Halfway down the street, he turned to fire at a Siren sailing through the sky. It swooped away from his gunfire and dropped into a nosedive, coming right at him. Holding in a breath, he squinted and fired a three-round burst into the creature's jagged spine. It crashed to the ground like a missile, throwing dirt into the air.

Miles was barking now, which drew the creatures' attention. Another Siren sailed toward the dog. Raising his rifle, the man fired two bursts that lanced through the creature's leathery flesh. Then he leaped over another toxic bush with the grace of a much younger man as tentacles reached up for him. One grazed his boot, needles slashing the worn leather. The tip broke through, burning his skin, but he breathed through the pain and limped for the doors. He would survive a minor sting as long as he could apply ointment in time, but he would not survive the Sirens. They would dismember him on the spot and fight over his remains. He had seen it before, years ago.

A memory of an old friend tried to surface in his mind, but he pushed the traumatic scene away and ran from the monsters.

Miles was pacing outside the door, his gaze trained on his master. The man wiped rain from his visor as he bolted for the entrance. He knew the final route better than any other place in Hades. But even with it memorized, he hadn't prepared for the wet asphalt. He hit a slick spot, slipped, and crashed to the concrete, losing the key in the fall. Pain swept across his battle-scarred body.

Miles barked and ran toward him, but the man yelled for the dog to get back.

He pushed himself up just as a network of lightning skewered a Siren in the sky, sending it windmilling to the ground. The smoking creature crashed into a cluster of the bushes. Tentacles clamped on, looping around it. The Siren wasn't dead, and it thrashed violently amid the pulsating red stems. Blood splattered, steaming in the cold.

The key. Where the hell is the key?

The man scanned the ground as the Siren twisted in agony, tentacles plastered to its body like cords hooked up to some monstrous machine. The screeching was so loud, it made the blood in his ears sing.

Fifty more steps—that was all he had left to go. Get to Miles; get inside the bunker. But first, get the key. He focused on the ground, searching desperately.

There it was, a few feet away, between him and the dying monster. Tentacles shot out at him as he approached. He parried them with his rifle butt and then bent down to scoop up the key. Another tentacle whizzed past his arm, and a second came from his left and smacked the visor of his helmet, sticking to the glass. He pulled his machete from the sheath on his thigh and slashed through the stem. A geyser of green blood jetted into the air.

Miles continued barking, frantically now. The man checked the sky to make sure none of the monsters were headed for the dog's position.

The trapped lightning-struck Siren stopped struggling and fell on its back, and the vines dragged it into the grasp of other vines, which pulled it into the heart of the thicket.

A final shriek followed the man as he turned to run.

Behind him, dozens of clawed, naked feet slapped the asphalt or slurped in the mud. Wailing Sirens filled the sky, and above the circling creatures there was something else: the beetlelike outline of an airship.

Raw memories washed over him like rain. Memories of a time before Miles, before this wretched hell. They filled his mind, and for a beat, Hades vanished, replaced by the brilliant sun. In the distance, the *Hive* was slowly flying away. Even as the balloon had pulled his body upward, his heart had pulled him toward the airship. He had drifted across the sky, hailing Captain Maria Ash over the comms as the helium in his balloon escaped and slowly lowered him back to the ruined surface. But his pleas for rescue had gone unanswered.

Lightning filled the cloud that he had mistaken for an airship.

Behind him, a Siren screamed. He pulled the blaster from his hip and shot a flare at the galloping beasts. The brilliant red light blossomed out across the street, and the monsters darted away from the glow. He holstered the gun, grabbed his rifle, and fired bursts at the retreating Sirens, then turned back toward Miles with the key in his other hand.

The dog trotted up to greet him, but the man pointed and yelled, "Inside!" He unlocked the door, and Miles darted through the opening.

In a fluid sequence of movements, the man shouldered his rifle again, turned, and squeezed off shots at the encroaching monsters. The flare was still coughing fire into the street, but there wasn't much light left, and he didn't waste it.

He fired a burst into a creature making a run for the door.

Rounds punched through its skull, making two neat holes where the eyes should be. Another Siren took its place, and he sent it spinning away with three quick shots to the torso. He leaned into the recoil, picking targets in the waning light. Blood pooled on the ground, and fallen bodies formed a perimeter around the ITC bunker entrance. Behind them, the tentacular arms of the bushes swayed back and forth like the dancing flames of candles.

Barking filled the passage behind him as he fired round after round.

"Hold on, Miles! I'm on my way!"

The bolt locked open on the carbine's empty chamber. He was reaching for another magazine when a torrent of lightning connected with the steel girders down the street. Dozens of skeletal, leathery bodies moved in the flickering downpour of sparks.

There were too many to fight. It was time to flee.

Lowering the carbine, he shouldered the door shut and barred it from inside. He flicked on his precious tactical light, shined it down the staircase, and loped down to a hallway below.

"Behind me," he said to Miles.

The dog trotted after him along the narrow passage that stretched under the ITC campus. These derelict arteries connected the basements of buildings designed to survive the apocalypse, though many had since caved in.

The man rounded a corner with weapon raised, but the beam from his light revealed an empty hallway. He knew this passage better than any other. The five doors all led to different rooms. In the first was a space that had been airtight until he opened it to discover food, water, and medical supplies designed to last five hundred years. When he first found this place, he had been dying from blood loss and radiation poisoning. The discovery had saved him, to the extent a dead man could be saved.

The second door opened onto an armory containing guns of all kinds, ammunition, equipment, and radiation suits for adults as well as children. One of the smaller suits, with a bit of alteration, had fit Miles well enough.

He passed the third door at a jog. It was a vault containing every seed that humans would have needed to start again on the surface. The man had spent many hours reading the information on each strain. He carried several of the sealed packets with him, though he wasn't sure why. Fruit trees couldn't grow without the sun.

The fourth door, marked by a sign that read CRYOGENICS, was sealed. This was where he had found Miles a year ago, in suspended animation inside one of the chambers.

When the man first came upon the space, he hadn't known what "cryogenics" meant, but when he took the elevator down and saw the silo of chambers, he understood. Humans, as well as animals unlike any he had ever seen, filled the capsules. Thousands upon thousands of them were hooked up to the backup power that would last another 250 years, but not all of them were preserved. An entire section of chambers was open, and several other sections had been destroyed. Whatever had broken into or out of the chambers was long gone by the time he arrived.

The man was not a god, however, and no matter how lonely he got, he never unfroze any of the other humans. But when he saw Miles suspended in cryo-sleep, he couldn't resist unfreezing him. He was a Siberian husky, like the dogs on the airship the man had once called home, but the man had quickly realized that Miles was different from those dogs. It was as if he had been designed to survive in hostile conditions. He could tolerate high doses of radiation, and his sharp senses had saved them from the monsters more times than he could count.

Miles ran ahead toward a blast door at the end of the hallway. By the time the man got there, the Sirens had found the door at the street above. The beasts pounded on the steel with their leathery fists. It wouldn't hold long, but the blast door would buy some extra time. It would also seal them in, and the only other exit was a highly radioactive crawl space. If their suits were uncompromised, they would live; if there was even the smallest tear, they would die.

He fumbled in his pocket for the other key and inserted it in the door, then used all his strength to push it open. Miles hurried inside.

Raising his gun, the man ran the light over a room furnished with metal tables and desks. Radio equipment and flat-screen monitors that no longer worked awaited users who would never arrive. He closed the door with a grunt, locked it, and hurried over to the only working radio.

The man leaned down and turned the knob. Static crackled from the ancient speakers as he scanned the channel for transmissions. But just as in all the other attempts, he heard nothing but static. No voices. No hint that there might be another human soul out there.

A high screech sounded from the hallway, and Miles let out a low growl. The monsters were here. They had never made it inside before. He didn't have much time.

He turned the knob slowly, straining his ears for any sound of survivors. A chorus of wailing Sirens drowned out the white noise, and he leaned closer to the speakers.

No one had responded to his SOS. He bowed his head, feeling defeated. For two years, he had sent his message out over every frequency, and for two years he had listened to silence. Help wasn't coming. There was nothing left for him here. Leaving meant abandoning the supplies that had kept him alive, but staying meant he would never see another human again.

Any conflict in his icy heart fell away.

It was finally time to leave this cursed place—finally time to leave hell. He had always wanted to see the ocean. Maybe, in a few more years, he would make it there.

"Come on, boy," he said to Miles. The dog whined as if he understood, and tried to wag his tail, but the ill-fitting radiation suit hampered his movement.

The Sirens slammed into the blast door, their electronic whines echoing through the space as he recorded his final dispatch from hell.

"If anyone's out there, this is Commander Xavier Rodriguez. I'm leaving Hades and heading east toward the coast."

ONE

EIGHT YEARS LATER

Captain Leon Jordan jerked awake from a recurring nightmare. He sat up slowly to avoid the aluminum bulkhead that curved over his bed. Sweat traced the scar from his last run-in with it.

The nightmare was almost always the same. In it, X would somehow be in Jordan's quarters, hovering over his bed with a combat knife in hand. What came next changed from dream to dream. Sometimes, X got his revenge slowly. Other times, he would kill Jordan with a quick slash across his throat. But every time, he would first ask Jordan one simple question: *Why?*

Jordan massaged his neck and shook off the fog of sleep. The buzz of an incoming transmission combined with the beeping of the alarm clock reminded him that he was already behind schedule.

He reached over Katrina DaVita, who lay sleeping beside him, to shut off the alarm.

"What time is it?" she murmured.

"Time to go over the night logs," he said, yawning.

"And time for me to go back to sleep." She patted the pillow and stuffed it back under her head.

Jordan studied her features in the faint glow of the computer screen across the small room. The rules on the *Hive* were clear—officers weren't supposed to sleep together. But he couldn't stop himself any more than he could stop himself now from staring at the beauty lying beside him. His eyes flitted down to the defined curves of her long, muscular legs. She was easily the most beautiful woman on the ship, and she was all his.

Good thing he was the captain. Rules could be bent when you were at the top of the pecking order. But with that power also came a heavy burden. Years ago, when Captain Maria Ash handed him the reins, he had realized just how heavy it was. This morning, he had a hundred things on his mind. They had just lost an entire harvest of corn, and power curtailments continued to cause unrest. Even worse were the whispers of a new illness on the lower decks. At times, it was almost too much to bear. Every minute of every day, there was a crisis somewhere on the ship.

He put a hand to his forehead. Not even fully awake yet, and already he felt exhausted just thinking about his to-do list. Years of sleeping no more than three hours at a time had resulted in a chronic migraine. But that was what it took to keep this rusting hulk of metal and helium bladders together.

With a sigh, he put his feet on the cold floor and crossed the small room, which was furnished with everything a person needed: a bed, a desk, a sink, and a shit can cordoned off by a faded curtain.

Jordan picked up a mug from his desk and took a slug of the cold coffee within. Better than nothing, but it still tasted terrible.

The incoming transmission alert was still buzzing.

"Will you turn that damn thing off?" Katrina mumbled.

He downed the rest of his mug and tapped the monitor. The screen flickered on at his touch, and he killed the sound with a swipe of his finger. He keyed in his security code and scrolled through the most recent messages. The first was from Chief Engineer Samson—something about a gas bladder issue that had already been solved. The next was an update from medical—a new case of the mysterious illness, and yet another stillborn baby.

He skimmed Dr. Tim Free's notes about a lower-decker admitted to the clinic, suffering from hallucinations, fever, and internal bleeding. It had to be from the radiation. That was also why they were losing so many babies. He had to get Samson to fix the damn leakage, but doing so meant another dive to the surface to collect parts.

Jordan cursed, reaching again for the mug before he remembered it was empty. Even the captain didn't get unlimited rations, but perhaps one of the junior officers would be willing to sacrifice for the good of the ship.

"What is it?" Katrina said. She sat up and brushed aside a wisp of hair that had escaped her braid.

"Another stillborn," he replied. "That makes two this month."

Neither of them said a word for several moments. Jordan discreetly directed his gaze at her stomach. She was three months pregnant now, but they hadn't told anyone. Soon, they wouldn't be able to hide her condition—or their relationship. Some people already knew, and he would just have to deal with any repercussions when the time came.

"Don't worry," he said. "Everything will be fine, I promise. Go back to bed. You need your sleep."

Katrina gave him a strained smile and laid her head back on the pillow. They both knew the odds of having a healthy baby were stacked against them. The last healthy child had been born six months ago. With the population of the Hive down to 443 people, it was vitally important that their baby be strong.

He read through the remaining messages. A fire in engineering, a fight in the trading post due to a price hike on tomatoes, and a dispute over rations, which led to a mini riot on the lower decks. Typical day on the *Hive*. The final message, however, made him pause. He read the subject line a second time.

Midnight.

Jordan glanced at Katrina to make sure she wasn't watching. Her naked back rose and sank rhythmically. She was already asleep.

He positioned his shoulders so she couldn't see the computer if she woke up again. She was his executive officer, but there were things that even the XO mustn't see.

"Midnight" was a top secret code for radio signals or transmissions picked up from the surface. Captain Ash had wasted a lot of time on them. She had believed there were survivors down there and that someday she would find a habitable place to put the ship down. Everything Jordan had seen proved otherwise. The only transmissions they picked up were decades, even centuries, old. Many of the bunkers below the blasted surface had generators and batteries that lasted far longer than the occupants, thus allowing messages to replay long after the last humans were dead.

The last time he had sent Hell Divers to follow up on a transmission, only one man returned. Still, part of his duty was to investigate any potential survivors, which meant listening to every radio transmission and signal they picked up, even if it was two hundred years old.

He put on his headset and hit the play button. A surge of static hissed in his ears; then a female voice.

"This is Governor Rhonda Meredith of the Hilltop Bastion, requesting support from anyone out there. The—"

Static.

"We are low on food and ammunition."

Jordan raised an eyebrow at that.

"We can't keep them back much longer. Please, *please* send support to the following coordinates..."

What were they fighting down there?

He cupped his hands over his headset. Flurries of static crackled across the line. The sound cut out. He clicked on the message again, but the signal was too weak. He would have to see whether Ensign Hunt could capture more of it. They had a deal: any messages picked up by the satellites came straight to Jordan. In return, he provided Hunt's young family with a few extra credits each month. The last thing Jordan wanted were rumors flying around the *Hive* about people down there—or about the monsters.

Jordan and Hunt weren't the only ones who kept the ship's secrets. The Hell Divers followed similar rules. Never speak about what you saw on the surface. Never give the population any more reason to worry.

But not even the Hell Divers knew what Jordan did.

He was pulling off the headset when he saw a second message marked "Midnight." Two in one night? The odds of that were basically impossible. The last time they heard anything from the surface was months ago, and that transmission had proved to be over a century old. It was the same one that cost him three divers.

Jordan settled the headset back over his ears. He clicked play and leaned closer to the monitor. This time, the message came through clearly. It was one he had heard many times, and he sighed as he listened to it yet again.

"If anyone's out there, this is Commander Xavier Rodriguez. I'm leaving Hades and heading east toward the coast."

Attached to the message was a note from Ensign Hunt:

> Sir, we have a potential problem. Someone has been poking around in the restricted archives, and they may have intercepted this message.

Jordan groaned inwardly. Only a few people on the ship were capable of hacking into the archives, and even fewer were stupid enough to try it. Whoever it was needed to be dealt with swiftly.

A hand on his shoulder made him flinch. He craned his neck to see Katrina standing behind him with her arms folded across her robe, revealing the tattoos of an angel and a raptor on her forearms.

Jordan quickly pulled off the headset and said, "What are

you ...?" Then he saw the militia soldier standing in the open hatch.

"Sorry to bother you at this hour, Captain." The young man's features were tense in the blue light of the computer monitor.

"Speak," Jordan said.

"It's a storm, sir. Came out of nowhere. Ensign Ryan says they need you on the bridge."

"I'll be right there."

The guard retreated into the hallway, where a second militia soldier held security with an automatic rifle. The passage outside was empty; most of the upper-deckers were still asleep. That would soon change when Jordan ordered his crew back to their stations.

Katrina frowned. "I guess I'd better get dressed."

While she put on her uniform, Jordan sat back down and typed a message to Hunt:

> I will deal with the security breach. Get me the coordinates for the Hilltop Bastion.

Jordan turned slightly to watch Katrina. She had made a damn fine Hell Diver, which was exactly why he had appointed her his second-in-command shortly after they started sleeping together. In doing so, he had saved her. He knew what was down there on the surface. The fate of every diver was always the same ... except for one man.

Somehow, Commander Xavier Rodriguez had survived on the surface all these years. There were other messages from X, noting his trek across the wastelands, but the most common was the recurring dispatch from Hades.

Jordan had made the decision to keep the information a secret, despite the nightmares and the guilt that tore at him daily. He knew he was condemning a man to death—or at the very least, the worst kind of life imaginable, for however long X could survive it. A man who, of all people, certainly didn't deserve that fate. But he couldn't risk the cost in lives and fuel to return to Hades for one man. Plus, Katrina had loved X once, and it had taken her a long time to move past her grief. How could he tell her X had survived all these years? He couldn't. She could never find out. He would do whatever it took to maintain order on his ship and protect his people from the truths they couldn't handle.

Looking over his shoulder, he checked to make sure Katrina wasn't watching. Her deep-brown eyes, the color of his coffee, focused on him.

"Is there something you're not telling me?" she asked.

Jordan shook his head. "No, everything's fine."

"I'll meet you on the bridge," she said. "I need to stop by engineering first."

As soon as she had gone, Jordan let out a breath he didn't know he was holding and turned back to the screen. He selected the SOS from X, tapped the message twice with his finger, and held it for a moment to delete it.

The voice on the transmission was nothing more than an echo.

A ghost.

* * * * *

Standing with his back to the wall in the launch bay of the *Hive,* Commander Michael Everhart watched the portholes on the starboard side of the ship. Rays of crimson shot through the filthy glass, filling the room with a warm light that showed every scratch, ding, and shoddy patch job. The ship was falling apart everywhere. It wasn't that the occupants didn't care. They just didn't have the resources, and every time they fixed a problem, another would pop up. Hell Divers continued to scavenge the Earth below, and the engineers on the ship continued to recycle and repurpose, but there was only so much they could do.

Michael remained in the shadows, away from the warmth of the sunlight—not because he liked the darkness, but because it hid the worry on his face. His Hell Diver team needed a heroic leader. Someone like X. Michael hadn't always liked or respected X growing up, but during the short time the man was his guardian following his father's death, he had learned some important lessons about honor, sacrifice, and courage.

Now, ten years later, a lot had changed. Michael had traded in his tinfoil hat for a Hell Diver's helmet, and the skinny kid was now muscular from countless hours working in engineering and training as a Hell Diver. With thirty successful jumps under his belt, he had quickly risen through the ranks to lead Team Raptor. His father had been a Raptor, and so had X. Could he live up to their legacy? At times like this, when the ship seemed to be hanging on by a thread, he wasn't sure.

The screech of metal doors pulled him back from the darkness, and a woman's voice reminded him that there was still light in the world.

"Sorry I'm late, Tin."

Michael turned to face the one person he truly trusted on this godforsaken ship.

"I told you not to call me that anymore," he said, grinning.

Across the room, past the rows of plastic domes covering the drop tubes, stood Layla Brower. She heaved the strap of a duffel bag higher on her shoulder and then closed the double doors to the hallway. They squeaked shut, sealing the room in shadows once again.

"The name's endearing," she said, dropping her bag and striding over to him. "As your girlfriend, I'm allowed to call you what I want, right?"

"Right," Michael said. "Except 'Tin.' You can't call me that." He stepped away from the wall and met Layla in the center of the vaulted launch bay. They stood under a small pool of red light from the emergency bulb overhead. He held her gaze, staring into her curious brown eyes. He had fallen in love with those eyes when he was just a kid, and sometimes he still couldn't believe that she felt the same about him. He never forgot how lucky he was, even when she was teasing him. Especially when she was teasing him.

"Fine, *Michael*," Layla said. She wrapped her arms around him and pecked his cheek.

"*That's* my good-morning kiss?" he asked. He leaned in and pressed his lips against hers. When he pulled away, her smile broadened and her cheeks glowed. She reached out to touch his shoulder-length blond hair.

"You really need a haircut, Tin," she said.

"Yeah, yeah." Michael rolled his eyes. No matter what he did, she was never going to stop calling him that stupid nickname. But that was okay, as long as the other divers kept calling him "Commander."

They walked together to the drop tubes. Layla stubbed her toe on the lip of a tube hidden in the dim light, and began muttering.

"I really wish they would extend the working hours," she said. "Can't get anything done with this stupid energy curtailment. I was hoping to cook us dinner tonight. I used our rations on some really nice squash, and now we probably won't even get to eat it before it goes bad."

"I'm not going to be home until late anyway," Michael said.

Layla halted and let out an exasperated sigh. "Why not?"

"Samson wants me to pull another shift."

"Again?"

"I'm sorry. You know how much I look forward to our dinners."

"We only get one night a week together, Michael. Just one."

He looked at his boots. He hated letting her down, but they

both had duties they couldn't neglect. He wasn't the only one with two jobs. Layla doubled as an engineer in the water treatment plant when they weren't diving to the surface.

Glancing up, he met her eyes. "Don't worry, I'll find a way to sneak away for dinner. Things will calm down soon."

"Maybe, but before they do, we're going back down there." She stalked over to her launch tube and looked through the plastic dome. Clouds hid the surface, but they both knew the dangers awaiting them below.

They stood for a few moments in silence, both of them likely thinking the same thing. The ship was running low on fuel cells again. There were never enough. For over a year now, Michael and the other Hell Diver teams had been scouring every known green-zone location for the ITC-manufactured cells, but they had come back empty-handed more often than not—those who had come back at all.

Something had to give. There weren't many green-zone locations left, and Jordan was going to have to start making some tough choices.

A sharp jolt rocked the *Hive,* throwing both of them against the side of Layla's drop tube. He steadied himself and helped her back to her feet.

"What the hell was that?" Layla huffed.

The room lit up with a cool blue radiance that answered her question. Outside the porthole windows, lightning jagged across the sky. A massive storm was brewing.

"At least we can see now," Michael said.

An emergency alarm barked from the public-address speakers in the corner of the room. The recorded female voice Michael had listened to his entire life repeated a message he had heard a thousand times.

He turned to watch the portholes.

"It never lasts, does it?" Layla whispered, leaning against him.

He didn't ask her what she meant. He already knew. The silence, the sense of peace—they never lasted long. On the *Hive*, calm was an illusion.

TWO

Magnolia Katib twirled her favorite knife, ignoring the annoying message on the public-address system as she watched the cards being dealt across the table. The game, a version of old-world poker, had evolved over the years. It was cutthroat and fast paced, much like diving. The only noticeable difference was that the high-stakes game couldn't kill her—unless one of the other players got mad...

The first dog-eared card glided over to Rick Weaver, commander of Team Angel. The second went to the commander of Team Apollo, Andrew "Pipe" Bolden. The third went to Raptor Diver Rodger "Dodger" Mintel, and the fourth came to her.

Despite the size of the blade, the knife spun effortlessly in her hand. Then the ship lurched, and she almost lost a finger. The metal bulkheads groaned as the *Hive* changed course, but none of her opponents seemed to notice. Storms were part of everyday life on the ship.

Magnolia sank her blade into the head of the Raptor logo someone had engraved long ago onto the faded wooden table. She formed a fort around her cards with her hands. Her mind was only halfway on the game.

"Yo, Mags," the dealer said. "You with us? The bet's twenty."

She shook away her troubling thoughts and focused on the dealer, a longtime dive technician named Ty. He looked at the knife and raised an eyebrow as if to say, *Don't mess with my table.* He was chewing vigorously on a calorie-infused stick—a habit he had picked up years ago and had never been able to break.

"Anyone ever tell you that you look like a horse eating straw?" Magnolia quipped.

That got a laugh from Andrew, but Ty just kept chewing.

Magnolia's eyes flitted to the other players, hunting for tells as they looked at their three cards. Andrew peeled the edge of his card up with a grimy fingernail. He wrinkled his beak of a nose and hunched his wide shoulders so that he loomed over the table. Magnolia considered cracking a joke about his thinning hair, but she would leave the snide humor up to Rodger.

Her eyes flitted to the skinny bearded man with black-rimmed glasses taped together in the middle. The frames accentuated his unusually large brown eyes. He was the newest addition to Team Raptor, chosen not for his fighting skills but for his keen intelligence and ability to cobble together useful tech from bits of scrap. Magnolia suspected that he was smarter than anyone else on the ship.

"Andrew, you look at me like you look at your food," Rodger said. "Please, don't eat me. I'd give you really bad gas, and these people have suffered enough."

"Whatever, man," Andrew said, scowling. "I heard you shat yourself in the launch tube on your first dive."

Ty chuckled, and Commander Weaver almost choked on a gulp of shine.

Rodger glanced at her, his cheeks reddening, then looked down at the table. Magnolia glared at Andrew.

"Shut it, Pipe," she said. She really hated that nickname. Layla had been the one to assign it to Andrew, because of his muscles. Tacky, to Magnolia's thinking. "Neanderthal" would have fit much better.

Her eyes flitted to Rodger. He gave her a brief smile that

revealed a missing front tooth. He had lost it on their last dive, when he tripped after wasting half an hour loading pieces of wood into the supply crate. He was smart, but he was clumsy. She also suspected he was nursing a crush on her, but she didn't have time for a boyfriend, and he didn't seem like the one-night-stand type. If she wasn't training or diving, she was in her quarters, going through the archives. Her main relationship was with history.

"Hurry this shit up," she said. She was anxious to get back to her latest find, an article about the farms that humans once cultivated on the surface. Maybe she could figure out a way to save the next corn harvest before they all starved.

Andrew checked his cards again, as if they were somehow going to change, and Magnolia used the moment to scratch at the newest tattoo on her forearm. For a while now, she had been working on a full sleeve of the extinct animals that fascinated her.

"What's a girl like you want with all that ink?" Andrew asked. "What is that gray thing, anyway?

She pulled her shirtsleeve down to cover her tattoos. "Something you'd never be able to recognize."

Rodger leaned forward. "That's a baby elephant, right?"

Magnolia tilted her head slightly, amused that Rodger could identify the image on her arm. Maybe he was more interesting than she gave him credit for. He was certainly more interesting than the Neanderthal sitting next to him.

"How'd you know?" she asked.

"My dad made an elephant clock once. It was beautiful."

Magnolia was intrigued. "Where is it now?"

"Are we going to play or talk about furry creatures all night?" Andrew asked.

"They aren't furry," Rodger and Magnolia both said at the same time. She chuckled at that.

"You kids are somethin' else," Weaver said. He shook his head and glanced at his cards. His hair and handlebar mustache seemed more salt than pepper these days, and his forehead was a maze of wrinkles. After losing his family a decade ago during the crash of the *Hive*'s sister ship, *Ares*, Weaver had dedicated himself to diving—and cards. He had mastered the game, but luckily, Magnolia had discovered the aging commander's tell. He lifted the edges of each card, one by one, and then squinted with his right eye when he looked at the final card.

Shit, he has a hand. She needed to shut her mouth and pay attention. She checked her credits to make sure she hadn't miscounted. Two hundred left. The blinds were chipping away at her stack. If she didn't make something happen, she was going to be begging Ty for some of those calorie sticks until her next payday.

Andrew folded, but Rodger ran a hand over his beard and said, "Ten credits."

Another rattle shook the aluminum bones of the *Hive*.

"Sounds like we're hitting some bad weather," Ty said. "Maybe we should—"

"Don't even think about it," Weaver said. "I call your ten credits and raise you ten."

Magnolia finally looked down at her cards and tried not to react when she saw they were all suited connectors: seven, eight, and nine of hearts.

She was on her way to a straight flush. Only one hand could beat that, but the odds against securing a ten and six of hearts were astronomical. Worse, if she wanted to play the hand, she would have to commit twenty chips just to see another card. She looked down at the faded, cracked chips in front of her. That was an entire week's pay on the line.

It was a risk, but it was only credits. The real risk was diving into the black abyss through an electrical storm, which Magnolia hadn't done for months. She missed the thrill of the dive. But for now, poker would have to do.

"I call Commander Weaver's bet," Magnolia said. She could make her decision after she saw her next card.

"You're not afraid of anything, are you, princess?" Weaver said. "The great Magnolia Katib. Fearless, fast, and—"

"Freaky!" Rodger said with a chuckle, his bushy brows raised over his glasses.

The smile on his face slowly turned to a frown.

"Can't do it," he finally said, tossing his cards into the muck pile with Andrew's.

Weaver eyed Magnolia. "Just you and me now."

She brushed a lock of electric blue hair back over her ear, trying not to let him get under her skin. It was part of the game. Everyone was a prick when playing cards, even nice guys like Weaver.

"Let's see another card," she said.

Ty peeled one from the deck and slid it to Weaver. Then he sent the next to Magnolia. She waited to check her card, focusing first on Weaver's face. There was no squint this time—only the hard eyes of a man who had lost everything in life except his honor. For the commander, the game wasn't just about credits. It was about being the best. After X sacrificed himself back in Hades, Weaver had taken his place as the top Hell Diver on the *Hive*. He didn't lose easily.

But neither did Magnolia.

The memories of that last dive with X were still raw. She had grown up without a dad, and ten years ago she had lost two of the men she respected most: first her own commander, Cruise, and then X. Their sacrifice was something she could never repay.

Keep your head in the game, Magnolia.

Another tremor shook the ship, and the unmistakable boom of thunder reverberated through the *Hive*. Magnolia lifted the edge of her fourth card, her breath catching when she saw it was a heart.

Not the six or ten she was looking for, but she was still just one away from a flush. A ten would give her a straight. Either would be a difficult hand to beat.

"You're first," Ty said to Weaver.

Weaver got out his old-world coin and flipped it while holding Magnolia's gaze. It was a trick, a ploy to make her think he was gambling. He brought the coin on missions with him, too, and used it when forced to make a decision with only lousy options.

He caught it in his palm, looked down, and said, "Twenty credits."

Now she had a decision to make.

She could raise his bet and hope she was wrong about him having a good hand. He might fold. Or, if she was right and he did have a made hand—say, two pair or trips—he would call and she would still have a good chance of beating him with the last two cards.

Ty looked up at the lightbulb hanging from a cord over the table. It winked on and off as it swayed.

"Your move, princess," Weaver said.

Magnolia didn't twitch as her sweep of blue hair fell over her right eye. She kept her gaze on the commander. She was really starting to hate it when he called her that.

"Call your twenty, raise you sixty more."

Rodger clapped his hands together. "This is getting good. I need more shine!" He took a long swig from his mug. After dragging a sleeve across his lips, he sat up straighter, opened his mouth, and let out a long belch that filled the room.

Andrew chuckled, Ty covered his nose, and Magnolia's eyes widened as the belch, reeking of cheap liquor and fried potatoes, continued with no sign of abating.

There was no reaction in Weaver's features. He looked at his stack of chips, then back at Magnolia. Without taking his eyes off her, he grabbed three columns of twenty chips and pushed them into the pot.

Shit, he's on a draw, too, Magnolia thought. Her eyes moved to Ty as he dealt their fifth and final card. Then he put a single card facedown in the center of the table. It was the community card, the one that Weaver and Magnolia would share to make or break their hands.

This time, she looked at her card first, allowing Weaver to study her.

Two of clubs. Damn.

She could feel the heat rising in her cheeks. If Weaver's tell was his squint, hers was a flushed face. She should have put on more fake rouge to hide her real blush. If she lost this hand, she wasn't going to be able to afford any more black-market makeup for a very long time.

Weaver glanced down at his card, then looked to Ty, who flipped the final card.

She saw the ten first, then the heart.

There was no way she could lose this hand. She would be drinking shine and eating chicken tonight! Her mouth watered at the thought.

Weaver reached out and plucked the stick from Ty's mouth and tossed it on the ground.

"You have no idea how annoying that is!" Weaver said.

Magnolia almost smiled. The commander was losing his cool.

"How much you got left over there?" Weaver asked.

She bit the inside of her lip and frowned, trying to play the part of a loser. "A hundred credits."

She felt Rodger's gaze across the table, and she automatically raised her hand to give him the bird. But when she saw the puppy-dog look on his face, she couldn't bring herself to do it. The guy was practically drooling. It was actually endearing, in a way.

"Has anyone ever told you that you look like Catwoman?" he asked.

"Who the hell's that?" Andrew said. He hit Rodger's arm out from under him, making his head fall toward the table.

"Hey!" Rodger protested, wiping his mouth off. "She's this total badass character from a comic I found in the archives." When Andrew's blank look continued, Rodger explained, "A comic book. You know, like *Superman*?"

"If you're looking for a super man, he's right over here," Andrew said, laughing.

"More like super *drunk*," Rodger grumbled.

Weaver snapped his fingers to shut them up and looked back to Magnolia. "I'll bet a hundred."

As he wedged the chips from his massive stack, Rodger wasn't the only one drooling. Magnolia almost salivated at the thought of all those credits. She was preparing to push in the rest of her chips when the *Hive* jolted violently to starboard.

Andrew grabbed the table, but too late. It slid across the floor, and with it went the chips, cards, and four mugs with varying levels of shine.

"NO!" Magnolia shouted, watching in horror as her cards joined the mess on the floor. The first straight flush in her life, and she couldn't even prove it now!

"What was *that*?" Ty asked.

Weaver scrambled over to the wall comm and punched the link. "This is Commander Weaver. What the hell is going on?"

Static crackled from the speakers. The ship lurched again, and a sound like a rifle shot rang out as lightning hit the hull. Magnolia joined Weaver at the comm.

"We're headed right for a massive storm, Commander Weaver," replied a voice from the wall-mounted speakers. "Report to the launch bay, ASAP."

The lightbulb swayed toward Weaver as he squinted in Magnolia's direction. She knew what the commander's tell meant. The pile of cards on the floor wasn't the worst thing that could happen today. If something had happened to the ship and they needed parts, there was a good chance she was about to end her hiatus from diving, in the worst possible conditions—right through the middle of an electrical storm.

* * * * *

"Where the hell did this storm come from?" Jordan shouted, though he already knew the answer. The weather sensors were 260 years old, like every other piece of equipment on the ship. Samson had run out of ways to repair them, which meant Jordan had a fraction of the time he needed to steer away from storms.

Jordan leaned into the spokes of the oak wheel to turn the bow away from the mountain of bulging clouds. A delta of lightning cut through the mass, branching out like veins from a throbbing heart.

"Ryan! Hunt!" he said. "How far out are we? I need a sitrep."

Ensign Ryan, moving slowly because of a worsening spine condition, got up from his station and pushed his glasses higher on his freckled nose. "Checking the data now, sir, but this one seems very ..."

Jordan could finish Ryan's thought for him. The storms, especially over the Eastern Seaboard of North America, were unpredictable. No one could explain why, but he had a theory. Some of the largest old-world cities had been on the East Coast: New York, Washington, Boston. All had turned into poisoned craters during a war that happened so long ago, no one remembered who started it. Even now, over two and half centuries later, the air above those scorched cities remained volatile and chaotic.

The same went for those cities on the West Coast: wastelands such as Los Angeles, Portland, and Seattle. But other than Hades, the Midwest hadn't been hit as hard during World War III. That was why the *Hive* and the ships before her had scavenged most of the known locations in the center of the continent. Jordan was now forced to search the more severely irradiated cities in the East for parts, fuel cells, and whatever else the Hell Divers could salvage.

Although he couldn't see it, he knew they were above the ruins of one of those cities now—a place the archives called Charleston.

"We're ten miles out from the nucleus of the storm," Ryan announced.

Another brilliant web of lightning flashed across the main display. The resulting boom of thunder rattled the bulkheads of the command center.

The ship was already too close.

"Your orders, Captain?" Ryan said.

Jordan felt the spokes grow slippery beneath his sweating palms. He continued to scrutinize the skies as if they might give him an answer.

"Sir?" said another voice before Jordan could reply to the first question. Ensign Hunt stood a few feet away, hands clasped behind his broad back.

"I have an update for you, sir."

"Can't it wait until later?"

"It's about that transmission from the Hilltop Bastion," Hunt said.

Jordan glanced over his shoulder to make sure none of the other crew had heard. "Keep your voice down," he said quietly.

Hunt took a step closer so that he stood right beside Jordan. "That signal you asked me to research is getting stronger, sir. I'm not sure how old it is, but I was able to identify the coordinates."

"And?"

Hunt jerked his chin toward the screen. "We're getting close." He hesitated and then added in a harsh whisper, "What about that other transmission? If word ever gets out that he survived ..."

Jordan shot him a stern look. He had been obliged to let Hunt in on some of the secrets aboard the *Hive*. Since he was communications officer, all transmissions from the surface filtered through him. Most were ancient recordings, playing on a loop. But if Hunt kept pushing, kept asking questions, Jordan would have no choice but to replace him.

Captain Ash had been too soft on security and information leaks, and look what had happened: an armed insurrection led by the lower-deckers. Six years ago, not long before Ash's death, she had discovered that one of her own officers was hacking into the restricted archives. The officer, a middle-aged woman named Janet Gardner, had been searching for information about the war that devastated the planet. That knowledge was forbidden for good reasons. There were things the citizens of the *Hive* didn't need to know. Things that would threaten their sheltered reality, like the truth about the surface and what dwelled in the darkness.

Ash had been too lenient with Officer Gardner. Jordan wouldn't make the same mistake.

"Sir, there's something else," Hunt said.

"What is it?" Jordan asked.

"I think I know who's been hacking into the archives."

Jordan scanned for any sign of eavesdroppers. The bridge wasn't the right place for this conversation, but he couldn't just walk away from the storm. The only people watching were several kids, all apprentices training for careers as the next generation of officers.

He took one hand off the wheel to wave them back to work. They would learn their duty fast or be kicked to a less desirable apprenticeship.

As they scattered, Jordan cocked an eyebrow at Hunt. "Proceed."

"It has to be Magnolia Katib, sir. She's logged more hours in the archives than anyone else on the ship."

Gritting his teeth, Jordan nodded and pivoted back to the view of the screen. Magnolia was a loose cannon, with no respect for the rules. He would deal with her soon.

On-screen, the storm appeared to have no end. The border of

the clouds stretched at least fifty miles east to west—a solid wall of black cumulus and flashing electricity.

Ryan cleared his throat to remind Jordan that the clock was ticking.

"I'm *thinking*, Ensign. Rash decisions get people killed. Patience keeps us alive."

"This could be it," Hunt said, his eyes bright. "This could be what Captain Ash was looking for. Perhaps this is what she was trying to say before—"

Jordan cracked his neck from side to side, silencing the man. Only Jordan knew what Captain Ash had been looking for—and what she thought she had found before she died. Magnolia was just like her: always curious, always searching.

Curiosity got people killed.

"Sir, I'm just saying it's worth checking out, don't you think?" Hunt said.

Hunt was a decent officer, but like Ash, he was also an optimistic dreamer. When Jordan took over command, she had told him to use his heart first, then his mind. And for a few years, he had bought that advice. But now he knew, the best compass wasn't in his chest. It was the one on the monitor to his right.

Math and science were the only things that could save humankind, not some delusion of a promised land.

There was nothing down there but death and monsters.

He made his decision. He would not risk the integrity of the ship by going through the storm, and he would not waste lives by dropping a Hell Diver team to the surface.

"Direct all noncritical power to the rudders and turbofans," Jordan ordered. He spun the wheel to the right, guiding the *Hive* away from the storm. The bulkheads groaned in protest.

Hunt looked as if he wanted to say something else, but he kept his mouth shut and returned to his station. That was good. Jordan didn't want to make a scene in front of his crew. He continued turning the wheel, but the more he pushed, the more it seemed to resist him.

Digital telemetry scrolled across his personal monitor, followed by a message: *Error 414*. It took Jordan a moment to recall the error code, but as soon as he did, he shouted, "Ryan, get Samson on the horn! We've got a problem with the rudders!"

"On it, sir."

"We're nine miles out, Captain," Hunt announced from the deck above.

The bow split through the southern edge of the storm, barreling northeast toward the towering monstrosity. Jordan tried to force the wheel, but it hardly budged. The turbofans allowed some movement, but without the rudders, they would veer into the storm.

The knot in his stomach tightened. There was no way the *Hive* would survive a trip through that. He couldn't drop a team down there even if he wanted to. This was exactly why he had tried to avoid the East Coast.

Cursing, Jordan twisted the wheel with all his strength. A shudder went through the ship.

He checked his monitor again, taking in the information with a quick sweep. The bow was turning at a forty-five-degree angle, but the rudders were now completely jammed. The *Hive* was spearing straight toward the flashing purple beast.

Jordan caught a drift of Katrina's herbal perfume, but he kept his gaze on the main display.

"Captain, I'm here," she said.

"About time, Lieutenant. Things are about to get very—"

The *Hive* lurched again, throwing Jordan into the wheel. His shoulder hit one of the wooden spokes. He caught himself, but Katrina hit the floor.

"Katrina!"

She smiled back at him from one knee.

"I'm okay."

"Go strap in," he said.

"But—"

"That's an order, Lieutenant."

Red lights flashed over her path as she made her way to her seat. The emergency alarm screamed from the PA system. Ensign Ryan had tripped and fallen on his way to another station. Letting out a grunt of pain, he put his hand to his unnaturally curved lower spine. Two other officers helped him up, and Jordan went back to steering the ship.

He grabbed the spokes and put all his strength into turning the wheel, pushing against the resistance.

"Lieutenant, Tell Samson he's going to be out of a job if he doesn't fix my damn rudders!" he shouted at Katrina.

An empty threat, Jordan thought grimly. If Samson failed, no one would have a job.

Katrina was already talking into her headset, relaying his orders. Jordan's eyes flitted back to the main display. He drowned out the chaos around him by drawing in steady breaths and exhaling through his nose. If the sky was the ocean, and the storm a rocky beach, then the *Hive* was racing toward the shoals faster than he could turn it away.

"Captain," called a voice nearly lost in the alarms.

Jordan glanced behind him and caught Katrina's gaze. Her sharp eyes told him things were about to get even worse.

"Samson says he can't fix the rudders from inside the ship."

Jordan closed his eyes in anticipation of what came next.

"We need to deploy a Hell Diver team to fix them," Katrina said.

Jordan pushed harder on the wheel. The aluminum struts creaked ominously.

"On this bearing, the heart of the storm will hit us in less than forty-five minutes," Hunt said.

Forty-five minutes. There was never enough time, but he had been in situations with less of it than he had now. Life in the sky was always coming down to the wire.

They were almost parallel with the storm now, but soon it wouldn't matter. Jordan knew the ship as well as he knew his own body. Without the rudders, they were, as Ash used to say, *dead in the air.*

"Sir, Samson is asking for your orders," Katrina said.

Jordan used his shoulder to wipe the sweat from his chin and then turned to his XO. "Direct full power to the turbofans—full reverse."

He made himself breathe deeply before he gave his next order. Every time he ordered the Hell Divers deployed, it was a potential death sentence. Their ranks were already strained by the losses they had sustained this year, but they knew the risks. On the bright side, perhaps fate would take care of his little blue-haired security problem, and he wouldn't have to take further action to deal with her.

"Send Michael and Layla topside," he said. "They're the best engineering divers we have left." He hesitated before adding, "And someone find Magnolia. I want her on this mission."

As his officers scrambled to carry out his orders, Jordan heaved a nervous sigh. Maybe one good thing could come of all this after all. He wasn't proud of the things he had to do as captain of the last airship in the sky, but the guilt was a burden he could bear if it meant keeping the human race alive.

THREE

Layla's hand brushed Michael's, and their fingers interlaced.

"Got bad news," Weaver said. "Samson sent a team into a tunnel connecting to the rudders from inside the ship, but the issue seems to be on the outside."

"So they're going to need us to fix it from ..." Layla's words trailed off, and Michael squeezed her hand.

"Afraid so," Weaver said. He hurried toward the launch bay doors, leaving Michael and Layla alone.

Most of teams Apollo and Angel stood near the portholes of the launch bay. Lightning illuminated their uneasy faces as they awaited orders.

All eyes were on Michael and Layla as they suited up. He pulled his chest piece from his locker and slipped it over his head. After putting his arms through the slots, he rotated for Layla to fasten the clasps on either side. The single piece fit snugly over his synthetic suit, but it was lightweight enough that it didn't weigh him down once his boots hit solid ground.

"We're still on for dinner later, right?" he said, smiling at Layla.

"Y-yes, of course," she said.

The hitch in her voice broke Michael's heart. He wasn't afraid to die if it meant saving the *Hive*, but the thought of losing her terrified him.

"Is there any chance," he said quietly, "that if I ordered you stay here, you'd listen to me?"

Layla grinned. "Why would I ever start listening to you now?"

She leaned in until they were so close he could smell the mint on her breath.

"You sure you know what you're doing?" she asked.

Michael nodded. Three years ago, he had fixed one of the ship's rudders, but that had been in clear skies. He hoped this would be another easy fix—say, an open circuit—but he wouldn't know until they were up there.

"Your turn," Michael said. He gazed into Layla's dark eyes. He was exactly her height now. When they were growing up, she had been a bit taller, but he caught up. He liked finally being on her level.

"What's our plan?" she asked.

Michael had to smile at her use of "our." Layla wasn't just his lover; she was his best friend. She was his person and always had been.

"Diagnose the problem." He cocked his chin at the coils of wire on the floor. "And fix it."

"And don't get fried," she added with a halfhearted grin.

"Right," he said. "Make a note: *don't get fried.*"

Michael secured the clasps on the sides of her chest plate, trying not to think about what she looked like without the armor. Oh, well, the prospect of climbing on top of a moving airship during a storm was more effective than a cold shower. He fastened the plates around his legs and pulled his helmet from the top shelf of his locker, then traced a finger over the Team Raptor crest for good luck, before slipping the helmet over his head.

Layla handed him his battery unit. If the armor had a heart, it was the battery. He clicked it into the socket on his chest plate, and it warmed to life, spreading a bright blue glow over the dull black armor.

"Well, look at that," Layla said. "Did you modify your battery again?"

He nodded. "It's got twice the power now. All I had to do was mess with the—"

Before he could finish, the double doors to the launch bay screeched open. Magnolia hurried inside the room, with Rodger and Andrew behind her. They all looked exhausted.

"Where've you guys been?" Michael said.

"Kicking Weaver's ass at cards," Magnolia said. "I was about to be rich!"

"'About to' being the operative phrase," Rodger said. "I've almost been rich about as many times as I've almost died on dives."

Ty and a couple of technicians carried bags of gear into the room. Weaver directed them away from the launch tubes and toward the control room. Then he jogged over to Michael.

"You almost ready, kid?"

God damn it, Michael thought. "Kid" was even worse than "Tin." Weaver seemed determined to be everybody's dad, but Michael wasn't interested in yet another father figure.

"Yes," he said stiffly.

Across the room, Magnolia was still ranting about the card game. "This is some horseshit!" she yelled. "I had a straight flush. You owe me two hundred credits, Weaver!"

"Save it for the rematch, princess," Weaver said.

Michael just shook his head. Weaver didn't call him *that,* at least.

Within minutes, the launch bay was full of personnel. Hell Divers, militia soldiers, technicians, and engineers from Samson's staff fanned out to perform their assigned tasks.

Another tremor rippled through the *Hive*. Outside the portholes, a skein of lightning filled the sky in front of the ship. Michael flinched as it licked the outer hull. The raucous crack rose over the screech of emergency sirens and reverberated in his ears for several seconds.

Forcing his gaze away, Michael punched his wrist minicomputer.

Digital telemetry appeared in the upper right corner of his heads-up display. He opened a private channel with a bump of his chin on the comm pad and turned back to his locker.

"Double-check your gear," he said over the channel. He followed his own orders and did a quick inventory of what he would need up there, going over all the potential issues in his mind. He stuffed the coils of wire into the cargo pocket on his leg, checked his parachute and booster a final time, and grabbed his duty belt.

By the time he was done, Magnolia had finished gearing up and Layla was rechecking her booster.

Ty dropped two bags of climbing gear in front of them. "Three hundred feet of eight-kilonewton-test rope. Should get you to the rudders."

Michael bent down and grabbed a handful of carabiners from one of the bags.

"Make sure you attach those to the hangers on the side of the ship every fifteen feet, and run the rope through it," Ty said. "That way, if anybody slips or gets hit, you won't go far."

"We *know*, Ty," Magnolia said, and Michael could almost see her eyes roll behind her visor. Her armor plates clicked together as she fidgeted.

Normally, Michael would have felt those same predive jitters, which brought with them the messy and addictive combination of adrenaline and fear, but this wasn't a dive through the clouds. Climbing onto the side of the ship during a storm was, in some ways, even more dangerous, since they would spend more time exposed to the storm and the threat of lightning strikes.

Get your shit together, Michael. Focus. You're not a kid anymore.

He summoned his most commanding voice and shouted, "Let's move it! We're working on borrowed time here."

With everyone in the launch bay watching, he clicked on his duty belt and led Magnolia and Layla to the ladder. Bumping his chin pad a second time, he opened a line to engineering.

"Raptor One to Samson, do you copy?"

He waited a second while Samson secured the line.

"Copy that, Michael. Where are you?"

"On my way topside. Any idea what the problem is yet?"

There was a frustrating pause.

They stopped at the bottom of the ladder, and Magnolia uncoiled the rope. She handed one end to Layla, who looped it through three steel clips attached to the bottom of her chest armor, just above her navel, and tied it in a figure eight.

Michael accepted the line when she was finished, and did the same thing. He didn't like the idea of being tethered to someone as unpredictable as Magnolia, but orders were orders. Captain Jordan wanted her up there with them, so he must think she would be useful on the mission.

Samson's voice came over the line as Michael secured the rope. He took the coil of slack and clipped it on his belt.

"We've troubleshot all three rudders from the back end," Samson said. "It's an electrical problem. You'll need to replace the wire and connect the rudders to a different grid."

Michael grimaced as he grabbed the first rung of the ladder. Rewiring the rudders was a lot more complicated than closing an open circuit. Ten years ago, he had patched a gas bladder from inside it while men with guns tried to lead a mutiny against Captain Ash. If he could do that, this should be easy.

He was no longer a little boy called Tin. He was the commander of Team Raptor, and he would fix the rudders no matter what it took.

"Roger that, Samson. We're on it." Michael swung up onto the ladder.

The ship trembled again as he climbed toward the narrow tunnel above. The slack came out of the rope connecting him to the other divers. With each step, he kept three points of contact on the worn metal rungs. If he lost his grip, he would bring Layla and Magnolia with him.

As soon as he reached the hatch, a transmission crackled from the comms. "Raptor One, Captain Jordan. I want Magnolia taking point once you're topside."

Michael held on to the rungs and glanced down at Layla and Magnolia. No way in hell was he going to let Magnolia take the lead. She would probably see something shiny on the other side of the ship and get all three of them killed when she chased after it.

"You're breaking up, Captain," Michael said. "I didn't catch your last." Switching off the frequency with a bump of his chin, he opened the hatch that led outside.

* * * * *

Magnolia was the fastest and most agile diver aboard, but walking on top of the ship while surrounded by the biggest storm she had seen in years was daunting all the same.

She had been *so-o-o-o* close to winning back the credits she lost to Weaver two weeks ago. Now she was up here, tied to a couple of lovesick kids.

Ahead, Michael battled the fierce winds. The glow from his weird red battery unit guided them across the top of the ship. They were right on the edge of the swirling mass, getting pounded by sheets of wind-driven rain.

Magnolia swore.

"You okay back there?" Michael asked.

"Fine," she lied.

Fearless, fast, and freaky. She liked Rodger's addition to Weaver's description of her. She did appreciate a man who could make her laugh. Hell, maybe if she survived this, she would share a mug of shine with Rodger and show him the true meaning of "freaky."

Nah. He's got to earn that.

She continued across the ship, ordering her priorities: fix the rudders, win those credits back, *then* decide whether to give Rodger a chance.

Ahead, Michael clipped a carabiner through the hole in a steel hanger and clipped the rope through the biner, then waved the team forward.

"Stay on the center line!" he shouted over the comm channel.

Magnolia could hardly hear him above the shrieking wind. Violent gusts slammed into the three divers as they worked their way aft.

Thunder boomed in the distance, like explosives going off in the center of the storm. A black fortress of clouds stretched across the horizon, blocking out the sun. If she hadn't seen it before, she might have wondered whether the sun wasn't just an invention from fairy tales.

Magnolia lowered her helmet and moved along the spine of the ship. The aluminum beam that ran along the top of the *Hive* was two and a half feet wide. To either side of the beam, the hull sloped away. Her boots had lug soles, but the surface was slick from the rain. A wrong step could send her sliding over the edge.

"Raptor One, you have thirty-five minutes to get us back online," Hunt said over the comms.

Rain pummeled Magnolia's armor. She wiped her visor clean, blinked, and focused on their destination. She could hardly feel any sense of motion beneath her, but she knew that the turbofans were whirring away under the ship's belly, helping keep them aloft. Jordan was backing away from the storm, but it was expanding, and without the rudders, he couldn't turn around.

Magnolia tightened her grip on the rope. The wind pushed against her, but she pushed back, fighting her way astern one step at a time. A spider web of lightning streaked across the sky, illuminating the scene.

Once, a long time ago, she had read in a book that there

were more stars in the sky than grains of sand on the faraway beaches of Earth. The idea had made her feel small and lonely. She felt that way again now.

Magnolia tried not to think of herself as a tiny figure moving along the top of the vast metal ship. A slap of wind reminded her that she was not a kid anymore. She was a Hell Diver, and if she didn't pay attention, she was going to end up as a very small and lonely splat on the ground four miles below.

"Almost there," Michael yelled over the channel. He twisted slightly and clipped another carabiner to another hanger.

Magnolia still couldn't see the rudders, but she could see the horizon of the drop-off that led to them. Michael clipped the rope into the biner, then clipped another bight of rope to the next hanger for backup, equalizing the tension between the two.

"I'll go first," he said. "We're going to have to rappel down."

A brilliant flash reflected off Layla's mirrored visor. Magnolia didn't need to see her features to know that the girl was scared. She had grabbed Michael's hand and was holding on to it as if it were the only real thing in the world.

"Be careful," she said. "I'll kill you if you die."

"I love you too," he said.

They pressed their helmets together. Magnolia groaned. This was exactly why she didn't have a boyfriend. Such cheesy, sentimental shit made her want to puke.

"Use a private channel," she grumbled.

With his back to the storm, Michael bent his knees and kicked off, rappelling down the sheer wall of the stern. Layla stepped closer to watch, but Magnolia reached out and pulled her back.

"Careful, kiddo." Magnolia winced as she said it. X had called her that, and she had hated it almost as much as being called "princess" by Weaver. Was she turning into one of those grumpy old Hell Divers who thought everyone under thirty was a kid?

"Okay, off rappel," Michael said over the comms, letting them know he had disconnected from the rappel rope. "Layla, you're next."

Layla grabbed the slack rope, clipped it through her rappel device, and turned her helmet toward Magnolia. "See you down there, *kiddo.*"

Magnolia almost chuckled, but a thunderclap focused her. She turned to face the storm, determined but terrified. Brilliant arcs of electricity left behind blue tracers across her retinas. Blinking them away, she turned back to the edge. By the time she looked down, Layla was gone.

She waited for the all-clear from Layla, who would by then be with Michael, anchored to the stern ladder that ran past the access tunnel and its three protruding rudders.

After clipping in to the rappel line, Magnolia took in a deep breath and pushed off into the darkness.

FOUR

Jordan kept his sweaty hands on the wheel, and his eyes on the storm. Either the team he sent topside would fix the rudders and save the ship, or they would die up there in the storm. Either way, there was nothing he could do now but stay the course he had set.

"Sir?" It was Katrina's voice.

Jordan looked over his shoulder at her. Commander Rick Weaver stood at the top of the bridge looking down, waiting for orders. He nodded at the Hell Divers and then glanced back to Katrina.

She unclipped her harness and staggered forward as another tremor hit the ship. Whatever she had to say, she didn't want others to hear.

He gripped the wheel tighter and glanced at the monitor to his right. A countdown ticked on screen. They had just over thirty minutes to get the rudders back online before the storm swallowed the ship. The *Hive* might survive for a few hours in the electric soup, but the divers would not.

"Sir, I just got word that we're picking up a transmission from the surface," Katrina said.

Jordan felt his heart kick. Who had leaked that intel? His eyes swept the bridge and found Hunt. The ensign avoided Jordan's gaze, answering his question. It was a reminder that he couldn't trust anyone but himself and Katrina. It seemed Magnolia wasn't the only person Jordan would have to deal with.

"What kind of transmission?" he asked calmly.

"An SOS, sir."

Jordan had prepared for this moment for years, ever since they intercepted the first transmission from X, but it had come at the worst time. She would hate him for keeping this secret from her. She might even leave him. He could endure a lot, but not the thought of losing her. "Kat, I'm—"

"I think this one could be the real deal, sir," she continued. "The Hilltop Bastion was an ITC bunker, one of the most advanced they ever built."

Jordan held back a sigh of relief. Hunt hadn't betrayed him after all. His secret about X was still safe. For now.

"Captain Ash marked the location as an area to explore if we ever made it this far east," Katrina said eagerly. "If their SOS is still transmitting, then maybe someone's still down there. I think—"

"Maria Ash is no longer captain, Lieutenant."

Several officers on the bridge looked up from their monitors. Katrina stopped talking, her lips a tight line as she stared at him.

"We're holding steady, sir," Hunt said. "Should I shut off the alarms?"

Jordan checked the screen to his right. They were sailing on the edge of the storm now. Warning sensors continued to beep, and the emergency alarm still wailed, but for now they were in the clear.

"Shut off the alarms, but instruct all noncritical personal to stay in their shelters," Jordan said, knowing that most of the citizens wouldn't listen and would just go on with life.

The wail of the emergency siren waned, and a recorded voice transmitted over the public-address system. "All noncritical personal, please remain in your designated areas."

Jordan used the moment of calm to scan the bridge. The entire room was spotless, from the white tile floor to the walls and the pod stations. His uniform, like those of his crew, was also white, continuing an age-old custom from the days when ships sailed on water instead of air. Unlike the rest of the ship, the bridge was lit with LEDs, although the lights were currently dim because of the energy curtailment.

Captain Ash had gone to great lengths to make sure this was a place of order amid the chaos. It was one tradition of hers that Jordan proudly carried on.

He breathed in air that smelled of bleach. As he turned back to the wheel, his eyes were drawn to the surface map displayed on one of the monitors. Where Ash had seen a new future, Jordan saw only a delusional fantasy. There was no hope for a new home on land. Their only hope for survival was in the sky, and right now it was riding on the work of three Hell Divers.

"Michael and his team are in position, sir," Katrina said. "Should we prep a second team to scout for Hilltop Bastion?"

"No." His voice was firm, and it drew a scowl from Katrina. "Once we fix the rudders and get clear of this storm, I'll consider allocating resources to investigate this mysterious signal."

"If you won't do this, Leon, I'll go down there myself," she said, unclipping her harness and standing up.

Jordan's eyes widened. She had always been feisty, but this was open insubordination.

"Sit *down*, Lieutenant," he ordered.

She took a step forward, then another, her lips quivering. Jordan felt the gaze of every staff member on the bridge watching them.

"If there is something down there, we need to check it out. For the sake of our child ..."

Jordan's eyes flitted to her stomach and then to the faces of his crew. They had heard. And within the hour, everyone on the ship would know.

He shook his head in frustration. "There is absolutely no evidence of human life on the surface. Captain Ash risked the ship and every soul aboard in pursuit of a fairy tale. I've kept us alive by not making that same mistake."

"We can't live up here forever," Katrina said.

"There is *nothing* down there, Lieutenant. But I'll tell you what: if we find a way out of this storm, I'll send a team down there to check those coordinates out, just to prove it to you."

*   *   *   *   *

Rodger Mintel was convinced he was the only one of his kind. He had always felt in his bones that he was different. Most of his friends and even his fellow divers thought him a little odd. For one thing, he loved to build things out of wood. Oak, if he could get it. Most softer woods had crumbled over the years. He had scavenged broken furniture from the *Hive* and even found whole planks on the surface during his dives. Once, trees had thrived on the planet below. Now they lived on in his creations.

He had just returned from the launch bay and was standing in the stall his family owned, looking at his creations: animals, figurines of people, and even a replica of the *Hive*. Most of the ship's inhabitants couldn't care less about his pieces, but he had a few customers who appreciated his art. Some of them even brought him furniture to fix from time to time. It wasn't how the Mintel family made a living, but it did add some extra credits to their account.

"You gonna tell me what's wrong, or just stand there?"

His father glanced up from the clock he was making in the workshop behind the stall, and took off his spectacles. The real family business had been passed on from generation to generation, but it would stop with his father. Someone else would have to become the ship's clock and key maker. Rodger had opted to become an engineer, and then a Hell Diver.

"You know I can't tell you anything, Pops. Besides, you're supposed to be in the shelter with the rest of the noncritical staff."

"Noncritical. *Pish.*" He laughed at the very idea. "I have clocks to finish. Without the sun, they're the only way to know the real time."

Another voice came from the back of their shop. "Cole, leave him alone. You know he can't tell us anything."

Both Rodger and his father turned to face Bernie, the matriarch of their little family. She walked into the workshop and set a wooden bowl of fruit down on Cole's desk.

"You're supposed to be in the shelter, too," Rodger said.

"Oh, stop, Rodge. The Mintel family doesn't cower." She smiled and pointed at the apples. "Eat something. You're as skinny as a pole."

Rodger grinned back. "Thanks, Mom."

He was one of the luckier citizens of the *Hive*: both his parents were still alive—although he wasn't sure how much longer this would be true. They both were in their fifties, and the years had not been especially kind to them.

Cole sat back down, moaning from the aches that plagued his body. Bernie took a seat at the desk beside his and brushed her thinning gray hair back over her shoulder. She was a two-time cancer survivor, and Rodger was perpetually afraid that it would come back and finish the job.

"Sit down, Rodge. You need your energy, especially if they're planning to send you back out there again."

Rodger sat, looking warily at his mother. "Who said anything about that?"

Without looking up from his clock, Cole said, "Your coveralls speak volumes."

Rodger glanced down at his black jumpsuit and laughed. "Oops." He plucked a small red apple from the bowl he had made for his mom on her fiftieth birthday. He had brought the wood back from a dive in a green zone. His team had discovered an entire warehouse filled with lumber, and Rodger had insisted on bringing some back. Magnolia had given him hell for that, rolling her eyes and telling him to leave the wood and grab something useful, such as plastic.

It was then that Rodger had taken a real liking to Magnolia. His thoughts were filled with the girl with blue highlights in her black hair—the girl who never seemed to pay attention to him. He wasn't going to wait any longer. As soon as she was back from fixing the rudders, he was going to tell her how he felt.

He picked up his carving knife, but instead of cutting into the apple, he went to work on a present for Magnolia. He had just the thing in mind.

* * * * *

As Commander Rick Weaver left the bridge, his mind was filled with questions about the transmission he had overheard Captain Jordan and his XO whispering about. Jordan probably wouldn't tell the Hell Divers anything, and he certainly wouldn't ask for their opinions. Everyone knew that the only reason he listened to Katrina's advice was because he was sleeping with her. It was obvious to most everyone but them, apparently.

Weaver trusted only one person on the ship for answers, and he had only a short time to sneak away and find her. Ten years ago, his home had come crashing to the ground, killing everyone he loved. He alone had survived, and it had changed him.

The hostile ruins of Hades had thrown everything at him, but in the end, he had beaten the wastelands. Captain Maria Ash had welcomed him to the *Hive*, and he had done his best to honor her memory and be a good role model for the other divers. But this place had never felt like home. It *shouldn't* feel like home. The human race belonged on the surface, and someday it would return.

Shortly after coming to the *Hive*, Weaver had heard rumors of a prophecy originating on the lower decks. He had traced those rumors back to their source. According to the prophecy, a man would come and lead them to their true home, on the planet's surface. For whatever reason, Captain Ash had believed in the prophecy. Weaver didn't know what to believe, and maybe that was why he kept coming back here.

He hurried through the passages, darting an occasional glance over his shoulder to make sure no one from command was following him. Jordan would have his head on a pike for going belowdecks. He dug in his pocket and felt for the old-world coin that seemed to bring him luck. He could use some right now.

The coast looked clear, but he drew up the hood on his sweatshirt and kept his head down to avoid inquisitive gazes. Most of the lower-deckers had emerged from their shelters and gotten back to their daily lives. For these people, the turbulence was just another interruption in their routines.

Weaver's fellow divers, when not working, usually stuck to the upper decks, playing cards and drinking shine. He had earned a reputation as a formidable card player, but few knew that he spent all his spare credits on food and medicines for lower-deckers who couldn't afford them. Helping the sick and needy, especially here in the third communal space, where the sickest and most disadvantaged people lived, was his way of holding on to hope. But today he wasn't here to help them. He was here for information.

As he climbed down the final ladder to the entrance to the barracks that housed over a hundred lower-deckers, a militia guard approached. Weaver kept moving purposefully, a worker intent on the task at hand. It seemed to work, and the guard didn't call after him.

Like the trading post, the communal area was one open space.

He pulled a bandanna over his mouth and nose before entering. Coughing and sporadic shouts echoed through the space. He walked inside and took a right at the first alley. Twenty families lived here in slots not much bigger than his launch tube, each habitation cordoned off by thin curtains hanging from cord or rusted drape rods.

Weaver knew exactly how many steps would get him to his destination. Because of the power curtailment, the banks of overhead lights were dark, and the heating units the engineers had hooked up to the boiler were dormant. The flicker of candles guided him through the cold space.

Stopping midway down the aisle, he pulled back a faded red curtain to reveal an empty bunk. The bed and the shelf next to it were covered with books and candles, but the woman he had come to see was gone.

"*Christ*," Weaver muttered.

"I thought you weren't big on him anymore."

Weaver spun around to see Janga, in a coat stitched together from colorful rags. Her waist-length gray hair was neatly combed. She made her living selling herbs and tinctures, but Weaver hadn't come here to buy a bottle of her "medicine."

"What can I do for you, Commander? I was just about to head up to the trading post before they turn the alarms back on."

"I can't stay long anyway," he said.

She sat down on her bed and spread the coat over her legs. Weaver checked outside for eavesdroppers. A boy and a girl, about five and six years old, peeked out of their stall across the aisle. Their parents or caregivers were nowhere in sight. Both had lumpy growths on their foreheads, and their curious eyes were centered on him. The girl waved at him with a hand missing all but two fingers.

He smiled and waved back, then reached into his pocket. The girl smiled when he pulled out two pieces of candy made from hardened jam. After tossing them across the aisle, he drew the curtain closed and pulled the single wooden chair up to Janga's bed.

He sighed. "I'm sure you know the ship's in trouble again."

Her thin lips stretched into a grin, and she lit a candle and placed it on the table in front of him. The light flickered over her wrinkled face.

"Did you come all this way to tell me what I already know?"

He kept his voice low. "It's more than the energy problem."

"The rudders," she replied. "I told you, I know."

Weaver's brows drew together, and he stroked his handlebar mustache. "How could you possibly know that?"

"You're not here to talk about rudders. You're here to talk about the past." She leaned toward him and put her hand on his knee. "Rick, you have to let it go."

He pulled away from her. She never called him by his first name. Hell, he hadn't even been aware that she knew it.

"I'm here to talk about the prophecy."

This time, Janga was the one to look skeptical. "I never would have thought a Hell Diver would be a true believer," she said.

"I need to know where the promised land is, Janga. Are we close? And how are we supposed to know the man who will lead us there?"

She shook her head slowly from side to side. "Rick, you know my visions are limited. I've told all I can."

"You need to try harder," he said. "I have to find this man."

She lowered her gaze to the candle and stared into the flame. Voices and coughing outside were the only sounds.

Weaver glanced over his shoulder and pulled the curtain back again to make sure no one was listening. Both kids were peeking through their curtain across the aisle again. The girl smiled, and the boy licked jam off his mouth.

Janga glanced up when Jordan turned back to the table. The gray haze of the cataracts made her eyes look eerie in the flickering light.

"I'm sorry, Commander." She closed her eyes and crossed her arms. "In my visions, I've seen the promised land, but it's not what you or anyone else would expect. There are fish there. Many fish. Fish of all shapes and sizes."

"Fish?"

She snapped her eyes open and smiled again. This time, her lips opened to reveal her two remaining teeth.

"Is this place near the ocean?" Weaver asked. "Because we're pretty damn close to the coast right now."

"Where?"

"If you're psychic, you should already know."

Janga let out a sigh that smelled like rot. Her robes didn't smell much better, but Weaver didn't flinch away.

"I'm only a little bit psychic," she said, a gleam in her rheumy eyes. "Just tell me where we are, Rick."

"A place called Charleston." He studied her for a reaction. She looked surprised, a bare flicker of emotion on her wrinkled face. "Does that name mean something to you?"

"Yes, but this is just another distraction from why you're really here. You said you aren't here to talk about your past, Commander, but we both know you're haunted. Until you face your ghosts, you'll never be able to enter the promised land."

The earpiece in Weaver's hand crackled. He put it back in his ear, his mind racing.

"Commander Weaver, report to the bridge immediately," said the voice over the channel.

"I have to go," he said to Janga.

The old woman dropped her arms and stood. "There's something else you should know."

Weaver hesitated, one hand raised to draw back the curtain.

"In my vision, I saw you with the man who will lead us to the promised land."

"Land or water?" Weaver said. "Because you mentioned fish. Last I checked, fish don't walk. Thanks for the chat."

Going back through the candlelit space, he shook his head. Maybe everyone was right about Janga. Maybe she was crazy after all. Maybe he was, too. Maybe they all were crazy for holding on to hope.

FIVE

Michael clung to the metal ladder on the vertical face of the stern. Wind lashed and tugged at his suit. Some of the rusted metal rungs were as old as the ship. But of the thousands of items that needed to be checked and replaced every six months during routine maintenance of the *Hive*, these were often overlooked. With resources stretched thin, who cared about a few metal rungs on the outside of the ship? Nobody—at least, not until lives depended on them.

The rung beneath his left boot creaked as he weighted it. The metal gave slightly, but it held.

The thunder was growing louder, the pauses between booms ever shorter. Each clap vibrated his armor and rattled his nerves.

The storm was getting closer.

Keep moving, Michael.

His stomach sank when he looked down to the next rung. The rudders were about ten steps below, to his left. All three were locked at a forty-five-degree angle, blocking his way into the tunnel—his only way in to reconnect them to the grid.

Another glance showed him the damage that had disabled the rudders. A black streak tattooed the hull. Lightning had ripped right through the ship's synthetic skin.

A boot hit the rung above his head. Layla was anchored to the ladder, with Magnolia just above her, their suits rippling violently in the wind and rain. Michael secured another carabiner to a steel hanger on the hull and clipped the rope. He pointed down.

"Holy shit!" Magnolia said over the comms. "Looks like the *Hive* got zapped."

"I was pointing at the rudders," Michael said. "We have to find a way around them to get inside."

"Are you *wacked*?" Magnolia yelled.

He looked again at the rudders but didn't see a better option. If they didn't do this, the ship would likely go down.

He took a slow breath to dispel the jitters from his voice before he spoke. In the upper corner of his HUD, a clock was counting down. They had twenty minutes to repair the rudders before the storm caught up with them—if they even managed to make it to the access tunnel. And if the increased power to the turbofans didn't blow the generators first.

This could end badly in a thousand different ways.

He fished another carabiner from the pocket on the outside of his armor. Only two left. Instead of clipping them every fifteen feet, as Ty had suggested, he decided to save the last two for later.

"Follow me," he said over the radio.

He stepped down another rung and pressed his boot against the slippery surface. The wind and rain rendered him nearly deaf and blind, but he was used to working in hostile conditions.

The rope tethered to the clip on his chest armor tightened as he took another step down. He nearly lost his balance when a voice hissed from the speaker built inside his helmet.

"Raptor One, Captain Jordan. Report."

Michael didn't respond right away as he struggled to keep his grip on the rusty, rain-slick metal.

"Raptor One, do you copy?" Jordan repeated, his voice taking on an anxious edge.

"We're working on a way down, Captain. Stand by."

Layla fed Michael slack, and he grabbed one of the carabiners from his pocket. He was about to clip the hanger just as the hair on his neck prickled. The lightning hit the surface of the ship an instant later. He braced himself as sparks blew past him. The hull, like their layered suits, had been designed to resist conductivity, and by the time the current reached the three divers, it had almost dissipated.

That didn't make it any less terrifying to see the white-hot electrical arc so close.

A jolt rocked the ship as they dropped into a wind shear. Michael gripped the ladder rail, but the carabiner slipped from his fingers, clanked off the side of the ship, and fell away into the darkness.

"*Damn it!*" he whispered. With only one biner left, he would have to choose the placement carefully.

He continued down the rungs until he was above the rightmost rudder. The pitted metal surface had more scars than a veteran Hell Diver. With utmost care, he reached with his left hand between the rudder and stern. The gap was a foot wide. Maybe a bit more, but not nearly enough to squeeze through.

He bumped the chin pad twice to open a line to the bridge.

"Captain, I've ... we've reached the rudder," Michael said, correcting himself to avoid a dressing-down from Jordan for not following orders and giving Magnolia point. "Still searching for a way past them into access tunnel ninety-four."

From this position, he couldn't get through to the tunnel. The only way in was down. They would have to climb underneath the rudders and then back up and through one of the vertical gaps.

A new sound emerged over the crackle of static and the rush of wind. The whine of the turbofans reminded Michael of another threat. They were getting closer to the turbines under the ship. If he got sucked inside, the eight-foot blades would turn him to mist.

Four more rungs down got him below the rudders, providing a view up through the gaps. There appeared to be enough room to squeeze through—if he could scale his way up there.

He reached out and grabbed the pocked edge of the first rudder with his left hand while holding on to the rung above him with his right.

"Be careful, Michael," Layla said over the comm.

"Just checking to see if I can move them manually."

As he pushed, a gust of wind slammed into his side, throwing him off balance as he pushed. Numbness rushed through his body as his left boot slipped off the rung. For a moment, he felt the same pure rush of adrenaline that prickled through him before a dive.

"Hold on!" Layla yelled.

Her upward tug on the rope helped center his mass, and he stepped back onto the ladder, grabbing the rail and the rung above him.

Drawing in a deep breath, Michael gave himself a few seconds to regain his composure. Sweat dripped down his forehead, stinging his eyes. He blinked it away and kept his visor pointed at the rudders. If he couldn't move them manually, he would have to step off the ladder, climb the side of the ship, and wedge himself between the first and second rudders to reach the access tunnel.

"A little slack!" he yelled into his mike. "I have an idea." He clipped the last biner to a hanger between the ladder and the right rudder.

"What are you doing?" Layla asked.

"Just keep me tight!"

The slack tightened around the clips above his navel, and he stepped off the rung, planting his left boot sole against the sheer wall of the stern. It slid several inches down the wet surface before the rope snugged. Next, he took his other foot off the ladder and pressed it against the stern. With his hands still on the rung, his waist was bent at ninety degrees. He bent his knees as if on rappel, while still holding on to the rung with both hands.

"Oh, hell no!" Magnolia shouted when she realized what he was doing.

"Tin!" Layla cried out a second later.

He let go of the rung with his left hand, then his right, so that he was now dangling entirely from the rope.

His boots slid another few inches, and he let the wind take him. The momentary sensation of weightlessness made his stomach flutter the way it always did during the first moment of a dive, when the launch tube opened and he plummeted earthward. This wasn't much different, he told himself. Heck, it was safer. Nothing but air separated his boots from the surface twenty thousand feet below, but at least he had a rope. He could do this.

"Hold tight!" he yelled.

Swinging from right to left, he studied the three rudders directly above him.

The countdown on his visor broke fifteen minutes.

How the hell was he supposed to get these things up and running in so little time?

Both X and Michael's dad had been in worse situations than this. They would have found a way. There was always a way.

He was stretching upward for the rudder when another blast of wind hit him, swinging him left. His fingers slipped across the wet surface of the first rudder. He tried a second grab and then a third as he swung back and forth. Each time, his gloves slid across without finding a grip, and the lump in his stomach grew heavier.

Lightning slashed through the sky behind him, firing the side of the ship with a brilliant blue glow. Water slid down the hull as if the ship were sweating.

The clap of thunder shook him so hard, he could feel it in his bones. Reaching down, he fingered through his tool belt for the clamp-locking pliers he kept there. Again he swung like a pendulum, this time dragging his feet on the hull to slow his growing momentum.

Bending his knees, he reached up with the pliers and clamped them onto the first right rudder. He repeated the process with a second pair on the middle rudder.

Ten feet above him, Layla and Magnolia clung to the ladder, looking down. Sporadic flashes of lightning glinted off their armor.

"When I give the order, send me some slack," he said calmly.

Layla's voice hissed in his ear. "I hope you know what you're doing, cowboy."

Michael wasn't sure what "cowboy" meant. Where did she come up with these words? No matter—he, too, hoped this would work. Kicking off from the side of the ship, he let the wind take him. He swung toward the rudders, walking his feet across the vertical hull, and grabbed the near pliers.

"Slack!" he yelled.

As soon as Layla fed out a foot or two of rope, he used the pliers to pull himself up and grab the second pair. Soon his head and chest were above the tools. His boots slipped on the slick surface, but he got enough traction to push his shoulders between the first and second rudders.

Boots pressed against the hull, and torso wedged between the two rudders, he held himself there like one of the muscular gymnasts that he had seen in the picture books.

Water sluiced down his visor, obstructing his view, but only a few feet remained between him and the access tunnel above the rudders. He just needed a little boost to get there.

He shoved off with his boots and swung his legs back. The wind pushed his lower body, and clenching his abs, he kicked forward, then back, then forward again. The pliers on the first rudder wobbled as he gathered the needed momentum to launch himself toward the tunnel entrance. Just as the pliers snapped free, his gloved fingertips grabbed the bottom edge of the access tunnel. His feet hit the hull, and he felt the force of gravity pulling him down.

The terrifying whine of the turbofans gave him new inspiration, and he pulled himself up and wedged his chest armor over the edge. Pressing the toes of his boots against the hull, he wriggled his upper body farther into the passage and kicked his way inside.

"I'm in," he gasped, and heard Layla's whispered prayer of thanks over the comms.

There was no time to waste. He pushed himself up and clicked on his headlamp. The entire area was only five feet wide, with a ceiling so low that his helmet nearly touched it. At the back of the narrow passage, a sealed hatch led into the tunnels that Samson's engineers couldn't access from inside.

Michael clove-hitched the slack around a vertical post in the tunnel. He had maybe forty feet left. Ty's calculations had been spot-on.

The hard part was over. Now that they had a ladder of sorts, Layla and Magnolia just needed to climb up the stern. He ran the rope through his belay device and cinched it snug.

"Okay, Layla, you're next," he said.

A minute later, Michael saw her helmet. Clamping her ascenders onto the taut rope, she stepped into the stirrups and pushed upward, first one side and then the other, until she reached the rudders. Michael walked up between the right and center rudders, grabbed her wrist, and hauled her inside. Magnolia came next, nearly jumping inside.

"We're inside, Captain," Michael reported.

"You have nine minutes," Jordan said.

As if to emphasize the point, the ship groaned as they passed through another bubble of turbulence. The rope kept the three divers tethered together, but they all wobbled. Michael reached out for Layla to steady them both. Magnolia grabbed the poles connecting to the first rudder.

"It's okay; we've got this," Michael said, trying to reassure himself as much as the other divers.

He let go of Layla and pulled the coils of wire from his cargo pocket. Then he took a screwdriver from his duty belt and staggered to the bulkhead. Unscrewing the rusted control panel for the first rudder, he stared at a bird's nest of colored wires.

Magnolia patted him on the shoulder. "Hope that makes sense to you, because it's noodles to me."

Layla was already working. She reached inside and began snipping while Michael prepared the new coil. They had done this a hundred times inside the ship, but never with so little time, and never in such harsh conditions.

Magnolia hovered behind Michael and Layla. "Come on, hurry it up!"

"I don't even know why Jordan wanted you here," Layla said. "We can do this fine on our own."

"Um, because I'm fearless, fast, and, um, have great hair?"

Michael ignored her. He pulled the wires that Layla had cut, dropped them on the floor, and handed her the end of the undamaged coil.

They worked for several minutes, Layla doing the splicing and Michael feeding the new wire to her.

"Five minutes," Magnolia reminded them.

"Shut up!" Michael and Layla said simultaneously.

Magnolia backed away, hands raised in surrender.

"Almost got the first one," Layla said. She used her multi-tool to strip the end of a coil and tie it to the connection. She stuck her arm farther into the control panel. "There, that should do it for rudder one."

Michael bumped his chin pad three times to open a line to engineering.

"Samson, Michael here. Try rudder one."

Over the crackle of static came a grinding noise. All three divers turned toward the huge fin as it slowly moved.

"Good job," Michael said. "Just two left."

"And four minutes," Magnolia muttered. When Layla turned to glare at her, Magnolia whistled and put her hands behind her back.

Michael shook his head and kept working. The ship would have some range of motion now, but they needed at least one more rudder to turn the ship enough to get away from the storm.

Michael and Layla moved to the next panel. They were a good team, working fast and efficiently together, especially under pressure. He honestly wished that Magnolia hadn't come with them. If he had to guess, Jordan had sent her because her claim to fame was her speed and agility, but so far, she had been no help whatsoever.

"I think ... yes! Got it!" Layla tightened a yellow wire nut down on the connection she had just made.

"Rudder two back online," Michael reported to Samson.

They moved to the final control panel. He unscrewed it and pulled it off. This time, the mess of wires was more of a lump, fried by the electrical strike.

"Shit," Layla said, leaning forward.

Michael pulled the rest of the wire from his cargo pocket. He was reaching out to give it to Layla when something flashed in his peripheral vision. Lightning lashed the side of the ship, and a heavy thud sounded as the stern suddenly plunged toward the surface.

Michael watched in horror as Magnolia fell backward, screaming. She windmilled her arms, striking the rudders as she fell between them.

The rope pulled Layla and Michael after her. He dragged his boots against the ground, but the ship dipped again and he lost his balance.

As he fell, the realization hit him like a gut punch. The lightning had severed the rope clipped above them on the top of the ship.

He hit the floor of the access tunnel knees first, sliding and reaching out for Layla. His fingers narrowly missed hers, and she flailed for something else to hold on to. The first rudder stopped her with a thump. She let out a squeak, and then she was gone, sucked into the void.

"Layla!" Michael yelled. He reached out for the poles connecting the rudders and grabbed them before he could slip through the gap. Looking down, he saw two battery packs glowing in the darkness. Layla was about ten feet down, and Magnolia was another ten below that.

He had to pull them back up before the turbofans sucked them in. Michael wrapped his fingers around the poles of rudders 1 and 2 and pushed himself to his feet, but the ship dipped again and he fell to his knees. The wind sucked him outside, and he fell helmet first toward the clouds.

They all dropped several feet before the slack caught on the clove hitch he had thrown around the vertical post. The rope went taut, and he came to a stop, arms and legs spread out as in a stable diving position. His heart stuttered when he looked down at Magnolia and Layla. Both were dangerously close to the turbofans.

A second later, a blast of wind took him, and he smacked into the stern. He braced himself with his palms and forearms, but his helmet whacked the hull so hard it rattled him.

Magnolia's screams came over the screech of the wind, and Michael quickly saw why. She was being pulled toward the turbofan directly beneath the stern, about ten feet below her.

The stern finally began to rise onto an even keel, pushing on him and sending him swinging back out into the storm. Pulling on the rope above him, he fought his way into a vertical position.

The ship was turning away now. The storm was almost on top of them, but he could see an end to the swell. They just needed to get around the outer rim of bulging clouds.

"Raptor One, what's going on out there? Please report," Jordan said over the comm.

"Captain!" Michael yelled. "You have to kill all power to turbofans nine and ten. They're pulling Magnolia in."

The brief pause felt like an eternity.

"Captain!" Michael shouted.

Jordan's voice came at last. "Negative, Raptor One. I *need* those turbofans to get us out of here!"

Michael could already imagine Captain Jordan justifying his actions at their memorial ceremony, explaining to the citizens of the *Hive* how courageously the divers had sacrificed their lives to keep the ship flying.

Not this time.

Michael wasn't going to let Magnolia and Layla die.

Squirming, he looked up. The bottom rung of the ladder was ten feet up and to his right. Clamping first one ascender and then the other onto the taut rope, he put his boots in the stirrups and began working his way up.

"Get in your stirrups and start jugging!" he shouted.

Layla followed his lead below, and when she reached the ladder, they rigged nylon pulleys from the bottom two rungs and started winching Magnolia up. The work was backbreaking, especially in the wind, but, inch by inch, they at last got her to the ladder.

The dark clouds on the horizon lightened. The end of the storm was in sight. The *Hive* was almost clear.

Michael hurriedly dismantled the makeshift rig and was stowing the pulleys in his side pocket, his other hand holding the ladder rail, when the ship lurched. His boots slid on the wet rung, and he lost his grip. Layla fell at the same time, yanking Magnolia off, and in the space of a second, all three were dangling below the rudders, right back where they had started.

"What the fuck are you doing up there?" Magnolia screamed. "Help me!"

"Hold on!" Michael shouted back. He felt for the rope and caught a wrap. It was eight-kilonewton test, so he wasn't worried about it snapping. But the hanger and the post that anchored them were another matter. If either broke, the other would probably give, too, and they all would get whisked right into the blades of the turbofans.

"Captain, you have to shut off the fans or we're going to lose Magnolia!" Michael said. "We're almost clear of the storm. Please. I'm begging you!"

"I'm sorry, Raptor One," Jordan replied. "I can't shut off those turbofans until we're *completely* clear."

The sound of the fans was louder now. Michael looked down to find Magnolia's legs being sucked toward the turbines, forcing her into a jackknife position.

He ran through their limited options. If Jordan was unwilling to shut the fans off, all Michael could do was rig his ascenders again and use the stirrups to haul all three of them a little higher until they cleared the storm. He needed only a few minutes.

There was, of course, one other option, which disgusted Michael even to think about. He and Layla *could* easily climb to safety if they didn't have Magnolia weighing them down. But he would never give that order. He wasn't like the captain. Either they all would survive this together, or no one would. Then Jordan could deal with the fallout from having killed three of his best divers.

Michael stepped into the stirrups and looked down at Layla. "Start jugging like your life depends on it—because it does!"

She nodded, and together they started upward again.

Magnolia's raspy voice rose over the whine of the turbines.

"Michael!" she yelled. "Tell Weaver I had that straight flush, you hear me? I want that on my fucking memorial plaque!"

Below, something glinted in the blue light of Magnolia's battery pack. She had pulled her knife.

"No!" Layla shouted.

"Magnolia, don't!" Michael said. "Just hold on! We're almost clear of the storm. We're going to get you home. Just hold on!"

He worked the ascenders faster, climbing as quickly as his exhausted limbs and the weight of three divers with chutes and armor would allow. Layla was doing the same thing below him. Sheets of rain hit the divers as they raced to save their friend.

They had pulled Magnolia a foot farther away from the turbofans, but it wasn't enough. The exertion was catching up. They would never get themselves and her to the ladder again. They would slide right back down the sheer face of the stern. He pushed with his boots and pressed his right foot into the stirrup with all his strength. The feeling that he was about to fail gnawed at the pit of his stomach. He pushed and pulled harder, unwilling to give up.

Lightning cracked, farther away now. The strikes were intermittent, and the sky was growing lighter. The storm was breaking up, but the turbofans continued to whir below them.

Michael felt something odd happening with the locking carabiner clipped to his chest armor. It was bending from the combined weight of Layla and Magnolia.

"Captain, please," Michael pleaded. "We're almost clear! Please just shut off turbofans nine and ten!"

This time, there was no response.

"It's been fun watching you kids grow up," Magnolia said quietly over the comms. "I'm sorry I can't be there to see you get married someday."

Before Michael could reply, the load beneath him suddenly halved. He looked down as the blur of blue that was Magnolia's battery pack got sucked under the ship. There was no scream, just the crack of thunder and the groan of the ship.

"Magnolia!" Layla yelled.

Michael closed his eyes and dipped his helmet in despair. Anger quickly replaced the pointless emotion. Was this how X had felt when Michael's father was killed due to a faulty weather sensor? Michael had blamed X, at least in part, and X had blamed Captain Ash. But now he realized the truth. Regardless of who was captaining the ship, divers always came last.

Layla was sobbing, and Michael kicked the taut rope below him to get her attention.

"Come on," he said. "There's nothing we can do for her, and we have to climb before my locker blows."

"I can't believe she's dead," Layla said. "She sacrificed herself for us."

"Maybe she made it past the turbofans. Maybe she'll deploy her chute and we can pick her up later." Michael knew how crazy that sounded. Even if Magnolia made it past the fans, she would be falling through the middle of an electrical storm. If she didn't get fried, she would have to use her booster after she landed, to go right back into that same storm, which would screw with her beacon and comms. Finding her would be nearly impossible, and Jordan would never risk the ship in a storm for a diver anyway.

Michael gave himself a few seconds to catch his breath and take in the reality that he had probably seen the last of his friend. Rain and wind battered him as he hung there. When he looked up, the sky had cleared. They had passed the edge of the storm.

"Okay, we're shutting the fans down now," said a new voice over the comms. It sounded a lot like Katrina.

Jordan didn't even have the guts to relay the message.

"Raptor One, what is your status?" Katrina asked. "Is everyone okay?"

Thirty seconds. Magnolia had needed only thirty fucking seconds, and then Michael and Layla could have pulleyed her up.

"With all due respect, no, we're *not* okay," Michael said. "Magnolia's gone." He wanted to say a good deal more, but he bit his lip and focused on his breathing.

Michael and Layla began climbing back to the relative safety of the access tunnel. Without Magnolia's weight, the storm, and the suction of the turbofans, the ascent went smoothly.

"Magnolia, do you copy?" Michael asked as he climbed.

Static crackled over the channel.

Layla tried several times, but the only reply was more static.

They worked as a team, and when Michael got back to the tunnel, he grabbed the side, hooked a heel over the top, and pulled himself up. Inside, he turned and grabbed Layla. Her hands were shaking, and he put his arm around her, pulling her helmet against his chest. For a moment, they just sat there, holding each other, neither of them saying a word. A delta of lightning split the horizon in the distance, but the rain had subsided.

Wearily, he stood and helped Layla to her feet. They still had the third rudder to repair before they could return home—without Magnolia.

SIX

Magnolia held her toggles in a death grip as she hung from the suspension lines of her parachute. Her entire body was numb from the mix of adrenaline and raw fear. This was the fifth time she had come within spitting distance of death, and it never seemed to get easier. She could still see the blur of the turbofans trying to suck her into a vortex of whirring blades. A sudden gust had sent her cartwheeling. She had become disoriented in the fall, making it difficult to move into stable position.

I'm not afraid of dying, she'd told herself.

That didn't mean she wanted to die. But she would gladly give her life to save her fellow divers, just as X had done for her many years ago. If she had to do it over again, she would have sawed right through the rope without blinking.

She wiped the rain from her visor for her first look at the postapocalyptic world below. From above, the terrain was split into squares, like the farms she had seen in the archives: corn, beans, wheat, all arranged like a giant game board across the land. There were also the great wooded areas of the Old World in those pictures. God, she wished she could have seen those endless fields and forests. The only vegetation she had ever seen was the toxic bushes that lit up like LEDs and ate anything that got too close. Everything else had either been incinerated in the blasts or killed in the radioactive fallout that followed.

Brilliant flashes of electricity filled the clouds to the east. The annoying chirp of the warning sensor continued to beep in her helmet, but she was too focused on the sky now to notice. The sprawling clouds looked … strange.

Different.

Unlike the typical storm clouds, these were wrinkly, like the leathery flesh of a Siren.

She tried to bump on her night-vision goggles, but the damn system was all screwed up from the electrical storm. The radio was still down, her electronics were malfunctioning, and her chute was pulling her toward the ruins of an ancient city.

Less than a half hour ago, when she was standing on top of the *Hive*, she had felt small and insignificant. But now, dangling over a radioactive wasteland, with no way of contacting the ship, she felt like a marble falling into a bottomless hole.

Captain Jordan would never send the ship to rescue her. The bastard hadn't even been willing to shut down two of his precious turbofans to save her life. That said a lot about the man, but nothing she didn't already know.

Lightning flashes split the darkness overhead, backlighting her canopy—and what looked like a tear in her chute.

"No," she muttered, twisting in the harness. "Please, *please* don't do this to me."

Another flash illuminated the rip, near the upper right edge of the sail. It wasn't from the turbofans, so what could have damaged her chute? It looked almost as if someone had deliberately cut the fabric, but that was crazy.

No one would sabotage a Hell Diver's chute.

Would they?

She squirmed again for a better look. The tear hadn't expanded much, but the air pressing on the sail would slowly open the rip. She thought back to the launch bay before she climbed the ladder. Ty had brought her gear, and she had no time to check the chute or the booster before the mission.

She looked hard at the tear. It was more of a slash, really, and it wouldn't be long before the entire cell collapsed and sent her to earth way too fast. She was surprised it had held this long.

With her system down, she had no way of knowing how far up she was, but if she had to guess, there was still another three thousand feet between her boots and the surface. She scanned the skies one last time for her home, even though she knew it was gone. Michael and Layla and everyone else must think she was dead.

She was very much alive, although that could change in a few seconds.

She raised her arm and checked her wrist monitor. The data showed her heart rate revving ... to an inhuman three hundred beats per minute.

"Seriously?" she yelled.

Even her wrist monitor was out of whack.

She was having one hell of a day. Her beautiful straight flush had ended up in a mess on the floor, she had been thrown from the ship and nearly pureed by the turbines, her chute had a rip from possible sabotage, and now her life-support system was malfunctioning.

If she somehow made it to the surface in one piece, she was going to have another problem. The radiation here could be astronomical. She didn't see any craters from the bombs below, but something had devastated this place. Her battery pack wouldn't keep her suit powered for long. Then it would be a toss-up to see what killed her: the radiation or the mutated beasts that thrived in it.

Lightning fractured the sky, casting its fleeting glow over a boneyard of flattened buildings. The city was one of the largest she had ever seen, and she wondered which of the great ancient metropolises it was. Atlanta, maybe? Whatever it had been, it was now just brown and gray and dead.

Magnolia pulled lightly on the right toggle, turning in a slow circle to scan the terrain. Roadways snaked through the decayed city, and the few buildings that still stood were nothing but skeletons held together by concrete and rebar. She had heard that the East Coast was hit hard, but this city was completely leveled. In her mind's eye, she imagined the citizens crowding the streets, their hands shielding their eyes from the inferno that incinerated almost everything in its path.

Another jagged hand of electricity cast a flickering blue wave over the city. Something in the distance caught her eye. Despite all odds, a cluster of buildings had survived. To the east, the terrain formed a shallow depression that seemed to have protected some of the larger towers.

She had seen scrapers before on dives, though never any as tall as these.

She pulled the left toggle to steer away from the debris field and toward the structures, searching for a clear drop zone. The damaged canopy pulled her to the right, and she gave it more left toggle to hold her bearing. The storm was rolling over the city, providing just enough light to reveal the ground now looming up at her.

Ever since she was a kid, she had always seemed to get the short end of the stick. She couldn't even remember her mom and dad. Both had died before she was old enough to talk. Since then, she had basically been on her own, passed from caretaker to caretaker until she landed in jail for stealing a scarf from the trading post. Diving had changed her life. The other Hell Divers were the only true family she had ever known. She had lost her only lover, Cruise, and X on that dive ten years ago, but without them, she would never have made it to the age of thirty. She was thankful for every minute she had spent with those men, with her fellow divers Michael and Layla, and even with Katrina. They were the closest thing to family she had ever known.

Now she was alone.

And that was what she had always feared most.

Her eyes went from the ground to her chute. She had done some lousy things in her life, but nothing to deserve this. Part of her wondered whether she even *wanted* to survive the landing. Then anger took over again.

"One time!" she yelled. "Give me some luck just one damn time!"

She chinned the pad in her helmet to open a channel to the *Hive*, but white noise hissed back. Next, she tried the NVGs again. On the third bump, a green-hued view of the city exploded across her field of vision. The electronics controlling her suit surged back to life.

Anger and frustration gave way to awe when she saw what lay beyond the outskirts of the dead metropolis. Those wrinkly clouds she thought she had seen earlier weren't clouds at all, and that valley wasn't a valley.

"My sweet Lord," she whispered.

Waves. Endless waves stretched across the horizon. The ocean seemed to go on forever. She held a breath in her chest and blinked rapidly. Was it an optical illusion?

She let go of the toggles to check her wrist monitor and pull up a map from the archives. Digital text rolled across the screen.

Charleston, South Carolina. Year 2029. Population 330,903.

Lowering her wrist, she scrutinized the city and the ocean beyond. It was hard to believe that so many people had once lived here. Hell, it was hard to believe that so many people were ever alive in the first place. Magnolia had grown up surrounded by hundreds of people, but *hundreds of thousands*? How could that be possible?

Her eyes shifted from the network of rusted girders rushing up to meet her, to her HUD. Numbers ticked across the display as her velocity increased. The chute wasn't catching enough air. The suspension lines twisted with her collapsing canopy. She grabbed the right cascade lines again and shook them, trying to coax the deflated cells open.

She couldn't die this close to the ocean. She didn't care that it was a toxic soup crawling with mutant monsters. Ever since she was a kid, she had longed to see the world as it once was, but she had fixated on two things that she wanted to behold more than anything else: the stars in the sky, and the vast sea.

It would take a change of luck, but she just might see one of them before she met her maker.

Or maybe not.

The rip had widened into a gaping wedge in the far right cell of her canopy, and the sail was sagging badly. At this rate, she would hit the ground way too fast. She had to land on top of a high building before her chute turned into a wad of garbage.

She scanned desperately for a place to land. There to the east was the enclave of towers she had spotted earlier. She was close enough to see the guts of the buildings. Staircases and sagging floors filled her view. Steel girders bore the structures up despite gravity's best efforts to bring them crashing down.

Rooms where people had worked or lived came into focus. She switched off her NVGs, hoping that maybe some of those wonderful twenty-first-century colors remained, but she saw the same brown and gray as always. Every other hue had been lost to time.

She toggled left, toward the first tower. Her altitude was two thousand feet, but she was dropping at an alarming rate. Even if she managed to put down on the rooftop, at this speed she wouldn't be walking away from the landing.

Magnolia shifted her gaze from the towers to her canopy. The tear was spreading, opening a gaping hole in the chute. She wasn't going to make it.

Yes, you're going to make it. You're going to run on the beach and dip your feet in the ocean, just like you dreamed of doing when you were a dumb little kid.

She almost laughed at how insane that sounded as she flew

over the edge of the valley, catching a glimpse of the sea beyond the scrapers.

A suspension line suddenly snapped, and the canopy slowly folded in two. Helpless, she sailed toward the first tower with only three lines attached to her disabled canopy. The lines twisted, and she twisted with them, her vision a blur of gray and brown as she spun.

She was falling with hardly any resistance, and although she couldn't determine her speed, this was not looking like a survivable landing.

Magnolia chuckled—a squeaky little sound that surprised her. Her whole life had been one shitty turn of luck after another, but today had been the absolute worst. It was enough to make her laugh. She wasn't going to spend the last seconds of this sorry existence screaming in fear.

"Fuck you!" she shouted.

The spinning made her queasy, and she caught the taste of bile and shine and greasy potato. She was coming in fast toward the roof of the tower. Bending her knees slightly, she pulled both toggles all the way down to flare what was left of her canopy and lessen the impact.

As she stopped spinning, she caught another glimpse of the tower. She had to move left, away from the top. Swallowing, she said her first prayer in years. She vaguely remembered the words that Weaver had repeated during an epic dive into an orange zone.

Lord, I am not worthy of your mercy, but I ask that you please grant me...

Her eyes fixed on the horizon. At least she had seen the ocean before she died.

A hard jolt rocked her as her canopy and lines caught on something and then snapped free, and she swung forward as if she had been shot from a giant slingshot back into the sky. It wasn't until her left arm scraped against steel that she realized she was actually *inside* one of the buildings. She had sailed right into one of the open floors, and something had snagged the mess of lines and canopy. But it wasn't enough to slow her down completely.

Her right boot hit a piece of rebar. The pain was instant, lancing up her thigh and hip. It felt as if her damn foot had come off, too.

She continued swinging upward until the risers and shroud lines caught and held. The force pulled her violently backward.

Something snapped. A bone, maybe, or a ligament? The burning pain was intense, and red encroached on her vision until she could see nothing but a bloody haze.

Magnolia struggled to take several deep breaths. Blood rushed in her ears, singing like an emergency siren. The extra oxygen entered her body, and the curtain of red slowly retreated. She fought the pain by biting down on her lip. Nothing like more pain to make you forget about other pain.

She could feel her feet again, and they weren't touching anything solid. She was hanging from a beam on one of the top floors of a scraper, and ten city blocks away was the most beautiful sight she had ever beheld. Massive waves ate at the shoreline, crashing on the beach before receding back out to sea. This close, the ocean was even more beautiful than she had imagined.

Maybe it wasn't luck she needed at all, she mused. Maybe what she needed was a little faith.

She hung from the beam, staring for so long she lost track of time. The rusted carcass of a boat lay on the beach. It wasn't nearly the size of the *Hive*, and its sailing days were clearly over, judging by the massive hole in the starboard side of the hull.

Past the wreck, a columnar tower jutted up from a rocky promontory. She had seen a building like it in one of the picture books in the *Hive*'s library. It was a lighthouse, built to warn ships away from the shore.

A flash arced overhead, backlighting the red dome of the tower. In this drab landscape, it stood out like a flame in the night.

Magnolia realized that being all alone might have an upside. With no captain or commander to tell her what to do, she was free to make her own choices. Her heart thudded with excitement. She was going to visit the lighthouse—right after she dipped her feet in the ocean.

A clatter and creak from the street below pulled her back to reality.

She held the air in her lungs and slowly twisted in the mess of lines to look for the source of the noise. Old-world vehicles littered the road. None had moved for a long time. She had to wait several moments before the sound came again. A flash of motion darted for a tunnel in the debris field.

Something was down there.

Maybe she wasn't alone after all.

SEVEN

Captain Leon Jordan leaned over the table in the empty conference room and took in a breath through his nostrils. The emergency sirens and the shouts of his crew had died away. He used the quiet to gather his thoughts.

The blisters on his hands stung from the sweat. That was what happened when you gripped wooden spokes for hours. The splinter that had pricked his palm didn't help. He was the twenty-second captain to bleed and sweat behind the oak wheel. If things ever calmed down, he was going to have Rodger sand it smooth and apply a new coat of varnish.

He reminded himself how lucky he was. The rudders were fixed, the ship was clear of the storm, and Magnolia's snooping was no longer a problem. Her death was an unfortunate accident. There would be those who disagreed with his decision to keep the turbofans going, but now he was faced with another major decision: Should he risk more Hell Divers on a mission to check out the coordinates of the Hilltop Bastion and keep his promise to Katrina, or keep flying south in search of parts and fuel cells?

A rap sounded on the door. He sat up straighter and flattened the wrinkles on his uniform as Katrina walked in and closed the door behind her. She was wearing an expression he knew all too well. The crow's-feet around her green eyes were more pronounced when she was angry.

"Captain, Commanders Everhart, Weaver, and Bolden are on the way here with their teams. Ensign Hunt has the ship on autopilot. We're currently sailing through clear skies."

"I know you're upset," Jordan began.

Katrina tossed her braid over her shoulder. "Magnolia was my friend, and now she's probably dead. And for what?"

"*For what?* Really?" Jordan knitted his brow and clasped his hands behind his back. "For the sake of the child inside you. For every life on this ship. She was a loose cannon, Katrina. You know that. It's not my fault she fell. She almost killed the other divers, too!"

"No, she cut herself free to *save* them."

He hadn't realized that Magnolia sacrificed herself to save Michael and Layla. It was an odd choice for someone that seemed obsessed with self-preservation, and also an honorable choice. But there was no denying she was also a thorn in his side and always had been. Magnolia had started her tumultuous career as a Hell Diver after she was caught stealing. Like many other citizens of the ship she was given a choice—spend her years in the brig, or spend her years diving.

Jordan sighed inwardly. Giving her life so Michael and Layla could live was a noble sacrifice and was the best gift Magnolia could have given the ship. It solved Jordan's problem, and it kept two of the best divers alive.

"You could have shut off the turbofans when Commander Everhart asked you. We still would have cleared the storm."

Jordan did his best to remain calm. This was why officers weren't supposed to sleep together. He was no longer just her captain, and she was no longer just his XO.

"I'm sorry," he said, reaching out for her hand.

"Don't apologize to me!" She jerked her hand back and rested it on her stomach. "I know you didn't like her."

He reached out hesitantly and touched Katrina's arm.

"I did what I thought was best, and I would do it again if I thought it would save the ship and our baby. That's why Captain Ash handed the reins to me. She trusted me to make decisions like this. If I let my emotions get in the way, we would have crashed a long time ago."

Katrina's lip quivered, and she looked away, tears welling in her eyes. A knock on the door snapped them both back to attention. She turned her back and wiped the tears away as Jordan opened the door.

The bridge beyond the conference room was dim, but he could clearly see the disconcerted looks of Hell Divers standing on the platform outside the room. Every diver on the ship had shown up. At the front stood Michael, shoulder-length blond hair pulled into a short ponytail. His blue eyes radiated anger. He was breathing like a wild animal ready to attack.

The militia soldiers on the bridge looked in Jordan's direction, but he refrained from calling them over. He could handle the divers on his own. Never in the history of the *Hive* had a Hell Diver and a captain had anything more than words.

"Come in, Commander Everhart," Jordan said curtly. "Bolden and Weaver, too. The rest of you can wait ..." He trailed off as he saw Xavier Rodriguez—grizzled beard, square jaw clamped shut. He stood at the end of the line of divers, his crazed eyes locked on Jordan. He had come at last for his revenge.

Jordan shut his eyes for a second.

When he opened them again, Rodger Mintel stood where X had been a moment ago.

The vision sent a chill up Jordan's spine. He often saw ghosts in his dreams, when X came to kill him in his sleep, but this was the first time Jordan had seen him while awake. Would he start seeing Magnolia's ghost now, too?

"Sir," Katrina said. "Should we get started?"

Jordan clenched his jaw. He was losing his edge. He had to maintain control.

"Yes," he said, more abruptly than he had intended. He saw the hurt and anger in Katrina's eyes, but he couldn't apologize now. Couldn't afford to look weak in front of the Hell Diver commanders.

He moved to close the door, but Michael stopped him by pressing his palm against it.

"Layla deserves to be here, Captain."

Michael held Jordan's gaze for a tense moment. The younger man was shorter by half a head, but his shoulders were broad and there was something in the set of his jaw. Jordan quickly calculated the possible outcomes of this scenario. If he forced a confrontation with Michael, the other divers would choose sides, exposing Jordan's weak position.

Jordan stepped aside a fraction of an inch.

Layla stepped inside, and he shut the door behind her. He strode over to the seat that Ash had sat in before him. Katrina took a seat to his right, and Weaver took the chair next to his, but Layla, Michael, and Andrew remained standing.

"I'm very sorry about Magnolia," Jordan said.

"All due respect, but screw that, Captain," Michael said. "An apology isn't going to bring her back. What I want is a search party to make sure she's really dead, or to bring her back if she survived."

"If she made it past the turbofans, she could have reached the surface," Layla said quietly, almost as if she herself didn't believe it. "Is it possible ...?"

Jordan looked to his XO. Katrina shook her head. "We haven't confirmed her death, but we aren't picking up a beacon or any transmissions."

Weaver laced his fingers together and bowed his head. "If we haven't heard from her by now, then we all know she didn't make it."

A voice of reason, Jordan thought. He nodded at the ship's senior diver.

"No," Michael said, "we don't. The electrical storm could be messing with the signals. It happens all the time. You know that, Weaver."

"I want to believe she could be alive," Weaver said. "I was hard on her, but I cared deeply for Magnolia. But I just don't see how she could have made it past the turbines. And even if she did, the storm would have finished her."

"I didn't hear or see anything after she got sucked under the ship," Michael said. "How about you, Layla?"

Layla, defiant, folded her arms across her chest. "Nope." Her voice was louder this time.

"And no one else did, either," Michael said. "You have to send a team down there to look for her. Every single one of the divers has already volunteered."

"We have to try," Layla said. "I'm with Michael."

Andrew nodded. "Least we could do, Cap."

Katrina cracked a smile and didn't bother hiding it from Jordan.

"I hate to be the old man here," Weaver said, "but we need to be cautious. The radiation levels in this area are sky high, and there will be creatures down there. We know that from the transmission."

"What transmission?" Michael asked.

Jordan pushed the captain's chair away from the table and put his palms flat on the surface again. "Listen, I know losing Magnolia is incredibly difficult for everyone. She was one of the best. Her final act was a truly noble sacrifice. She's a hero."

"No," Michael said. "She's a Hell Diver. That's what we do. You'd know that if you ever left—"

"Watch yourself," Jordan said. "I've been helping keep this ship in the sky since the days when you were wearing a tinfoil hat."

Layla and Andrew stood behind Michael, their expressions

thunderous. Weaver looked between the two groups and slowly ran two fingers over his gray handlebar mustache.

"What transmission?" Michael asked again. His voice was calm, steady, but Jordan could see he had gotten under the diver's skin with the last jab.

There was no way to avoid telling them now. Better to let them in on part of the truth than risk their digging into the rest of his secrets. "A few hours ago, Ensign Hunt picked up a radio transmission from the surface. It was a distress call from someplace called Hilltop Bastion."

Layla reached over and grabbed Michael's hand. The gesture made Jordan glance in Katrina's direction. She still wouldn't look him in the eye. Instead, she leaned over the table and activated the monitor. A holographic display emerged over the table. She typed at the keyboard, and a topographic map of Charleston spread over the white surface.

Michael, Layla, and Andrew all took seats and studied the blue contour lines that described the location of Hilltop Bastion.

Jordan couldn't believe he was considering a mission to scout the coordinates. He tried to keep his face expressionless as he cut in before anyone could ask the questions he knew were coming.

"Captain Maria Ash listed the settlement as one of many potential areas where there could be survivors. But we all know, the odds are next to nothing. We're talking two hundred and sixty years, folks. No one could survive on the surface that long."

"We've been in the air that long," Michael said. "What makes you think people couldn't survive underground if we can up here?"

"Because we don't have monsters in the sky," Jordan replied. He nodded at his XO. "Go ahead and play the audio file, Katrina."

She typed in a command, and the wall speakers crackled.

"This is Governor Rhonda Meredith of the Hilltop Bastion, requesting support from anyone out there. The—"

Static.

"We're low on food and ammunition. We can't keep them back much longer. Please, please send support to the following coordinates..."

Jordan raised his hand, and the audio stopped.

"Ensign Hunt was able to decipher the rest of the message and provide the coordinates," Katrina said, "but we have no idea how old this SOS is."

"Even if the people are gone, this place sounds like a potential treasure trove of supplies and fuel cells," Layla said.

"And potential threats." Jordan looked at each diver in turn. "You heard the audio. Something was trying to get in."

He gave the team leaders a moment to digest the information, hoping they would change their minds about the mission. But he could see they were ready to climb into their launch tubes.

Michael and Weaver exchanged looks. "Worth a shot," the older diver said.

Jordan stood and pulled on his cuffs. Everyone else stood up in unison.

"I've made my decision," he said. "I'll agree to send two—and *only* two—divers to the surface to scout the facility for supplies."

"I'd like to volunteer, sir," Michael said immediately. "I can look for Magnolia while I'm down there."

"Then I'm going, too," Layla added.

Jordan shook his head. "That's precisely why I'm sending Weaver and Bolden."

"Sir, please," Michael said. "It's the right thing to do. If there's even a small chance that Magnolia could still be alive, then we have to look for her. Like we should have done for X."

Jordan glanced at Michael. Was that a dig to pay him back for the foil-hat comment, or did Michael actually know something about X?

"I saw X die," Weaver said. "So did Magnolia and Katrina. You think we didn't do everything we could?"

Katrina hugged herself, her eyes shining.

"I know ..." Michael said, his voice trailing off.

Jordan scrutinized the young man for a second. He could read people well, and his instincts told him that Michael didn't know anything.

"I can't risk you two going on a futile search for Magnolia. She's dead. So is X. The dead don't come back. Is that understood?"

The room fell silent, the words stinging everyone in it. Jordan cursed himself. He had slipped, and badly. He had to mitigate the damage he had just caused with his insensitive words.

"If Weaver picks up her beacon after he lands," Jordan said, "then he has permission to look for her. But that is not the primary mission. We're already on an energy curtailment, Commander. Weaver's priority is to find fuel cells."

"With all due respect—" Michael began again.

Jordan held up his hand. The diver might not wear his ridiculous tinfoil hat anymore, but he was still barely more than a child. "Commander Everhart, I recommend that you not finish that sentence."

"I'll check out the coordinates, Captain," Weaver said. He scratched at his gray mustache. "If there are supplies down there, I'll find 'em."

"Good." Jordan looked toward the door and said, "Dismissed."

Michael was the last to leave. He hesitated in the doorway.

"That is all, Commander," Jordan said.

"Captain, I'm talking to you man to man here. Do you promise me that if Weaver finds her beacon, he can search for her?"

"I'm a man of my word," Jordan said with a brusque nod.

"Thank you, sir," Michael said.

He shut the door, leaving Jordan alone to contemplate the

mission. As Captain, Jordan prided himself on his word, and on keeping the secrets that kept the ship in the sky. Sometimes, those things conflicted, but not today. Weaver was welcome to search for Magnolia, but he wouldn't find her alive.

EIGHT

Michael placed his helmet in his locker and traced his finger over the Raptor logo. Nothing in his young life had ever meant so much to him. The symbol represented more than his team—it was the seal that bound the divers together in life and death. His father and X had been Raptors, and when Michael dived, he felt as if they were with him.

He shut the door and looked for Layla. The launch bay was teeming with activity, and it took him a moment to find her, standing at the edge of the growing crowd of techs and divers. Michael wasn't the only one anxious to get back out there. He caught her eye and waved her over to the lockers.

"*We* should be going," she said. "Not Weaver and definitely not Andrew. She's our teammate, not theirs. They don't care if she lives or dies."

He shook his head. "They care."

She reached out and grazed his arm with her fingers. "I'm sorry, I shouldn't have said that. I know they care. I'm just so frustrated and confused."

They stood there in silence for a few moments, watching the activity in the bay. It had been a few weeks since the launch tubes last opened. Divers tended to get antsy between dives. Everyone here was on edge and eager to get started. Even the civilians in the corridor beyond the launch bay were asking questions—questions that no one was going to answer.

While Weaver and Andrew geared up, Michael made his decision. He might not be able to rescue Magnolia, but there was something he had to do.

He kissed Layla on the cheek and turned away.

"You're not going to stick around?" she asked. She scuffed the floor with her boot, and her eyes flicked upward. Layla didn't play poker with the other divers, but if she ever did, Michael would be able to read her like a book.

He knew what was coming next.

"You're running away, aren't you? Going wherever it is you go when you're upset. Without me. You should be telling Jordan to fuck himself and then leading a full team to the surface." She was speaking faster now. "You're the commander of Team Raptor, Michael."

Michael closed his eyes to rein in his temper. It always came back to some variation on the same old fight. Layla was passionate and impulsive. She did whatever she believed was right, and thought about the consequences later if she thought about them at all. He admired that about her, but sometimes it made him want to scream. Disobeying the captain could result in their both being recalled from duty—or worse, get them a stint in the stockade.

"I'm talking to you, Michael Everhart," Layla said.

"And you're being unreasonable, Layla Brower. We have to pick our battles. You and I both agreed to that."

Apparently, his calm, logical approach had been the wrong tactic. Her eyes were bright with anger, but she didn't answer.

"There's something I have to do," he said, running out of both time and patience. "I'll be back in an hour or so."

"Whatever," Layla said. Her eyes homed in on her launch tube. That made Michael pause. He couldn't leave her here. No doubt, she would bribe one of the techs to let her dive, or stow away in one of the drop crates, or do something else equally rash.

"You want to come with me?"

Layla's eyes flitted to his. "Where are you going?"

"Trust me?"

She hesitated less than a second. "Yes."

He smiled, relieved. "Okay. I ... okay. Let's get out of here."

They walked through a throng of variously colored coveralls: engineers in red, technicians in yellow, Hell Divers in black. Several militia soldiers stood at the doors, but a crowd was already forming outside. Launches were always off-limits to civilians, but that didn't stop them from trying to sneak a glance.

Michael scanned the room for Captain Jordan. It appeared that he hadn't shown up for this one. Unlike Captain Ash, he didn't like venturing outside the bridge, especially to the lower decks or the launch bay. Michael couldn't even remember the last time the captain had been present for a launch.

In Captain Jordan's place, Katrina walked into the bay and ordered the doors shut. She was an older version of Layla: tough, smart, and stubborn. He had heard that Katrina was once romantically involved with X, but looking at her now, in her sleek white uniform and with her hair pulled back in a severe braid, Michael couldn't imagine it.

He and Layla walked around a cluster of technicians working on Weaver's tube. Weaver was loading a shell into the open break of his blaster. Extra shells and magazines for his assault rifle stuck out of his vest. Michael didn't need to ask why he looked as if he was preparing to go to war. They all had heard the audio from the Hilltop Bastion.

Weaver regarded them both with a nod. He dropped a flare into the weapon and snapped the break shut.

"Don't worry," he said. "If Magnolia's down there, I'll find her. But don't hold your breath. Even if she survived the turbofans ..."

Layla dropped Michael's hand and cut Weaver off. "She's alive, I know it. I can feel it in my heart."

Weaver holstered the blaster and scratched the back of his ear. "I hope you're right."

Michael reached out to shake Weaver's hand. "Good luck, sir."

"Damn, I hate it when people say that. Son, it's not luck. It's experience."

Michael wanted to remind Weaver how his father had died, how X had been lost despite being the most experienced Hell Diver in the history of the *Hive*, but now wasn't the time.

They shook hands and parted. A few tubes down, Andrew was bending over a box of supplies. He held up an assault rifle with the Raptor logo on the side.

"Yo, Mikey. Mind if I borrow your gun?"

"As long as you bring it back," Michael said. He didn't really want to say yes. He hadn't forgotten the way Andrew used to bully him when they were kids. Then again, if Andrew hadn't kept flicking Michael's tinfoil hat off his head, Layla wouldn't have lost her temper and kicked him in the nuts. Michael almost smiled at the memory. That had been the day he realized that Layla liked him.

They all had matured over the past decade. Mostly. Andrew was still a meathead, but they were all Hell Divers now. Diving had a way of bringing them closer together. They trusted the man or woman in the next drop tube with their lives. Magnolia had proved that when she chose to sever the rope rather than pull them all down.

Andrew was pulling extra magazines from the crate and stuffing them into his vest as Michael and Layla approached.

"You think there are Sirens down there?" he asked.

"*Something's* down there," Michael said. "Let me check one thing before you go."

He held his hand out, and Andrew handed it over. He raised the rifle toward the bulkhead. On the last dive, his shots had been ever so slightly wide left. He twisted the knob and handed the rifle back to Andrew.

"You see Sirens, you run. You got it?"

Andrew gave a toothy yellow grin. "Don't worry, I'll bring your gun back, Mikey."

"And Magnolia," Layla said. "Bring her back, too."

An enthusiastic voice called from the crowd of technicians and divers. "Hey, wait for me!"

It was Rodger Mintel, carrying his helmet.

"Whoa! What the hell are you doing, man?" Michael asked.

"What it looks like." Rodger stopped at his launch tube. "I'm going with them."

Andrew stepped in. "Cap said only Weaver and me get to go."

"Captain Jordan changed his mind." Katrina was standing behind them, her arms crossed firmly over her chest. The tattooed head of a raptor showed on her forearm.

Layla took a step toward Katrina. "If he's going, then so am I!"

"We've authorized a third diver and selected Rodger," she said. "We need his engineering experience."

Rodger tucked something into his vest pocket so quickly that Michael couldn't see what it was. He didn't have to guess why Rodger had volunteered to dive. If Layla were stranded on the surface, nothing short of death would keep Michael from diving. He and some of the other divers had a pool going about when Rodger and Magnolia would finally get together.

He turned his attention back to Katrina. "And what about *my* experience?"

"Don't worry, Commander." Rodger flashed a nervous smile. "I got this."

"I hold rank," Michael said, "and I'm respectfully requesting you send me instead."

Katrina's sharp gaze fell on him, but he wasn't intimidated by her tattoos or her reputation. Or the fact that she was the captain's mistress.

"Captain Jordan has made his decision, Commander."

"Come on, LT," Michael said. "We all know you have special powers of persuasion when it comes to the captain."

"*Excuse me?*" Katrina said. She put her hands on her hips. "You're way out of line, Commander."

Layla squeezed his hand. "Don't," she whispered.

Biting the inside of his lip, he held Katrina's gaze for a few seconds before finally backing down.

Katrina nodded. "That's what I thought." She turned away from the divers and cupped her hands over her mouth. "Everyone out! We're clear for launch!"

The technicians finished their final checks on the three launch tubes while Rodger, Weaver, and Andrew fastened their helmets.

Michael patted Rodger on the back as he stared wistfully at his usual launch tube. This was utter bullshit, but there was nothing he could do about it. They left the room with everyone else and piled into the dark hallway. Michael could hardly see the grimy faces of the lower-deckers in the dim light. Bodies that hadn't been washed in weeks pressed up against him as he and Layla walked away from the launch bay.

"Where are they diving?" one man asked.

"Why aren't *you* going, Commander?" asked another.

Michael turned back to the bay just as the militia guards pulled on the massive doors to seal them shut. Through the narrowing gap, he saw Rodger climb into his tube and throw him a thumbs-up.

Knowing that Rodger cared for Magnolia was reassuring. Perhaps a little bit of love was exactly what this mission needed. That and a miracle.

* * * * *

Rodger stood in his drop tube, listening to the countdown. This was his tenth dive—five short of the magic number. The average was fifteen dives before ending up as a splat on the surface, or a lightning fritter on the Hell Diver highway. Of course, X's legendary ninety-seven dives had thrown the curve way off. A lot of men and women had to get dead their first dive to balance out his record.

But Rodger didn't plan on being one of those. Nope, he had two missions right now. One: locate a special section inside the Hilltop Bastion that Jordan wanted him to search. Two: rescue Magnolia and sweep her off her steel-toed boots, if possible. The wood carving inside his vest pocket was supposed to help with the second objective. The piece fit nicely next to the ITC access card Jordan had given him.

In the tubes on either side of his, Andrew and Weaver were likely feeling what Hell Divers described as "the rush." The other divers were all addicted to it, to varying degrees, but Rodger had never experienced the heady blend of fear and adrenaline. The fear was too strong. Today, though, he felt different as he waited for the glass doors to whisper open and drop him into the hell below. Because today Magnolia was down there, and he was going to bring her home or die trying.

"Thirty seconds," Ty announced over the channel.

"Copy that," Weaver replied. "Ready to dive."

Rodger tried to hold in a belch. He was hungover—or, more accurately, still a little drunk—after last night. The stimulant he had taken this morning was keeping him awake, but it had soured his stomach.

Captain Jordan hadn't seemed to care, or even notice, when giving Rodger the mission to find the room that housed cryogenic chambers. Jordan hadn't been forthcoming about what he expected him to find there, but the captain had insisted that he tell no one of the mission until he was on the surface.

Rodger let the belch escape as he contemplated whether being privy to secret information was a good or a bad thing. While he didn't like Jordan, it was nice to be entrusted with a quest. Never in his life had he been in charge of anything like this. He wouldn't let the captain down. Nope, he would find this bunker and whatever prizes it held. But first, he would rescue Magnolia.

The red glow swirling in his tube shifted to a cool blue. Klaxons faded in the background. Rodger clamped down on his mouth guard and checked the Velcro flap of the pocket containing Magnolia's present. His vest was stuffed with magazines for his rifle, flares and shotgun shells for his blaster, and his engineering gear. He wore a duty belt containing everything he would need on the surface.

The voice of Captain Jordan fired over the channel. "Good luck, divers. Remember your objectives and complete the primary mission first."

Yeah, yeah, Captain. No scavenging for lumber and no searching for lost girls. Asshole!

"We dive so humanity survives," Weaver said.

Andrew and Rodger both muttered the words along with him.

Rodger's thoughts turned to his parents, as they always did before a drop. They had hugged him goodbye, but they hadn't said the actual word. They never said goodbye; they always said, "Catch ya later."

He smiled. Pop's birthday was coming up soon. Maybe Rodger would bring him back something from the surface. In his heart, he was hoping to bring back his future bride, but it was too early even to voice such hopes. Still, he hoped that someday soon he would be able to introduce Magnolia to his folks. He was sure they would love her as much as ...

"Prepare for launch," said Ty's voice.

Rodger wrapped his arms around his chest as the final warning beeped. The glass floor opened just as he locked his gloved fingers together. It was an effort to keep from flailing at the sides of the tube as he fell—something he had done the first six dives.

He felt a moment of numbness as the sky opened up below him. He clenched his muscles—a reflex the other divers had tried to train out of him. No matter how many times they told him to dive loose, he tensed up like a wound clock spring.

As he fell, he arched and positioned his body on the mattress of air so he could see the *Hive*. The turtle-like hulk seemed to float effortlessly. He scanned the turbofans, almost afraid to look, but they whirred too fast for him to spot any blood on them. An instant later, crosswinds sent him tumbling away from the view.

To the east, lightning cut through the darkness. It was hard to gauge how far away the storm was, but the bolts were impressive. Long ago, when he was in school, he had read that lightning could be hotter than the surface of the sun. He hadn't believed it until he saw his childhood friend Hal struck on a dive. The blast had raced through his body, blowing out his fingers and the bottoms of his feet and taking off the top of his skull.

Rodger blinked away the memory of Hal's smoldering remains and craned his neck one last time to see the airship.

"Catch ya later, Mom and Pop," Rodger whispered as the ship vanished.

He shifted his attention to his HUD. The readings were all normal. They were at eighteen thousand feet and falling through clear skies.

Weaver and Andrew had fanned out in intervals of a thousand feet. Rodger saw the glow of Weaver's battery unit to the west. They all were diving in the stable falling position that divers used in fair weather: arms loosely out, elbows and knees bent at right angles. As Rodger blasted through the clouds, he caught a glimpse of lightning below. The wall of black clouds disguised the strike, and the visible bolt quickly waned, leaving a residue of blue light.

On his HUD, the altitude ticked down. They were already down to fifteen thousand feet, and he was falling at just under a hundred miles an hour.

Static crackled over the open channel. "Rodger Dodger, Pipe, be ready to nosedive. Looks like a layer of electrical activity pushing in below."

The dark clouds were deceiving, like a clean bandage hiding an infected wound. Sometimes, it was hard to tell exactly what you were falling toward, until it was too late.

Another pocket of crosswinds took Rodger, sending him spinning toward Weaver.

"Watch it!" The words were difficult to make out over the crackling static.

Rodger brought his arms to his sides, kicked his boots together, and speared through the sky in a headfirst dive, veering away from Weaver, who was still getting head-down.

As Rodger looked down, the floor of clouds lit up with bright strikes. His electronics suddenly turned to gibberish. His HUD winked on and off.

Shit. NOT good!

A wave of nausea boiled up from his guts. He could taste the bile. It was almost as nasty as the herbal slime his mom forced him to drink whenever he was sick. The comm channel broke into a jumble of words and static. Whatever Weaver was trying to say, Rodger couldn't hear him. He focused on trying not to puke as he cut through the clouds like Superman.

"We dive so humanity survives!" he cried. "I'm coming, Magnolia!"

NINE

Magnolia hung from the tangle of canopy and shroud lines, hardly daring to move. She wanted to look at her left arm, but she was too afraid—if the girder had cut through her suit, she wouldn't last the day.

She had heard noises in the street below. Whatever had made them was gone now, but she could see shadows moving around down there.

They moved with stealth, as if they were hunting.

If this were a normal dive, she would have had weapons and supplies. She would also have had her Hell Diver brothers and sisters for support. Instead, she had a ripped chute and a mean headache.

Another shadow below snaked around the shells of vehicles. She looked closer, but it melted away. She activated her NVGs with a bump of her chin. The vivid green bones of the building filled her visor, but she still couldn't get a lock on the moving shapes.

She tried to open a line to the *Hive* by tapping the comm link. White noise filled her helmet.

"Command, this is Raptor Three," she said as loudly as she dared. "Does anyone copy?"

More static hissed from the speakers.

The storm was still blocking out her signal, or else the *Hive* was too far out of range to pick it up. Another flash from the dark clouds filled the street with even more slinking shadows, which began to fan out like a cloud breaking apart in the sky.

She felt for her tactical knife and remembered that she had lost it in the fall. Leaning down, she stretched to grab the spare tucked inside her boot. Her fingers gripped the handle but slipped off. She breathed out to make her belly smaller and stretched again. This time, she pulled the blade free.

The girder holding her tangled chute and lines groaned in the wind as a flurry of dust and soot came swirling through the scraper's skeletal remains.

Magnolia froze, holding the blade to her chest, eyes combing the terrain. A shadow darted across the asphalt below. Another shifted on the sidewalk. She leaned forward, straining to identify what was down there.

In the green hue of the night vision, she saw that the shadows weren't Sirens or some other mutated monsters after all. They were just ... ghosts. Optical illusions caused by the flashes of lightning.

She checked the layout for an exit route. This place looked as if it had been through hell and never left. Deep burns marred the structural steel, and a carpet of ash and grime covered the floor. Concrete columns, black and heat-chipped, supported the upper floors, but she couldn't fathom how they were still standing. The tower's foundation had settled to the point that the floor sloped at a ten-degree angle. Once she cut herself free, she would have to be careful not to slide down it and out into thin air.

Her exit was an enclosed stairwell a hundred feet away, past one of the pillars. From there, she would make her way down to the street and try to find cover to run a diagnostic test and check the integrity of her suit. Perhaps, on the way, she would find some sort of weapon more substantial than her dinky little knife.

She used the blade to cut her lines one at a time, leaving the left-rear suspension line for last. Then she bent her knees to prepare for the three-foot drop. This was going to make some noise.

She touched the knife to the weighted line, and it parted

with alarming ease. Even favoring the injured ankle, the impact with the floor sent a painful jolt up her leg. She didn't let the pain keep her from moving, though. She ran for the stairway, aware that she was leaving tracks behind her in the ash. Vivid green snags of rebar reached down like tree branches from the ceiling. She ducked them as she ran, trying to balance speed with stealth, supremely aware that a single misstep could put another tear in her suit. Approaching the stairwell entrance, she held the knife loosely, ready to slash and stab.

She scanned the passage leading down to the next floor. Cracks ran everywhere across the floor and walls. At some point in the past 260 years, the stairs had shifted out of true. The top two treads sagged, and the third was broken in two. She leaped to the fourth step and stopped to listen.

The whistling of the wind and the distant crack of thunder echoed through the dead city. It was an eerie and beautiful sound, a change from the everyday noises aboard the airship. This was the real world. This was where humanity was meant to live.

For Magnolia, the greatest wonder of the surface world had been all the different colors to be found. On the ship, almost everything was gray, black, or brown, just like the desolate city outside this scraper. But once, there had been more colors than one could even name. That was what kept her scanning the archives on the ship each night into the morning hours. Whenever she was exploring the surface on a dive, she searched for pastels in particular. Those were her favorites: pink, baby blue, lavender. Those shades soothed and fascinated her, but she was drawn to any scrap or fragment of color. She couldn't wait to see what she would find in the lighthouse, with its fiery red dome.

Another distant crash rolled across the city, echoing through the tower. It was powerful enough to rattle her visor. Though she couldn't see it, she knew that the storm was rolling east over the city.

She continued down the staircase, carefully navigating the skewed and broken steps, knife at the ready. The walls seemed to narrow as she proceeded. Or was that just a trick of the light? She couldn't be sure.

At the first landing, she finally stopped to check herself. A quick glance revealed what she had feared all along: the girder's corner had scraped her armor—and torn her suit. She craned her neck to assess the damage. It had sliced through the layer that insulated her from lightning. Beyond that, she couldn't see whether the secondary layer, the radiation shield, was compromised. At least, the alarm sensors had stopped beeping, although that didn't mean she was in the clear.

She tapped at the screen of her wrist monitor and brought up the control panel. A diagnostic should tell her the status of the suit's radiation shield. Digital telemetry scrolled across the screen. The battery unit was at 50 percent—only about twelve hours of juice. She scrolled through the data, heart rate increasing with each swipe of her finger.

A clatter and snapping from deep in the building distracted her. She lowered her wrist and raised the knife in her other hand.

The sound faded, and silence reclaimed the space. Magnolia waited in the safety of the enclosed stairwell, where the wind couldn't reach her. Listening for the barest creak or rustle, she raised her wrist monitor and continued swiping through the data. The radiation level here was in the red—high enough that Sirens might nest here. The divers still weren't any closer to understanding the monsters' habits or biology. Hell, they didn't even know what the things were or where they had come from. Maybe they were mutant animals, changed by radioactive fallout after the war, though they didn't look much like any of the creatures she had studied in the archives. They couldn't very well bring a specimen back to the *Hive* to examine, either. The ordinary people aboard the ship had no idea what was down here, and it was probably best left that way.

She finally brought up the diagnostic controls for her suit. Across the screen rolled the first good news she had gotten all day:

Suit integrity, 100 percent.

"Thank—"

A clatter like dishes falling on the floor cut her off. A creaking and snapping joined the sound, followed by a crack and a thud.

Something alive was inside the building.

By now, her nervous tension was rising at roughly the same rate the thing below was climbing the stairs.

The noise stopped just as Magnolia turned to run. A cardinal rule of surviving on the surface was never to draw attention to yourself. If she ran now, anything in the building with her would hear it.

The knife in her hand suddenly looked more like a nail file. Sweat dripped down her forehead, but she didn't bat an eye.

Part of her wanted to find a cubby to hide in, but the other side of her nature told her to run. That was the side that had always goaded her into taking risks, such as stealing from the market, or jumping out of a freaking airship onto a planet filled with monsters.

Remember, no dying before you dip your toes in the ocean. That was the deal.

A minute passed in silence.

She had a decision to make: go back up the stairs and look for another way to climb down, or keep moving forward.

Her curious side won, and she moved down to the next step. Her footfall was soft enough that she couldn't even hear it. In another lifetime, Magnolia had been a thief, with a reputation for sneaking in and out of places. It was time to put those skills to work.

Pausing every few steps to listen, she made her way down the flight of stairs without attracting any attention. The next landing opened onto another story. Debris littered the dark tile floor.

A metal chair arm protruded from a pile of concrete rubble. An upside-down table, its legs bent in opposite directions, lay in the dust a few feet away.

Magnolia remembered the Pepsi machine she had discovered in Hades, on X's final dive. The freezing temperatures there had preserved the ancient artifact, but Charleston's climate was much warmer and wetter. Nothing of value seemed to have survived the years.

She continued down the cracked and twisted steps, holding her knife as if she were about to spar with the darkness. Her breath fogged the inside of her visor with every step. The pane was so blurry, she almost didn't see the strange ivy clinging to the wall.

She took another wary step and raised the knife, staring at the first living thing she had seen on the surface in months. The vines grew thicker on the next landing and snaked around the corner.

The sinewy vegetation covered the wall like gigantic cobwebs, each strand ending in barbs as thick as her hand. Magnolia knew better than to touch one of them. Half the shit down here was poisonous, and the other half was carnivorous. She proceeded cautiously down the steps, listening for movement and hugging the rail to keep her distance from the vines.

Halfway down the next flight, the entire stairwell lit up with a pinkish glow. Magnolia flinched and then froze as the barbed heads of stems snapped free of the walls. The labyrinth of vines pulsated and came to life, dozens of them, each twisting and undulating independently of the others.

More pink lights flashed across her path.

This wasn't exactly the sort of pastel she was hoping to find.

Two years ago and a thousand miles to the west, she had come across groves of glowing, tentacled plants like these. Matt Shaw, a diver on Team Angel, had wandered too close. It cost him a leg.

Magnolia had helped hold him down while Andrew sawed through flesh and bone to stop the spread of the venom. Matt had survived, earning himself a cushy job in the water reclamation plant, where he sat and stared at monitors most of the day.

After the accident, Magnolia had visited him. Privately, she had felt that a desk job was the last place she wanted to end up. But right now she would gladly trade with him.

She hugged the opposite side of the stairway as the flora continued to move. The ends waved about as if searching for her. The monstrous vines stretched across the next landing, too, and into the open room beyond. She peered inside, where the pulsating stems all connected to a central trunk growing in the center of the space.

It looked almost like an old-world tree, but twisted and wrong.

Magnolia spotted the cracked hole in the center of the room. The tree thing had grown right up through the floor. But could it really be that big? The tower had to be thirty stories high, and she was still a long way up.

She pressed her back against the wall and steadied her breathing. Never in her forty-seven dives had she seen anything like this.

Keep moving, Mags! You want to see the ocean or not?

Fear crawled through her. She forced herself to take another step. Then a second and a third. With each step, the glowing foliage grew thicker. As she worked her way deeper into the guts of the tower, the vines grew harder to avoid. She plastered herself against the far wall, sidling carefully.

Above the next landing, she could just make out the stenciled characters that read FLOOR 6.

She still had a way to go.

Holding the knife in front of her, Magnolia moved around the next corner. The pinkish lights were blinking frantically now. It was almost as if… but no, that was crazy. The vines couldn't be talking to each other. It was just a plant—a very weird, very big plant.

Her next step made a squishing sound. It was enough to make her cringe, but as she backed up, she saw that she hadn't stepped on one of the vines. The sound came again as she stood still, holding in a breath and tingling with adrenaline.

A noise like a dog chewing on a bone echoed off the walls. The web of vines glowed an angry red, filling the staircase with a ghastly light.

Frozen in place, she breathed silently and did her best not to move. The crunching turned to cracking and then a guttural choking.

She took a cautious step backward at the same moment a shadow flickered across the wall below. The sound of creaking ligaments and bones filled the stairwell. It reminded her of the Sirens, but the thing that emerged was nothing like one of the creatures from Hades. This time, it wasn't an apparition. The thing stretched furry skeletal arms lined with thorns, and raised something over its bulbous head.

Magnolia stumbled backward, falling on her butt. She scooted out of view as the creature skittered up the stairs.

A huge eyeball on a stem poked around the corner. The leathery eyelid snapped over the black pupil several times like a camera shutter before the stem retreated.

Raising the knife in one shaky hand, Magnolia pushed herself up with the other. As soon as she was on her feet, she backed up the steps. The sound prompted a screech, and the furry creature connected to the eyeball bounded around the corner on two peg legs and a third limb connected to its bony chest. The webbed feet and hand slapped the concrete.

Magnolia backed up several more steps, and the creature halted. A vine, dripping pinkish goo, hung from the long, curved beak on its feathery face. Swinging the stem from side to side, it rolled back its head and slurped down the snack.

She finally understood. The vines weren't reacting to her. They were reacting to the beast that was feeding on them.

"Stay back," she said, angling the blade toward the monster. It tilted its eyeball at her as if trying to understand.

"Don't come any closer."

It was the tone, not the words, that mattered. She had often employed the same tone when one of the junior Hell Divers tried to get a little too familiar with her on the night before a dive.

She took another step backward. The creature blinked again, its eyelid snapping open and shut like a hatch. She poked at the air again with her knife. If forced to, she would kill it. The beast was only half her size, but the sharp hooked beak and long talons gave her pause. A single strike from any one of them could tear her suit wide open—and maybe her flesh, too.

A cackle escaped from the open beak. She lunged with the knife to scare it off, but that only seemed to make the creature even more curious.

Magnolia staggered back up another step, brandishing the knife. The foliage continued to glow, filling the passage with pulsing light. The subscreen on her HUD showed that her power was already down to 45 percent.

She was wasting time.

In a swift motion, she swiped at the beast. The blow didn't connect, but the creature flinched and the eyeball reared back. She took off running, back up the stairs. She wasn't sure where she was going, but she could hear the creature chasing her. Another eerie cackle followed her. It sounded as if the creature was trying to speak and throw up at the same time.

She loped up the stairs, her injured ankle hurting but not slowing her down. At the next landing, she went left into the main room. The vines there flared red as she stomped all over them in her haste.

Magnolia leaped over clusters of thick roots. The beast was inside the room now, trying to flank her on the left. She kept moving, matching its pace, keeping it in sight. She could not allow it to get behind her.

Wind rustled her suit as she crossed the room. It was rushing in through the missing windows. She pivoted her helmet slightly so she could see the ocean lapping at the shore less than a mile away. The move cost her dearly. Staggering, she fought to regain her balance as she tripped over a vine. She managed to fight her way upright and continued running, but the floor ended in a sheer drop. The seven-story fall would kill her outright or at least break her legs—in this place, a fate worse than sudden death.

Two options remained: turn and fight, or jump.

Magnolia eyed the nearest building. It was close enough that with a running start, she might make it across. Assuming that the beast wouldn't follow, it was her best way out.

The monster screamed, and she screamed back at it. It was galloping toward her, the stalked eyeball leering.

Magnolia pushed hard, trying not to second-guess her decision. The winking red stems guided her path. In the glow, she saw the vines shifting and breaking away from the surfaces they had grown on. The central trunk creaked and groaned behind her, as if it was coming to life and might attack at any moment. She had thought the one-eyed creature was the biggest threat in the room, but what if she had been wrong?

She shoved her curiosity aside and sprinted toward the ledge. About ten feet lay between her and the sloping edge of the next tower. To clear the gap, she would need to leap as she never had before.

One of the stems snapped free of the concrete and shot

through the air past her helmet. She moved to the right at the last instant. The ground raced by below her as, arms flailing, she jumped. A screech followed her across the gap between the buildings, but that didn't concern her right now.

She was not going to make it.

Her momentum quickly dissipated, and gravity took hold. She reached out for the ledge of the building, but she was still a good five feet away, and then she was falling headfirst toward the pavement.

Time seemed to slow and speed up at the same time. Lightning surged above the city, giving her a snapshot of her landing zone. Derelict vehicles littered rubble-strewn asphalt. Would it hurt more to land on one of them, or should she aim for the bare ground?

Something wrapped around her left ankle, jerking her upward. The abrupt motion put her stomach in her throat. Blood rushed to her head as she stared at the ground, which was now falling away.

Magnolia twisted to look at the vines that had caught her boot. They had snaked up to the floor she jumped from. She caught a flash of movement between two broken pillars. She wasn't the only thing the vegetation had caught. The beast fought the vines wrapped around all three of its limbs. They pulled from all directions, as if determined to tear it apart.

Magnolia did a midair sit-up and grabbed the stems so she faced upward. She hacked at the vines just as the creature above came apart. Stems snapped the two legs and single arm away from the body, carmine blood gushing from the wounds as more vines pulled the torso away from the ledge.

Her heart was beating at double speed now. Red sap oozed as she sawed through one of the vines holding her left boot. It snapped free, and the wounded vine writhed back to the floor above.

She grabbed the remaining stem with one hand and sawed at it with the other. If she cut herself free now, she would fall to the street. Her only chance was to wait until she was close enough to the building she had jumped from to grab on to something.

Above, dozens of the stems waited at the ledge, their snakelike heads weaving back and forth in search for prey.

Magnolia waited for the right moment, then gripped the vine right above her saw marks and cut herself free.

The shortened tentacle pulled her back to the floor she had jumped from. Her helmet and shoulders rose above the ledge, and in the hellish red glow she saw something that took her breath away.

Hundreds of vines were squirming around the central tree, which had split down the middle. Something that looked horribly like a mouth surrounded the torso of the one-eyed beast, and jagged teeth the size of her hand chopped the creature to pieces.

A dozen of the vines shot toward her, and she let go of the one she had cut. She was dropping again, this time not to the ground but to the next floor. The vines there pulsated at her presence, but Magnolia was off and running by the time they started crawling toward her.

Nothing was going to stop her from reaching the ocean—especially not some big, ugly tree with teeth.

* * * * *

Weaver had pushed all his thoughts and worries aside the moment the launch tube doors opened.

He led the other two divers through the clouds, constantly checking the subscreen in the upper right corner of his HUD. The data was a jumble of meaningless characters because of the electrical currents they were passing through. The hair on his body prickled. He was giving the storm a run for its money, as he always did.

One day, the storm would win, but maybe not today.

Weaver was falling at 150 miles per hour. This was his eighty-ninth time reaching terminal velocity in his career as a Hell Diver. He had shattered all records but the one held by Xavier Rodriguez. And somehow, he continued to make it back from each dive. But part of that was due to the so-called safe dives Captain Jordan had assigned them. Jordan favored green-zone jumps, where the biggest threat was lightning. This was the first dive into a red zone in over a year, and now he wasn't sure he would ever break X's record.

Thunder boomed, farther away now. The storm had weakened, but sporadic lightning still flashed across his flight path. He bit down on his worn mouth guard. The piece of plastic should have been jettisoned from the *Hive* with the rest of the trash long ago. But he had kept it for sentimental reasons ever since the last dive from his home ship, *Ares*, when he lost everyone and everything but the equipment he was carrying.

He searched the clouds below for a glimpse of the city that could possibly harbor survivors. Janga had said that a man would lead them to the promised land, but the transmission from Hilltop Bastion had been a woman's voice. Weaver hadn't told any of the other divers about his visits to Janga. They wouldn't understand. Worse, they might laugh at him. Hell, right now the prophecy looked silly to him, too.

The bed of wind pushed up against him as he slowly turned his body in the air to look for Andrew and Rodger. Both divers were to his east, the cool blue of their battery packs sparkling in the clouds. Weaver was glad Jordan had sent Rodger, but he feared that an extra team member wouldn't be enough. He had no idea what they would find on the surface. Maybe there was a bunker full of supplies. Maybe Magnolia would be waiting for them, wondering why it had taken them so damn long to show up. Maybe Rodger would give her the toy he had made her, or whatever it was, and they would live happily ever after in the promised land. But for now, Weaver just needed to get his team safely to the surface.

As the storm weakened, the data on his HUD sorted itself out, and he bumped his chin pad. "Apollo One and Raptor Two, you guys okay?"

"I'm good," Andrew replied.

Rodger let out a belch. "I don't feel so good, Commander. I think I'm going to have—"

"Keep your cheeks clenched. That's an order." Hadn't he just been thinking how glad he was about having Rodger along? The guy was brilliant, but he needed to figure out when it was time to be serious.

As the thunder waned, Weaver turned his mind to the next hazard. The landing could be just as deadly as the lightning. His neck ached as he tilted his head. Everything hurt when you were over fifty years old, especially if you had spent most of those years trying to get yourself killed.

His HUD showed an altitude of four thousand feet. They had to be getting close.

All at once, the city bloomed into view, outlined in green by his night-vision optics. He brought his arms out to his sides and bent his knees to pull up out of the nosedive and slow his descent.

The coordinates for the Hilltop Bastion were two miles east of here. Two miles of uncharted terrain in the middle of a red zone—a trek that didn't exactly buoy him up with confidence.

At two thousand feet, he pulled his rip cord. The suspension lines tightened as the chute inflated and slowed his fall.

He licked the bottom of his handlebar mustache—a nervous habit he had developed over the years. He switched off his night vision to study the city with unaided eyes. He instantly saw something he had missed with the optics.

Andrew's deep voice boomed over the comms. "Angel One, do you see what I'm seeing?"

Weaver blinked just to make sure his eyes weren't playing tricks.

"Angel One?"

"Roger that, Pipe," Weaver muttered. He blinked twice more. To the east, waves slapped against a rocky shoreline, but it wasn't the ocean that Weaver was staring at. It was a tower not far from the water. A scraper pulsed red from the inside, as if it had a massive battery unit for a heart.

"What the hell *is* that?" Rodger said.

"I've never seen anything like it," Andrew replied.

The numbers on Weaver's HUD ticked down. They were at one thousand feet now.

"We're two miles off course," he said. "Follow me."

He grabbed the toggles and headed west, away from the ocean, but he couldn't force his gaze away from the tower. The groves of glowing bushes were the only thing even remotely close to what he was witnessing, but even those didn't compare to this.

"Commander, you think we should check that out?" Rodger asked. "What if it's some kind of settlement?"

"Aw, hell no, man," Andrew said. "That scraper may be a settlement, but it sure as shit ain't humans."

"Sir?" Rodger repeated.

"Negative. We proceed to the coordinates."

The three divers came together in a V formation as they sailed over the ruined city. Weaver finally pulled his gaze away from the tower and did what he had promised he would do. Bumping his chin pad, he selected the open frequency. If Magnolia was out there, she would have her set tuned to the channel.

"Raptor 3, this is Angel One. Do you copy?"

Weaver raised his wrist-mounted monitor to check the coordinates again as a wave of static crackled inside his helmet. The noise didn't surprise him. He had already resigned himself to the idea that Magnolia was dead. It was easier that way. Hope hurt.

"Princess, you out there?" he said, trying one last time.

White noise was the only reply.

"Magnolia," Rodger said over the comms. "Please."

They sailed over girders and piles of debris. Vehicles littered the streets below like the carapaces of dead insects. It was a sight all too familiar to Weaver. There was no way humans could have survived down there for centuries among the monsters and bombarded by all those rads.

There was no one to rescue down here. If they were lucky, they might find some salvage or a couple of fuel cells, but Weaver had already written this dive off as a waste of resources.

A wave of static broke, and a voice rang out over the channel.

"I'm here!"

Heavy breathing sounds filled the speakers, as if the person on the other side of the comms was running.

Weaver's heart skipped.

"Princess, that you?"

"My name," the voice panted, "is Magnolia Katib."

There was a pause, and before Weaver could reply, she said, "I hope you brought me my two hundred credits, Angel One."

He felt the smile crack below his mustache. "You'll get a chance to win 'em back," he said. "Relay your coordinates, and we'll rendezvous."

Several agonizing seconds passed before she replied, her words garbled by static.

"Vines are everywhere ... I can't get away ..."

"Magnolia!" Rodger shouted. "We're coming. Just hang on!"

Weaver snapped out of his trance. They were halfway to the coordinates of the Hilltop Bastion. He could see the raised earth in the distance, but Magnolia's beacon wasn't showing up on his minimap.

Weaver dipped his finger and thumb into his vest pocket and rubbed the old-world coin. He couldn't very well flip it in the air right now, and it wasn't going to help him decide what came next, but he found massaging the smooth surface with a gloved finger and thumb calming.

"Magnolia, relay your position," Weaver said.

"I'm in a tower, but my monitor isn't working!"

"What do you see? Give us something."

"Vines. All I see are vines ... and ... the ocean. I can see the waves."

Weaver's eyes flitted from his HUD to the ground. Forced to make a decision, he said, "Pipe, you and Rodger head to the target. I'll go find her."

"Yes sir," Andrew replied.

Another silent pause over the comms.

Rodger spoke next. "Bring her back, Commander, or I'm coming for you!"

Weaver pulled his right toggle and turned east toward the glowing tower. Magnolia didn't need to respond with her coordinates. He had a feeling he was already looking at her position.

TEN

Michael and Layla walked through the hallways of the *Hive* in silence. She didn't ask where they were going, and he didn't tell her. They passed through the wing where most of the upper-deckers lived. Intricate drawings marked the floor and the bulkheads, providing a glimpse into the lives of those who had lived here over the centuries.

Utility pipes snaked along the ceiling, carrying helium, water, and sewage. Ahead, an engineer stood on a ladder, working to seal a leaking joint in a red helium pipe. Michael nodded at him as they passed underneath.

Open hatches allowed a glimpse into life on the *Hive*. Inside the first quarters, a stained couch missing all but one of its pillows was nestled against a wall. Deborah, a staffer who worked on the bridge, sat on it reading a book with no front cover. She looked up and smiled at them. Layla waved back.

Next was the room where Michael had spent many of his younger years. Layla picked up her pace as they neared the hatch marked with a drawing of the sun.

"You don't want to stop?" Michael asked.

"For what?"

He shrugged even though he wanted to encourage her to stop. Ever since her parents died, she had avoided this place. She didn't even look at the smiling yellow sun that she had drawn when she was a little girl.

They had reached an understanding that certain areas of the ship were no-go zones. For Michael, it was the farm. That place triggered too many painful memories. The sight of the room Layla had grown up in was her trigger. She dropped Michael's hand and hurried down the hall, clearly unhappy that he had brought her this way.

Ahead, a sign for the water treatment plant hung from the bulkhead. Layla waited for him at the junction. He jerked his chin to the right, and they continued past two militia soldiers guarding the upper-decker wing. Two more stood outside the entrance to the plant.

Michael kept moving. They were almost there. He felt for the sealed envelope in his pocket and tried not to think about anything but what he needed to do.

Raised voices echoed down the hall as they approached the trading post. Several civilians loitered in the open space outside. A thin man with a sharp jawline and a shaved head approached Layla. He wore a brown coat, and black trousers that were two sizes too big.

"Not interested," she said.

He looked to Michael, but then scurried away when two militia soldiers approached.

"You at it again, Jake?" one of the guards said. "I told you, you can't loiter here."

The man held up his hands and grinned. "What? I didn't do nothin'."

Michael kept walking, through the throng of people filing out of a hatch at the end of the hall.

"When are you planning to tell me where we're headed?" Layla asked.

He glanced toward the entrance to the lower decks. She reared back.

"What the hell are we going down there for?"

A woman holding a basket of potatoes stopped beside them.

"Would either of you like to—"

"No," Layla snapped.

She grabbed Michael's arm and dragged him to the edge of the corridor.

"Tin, what's going on with you? Why won't you tell me anything?"

He ran his hand through his hair to comb it back out of his eyes. "Because I know you wouldn't come if I told you."

She traced a finger across his arm—a gentle movement. "You can always talk to me."

"You said you trusted me."

A nod. "I do, but we should really be with the other divers, monitoring the mission below."

Michael pulled an envelope out of his pocket. She tilted her head to one side.

"Is that why we stopped in our room?"

He nodded.

"Well, what is it?"

"Something Captain Ash gave me before she died." Michael felt the smooth paper. He had spent hundreds of hours staring at the envelope when Layla was sleeping, wondering what it contained. But he had kept his promise to the captain and never opened it.

Until now.

"Captain Ash said not to open it unless we heard a legitimate radio transmission from the surface."

Layla's forehead creased. "You've got me intrigued, but why are we going to the lower decks?"

"You keep saying you trust me, right?"

She nodded.

"Then follow me."

* * * * *

It could have been a minute or an hour. All Magnolia knew was that she felt as if she had been hiding forever. She held her battery unit in her gloved hand. The warmth bled through the worn fabric. Her comms, night vision, and life-support systems were all down.

The other divers had come for her. She couldn't believe that Captain Jordan would risk lives to save her sorry ass. She wasn't going to make him regret that decision. It still didn't explain who was trying to kill her, but it did seem to rule him out as a suspect.

She heard scuffling sounds. The vines were searching for her again.

Red lights throbbed around the entrance to her hiding spot. The light blossomed over the room like an expanding puddle of water. She squirmed farther under the concrete platform where she had taken shelter, careful to avoid the raw end of rebar sticking out from the edge of the slab.

The sound grew louder. There were two vines inside now. The shadow of a third wiggled across a concrete pillar.

A barbed end suddenly darted forward. Watching it move, she held the knife a little tighter. Pale red sap trailed from the thick vine, and gashes marked the stem where something had fed on it. Directly in front of her visor, the barb split open into four small mandibles.

Instinct took over. She snapped her battery pack back into its slot in her armor and jammed the knife into the open maw. The jaws clamped shut around the hilt, and she yanked her hand out just in time. The vine twisted away, the knife still stuck inside its mouth.

Magnolia left it behind and ran for the staircase. She halted when she saw the dozens of vines creeping blindly up the steps. The only other escape route was to jump, but she had tried that already. She would never clear the gap to the next tower, and the four-story drop would telescope her legs.

What the hell. She decided to take her chances with another leap of faith.

Her battery glowed a cool blue amid all that flashing red. Dozens of stems snaked into the room, surrounding her. She turned toward the open area where windows had once been, and for the first time, she could see more trees growing through the floors of the adjacent tower.

This was it: the moment when she must make a decision that would probably kill her anyway. A flashback to the cyclops beast convinced her there was only one option.

Magnolia crossed the room at a sprint, weaving around the stems that whipped through the air. One of them wrapped around her arm, jerking her to a halt. The mandibles clamped down on her wrist monitor. Glass crunched. The screen was destroyed, and her hand was about to be next. She used her other hand to pry the thing off, ripping the plant's jaws away from the monitor and freeing herself.

In seconds, she was running again.

She bumped her chin comm. It didn't matter if these things heard her now, assuming they could even hear at all.

"Weaver, do you copy? I'm at the glowing scrapers just west of the ocean. Trust me, you can't miss 'em!"

Magnolia could see the inside of the next building clearly. The vegetation there was flashing pink. Pink seemed a slightly less dangerous shade than red. She slowed as she approached the edge. The vines writhed across the dusty floor.

She turned to face them and backed down the sloping floor until she was at the edge.

"Weaver," she said. "I could use some help!"

"I'm on my way," he said. "Just hold on."

Magnolia took another step back and looked over her shoulder. It was too far to jump. She raised her arms and shielded her body as the vines whipped toward her.

A sparkle came from the west—a battery unit in the clouds.

Then a canopy flying toward her at a low angle. And with that sight, an idea emerged in Magnolia's mind.

Reaching behind her back, she hit her booster, hoping it hadn't also been sabotaged. The balloon exploded out of its canister, and as it filled with helium, she turned and jumped into the air.

The booster pulled her into the sky just as the barbed mandibles reached up for her boots.

She glanced up to see Weaver threading between the two towers. He steered toward her and reached out.

"Grab on to me!" he yelled.

Magnolia opened her arms wide. She was above the ninth floor now and climbing slowly toward the storm clouds. Weaver swooped in, and she wrapped her legs around his waist.

"Hold tight, princess."

"Don't think that saving my life will get you out of paying me," she said, her voice ragged as she tried to catch her breath.

"Still on the straight flush, are we?" Weaver let out a chuckle that was almost lost in the noise of the wind. He looked toward the buildings below. "You wanna tell me what happened in there?"

Magnolia shook her head. "Freaky-ass shit is what," was all she said.

This time Weaver didn't respond. He reached up with a blade toward the lines connected to her helium balloon.

"What are you doing?" she asked. "Why aren't you punching your booster, too?"

A voice crackled over the comm before Weaver could reply to Magnolia.

"Angel One, this is Apollo One. Do you copy?"

"Roger that, Apollo One," Weaver said. "I've got Magnolia, and we're en route."

"En route?" Magnolia said. She tightened her grip around Weaver.

"I'm sorry," he said. "We haven't met our mission objectives yet."

"You didn't come down here to save me, did you?" she asked.

In answer, he sliced through her booster lines. The balloon soared away into the sky while his chute carried them gently back toward the surface.

* * * * *

Secrets ran deep on the *Hive*, and the officers who kept those secrets did so with a sense of honor and duty. And yet, the burden ate at Jordan's mind as he sat alone in his quarters, watching a classified video from the restricted archives.

He could picture Captain Ash vividly, her eyes glued to the screen, mesmerized by videos just like this one even as her own body was wasting away.

Jordan slipped on his headset and hit play. The deep, resonant voice of the narrator filled his earpiece.

"Industrial Tech Corporation, leading humanity into a bright future," the voiceover said as an image of a bustling city appeared on-screen.

Scrapers with glass walls filled the skyline. Vehicles of all shapes and colors buzzed around the streets, and the sidewalks thronged with thousands of people dressed in the fashions of 260 years ago. Most of these people seemed to be speaking not to one another, but to small handheld devices. Jordan had seen one of these "smart phones" years ago. Captain Ash had kept it in her desk, but Jordan had given it, along with various other relics the captains before him had kept in the office, to Samson, to cannibalize for parts.

"The future has never been more exciting," the narrator continued. "Advances in medicine and technology have allowed humans to live longer and better lives than ever before."

The video feed was now of the countryside. A clear stream meandered through a thick forest. The collage of colors filled the screen. It seemed unreal that the world had ever been so vibrant and beautiful. A man and a woman strolled with their daughter on a stone path around a lake. Leaves drifted to the ground around them.

"Industrial Tech Corporation believes in a better future for all," the narrator said. "We also believe in safeguarding your future in this time of unprecedented growth. That's why we are taking steps to protect what we value most."

The next section of the video was shot inside a huge warehouse. The *Hive* and several of her sister ships filled the space, resting on platforms that stood five stories high. Ladders and scaffolding surrounded the airships, and hundreds of workers in gray uniforms worked on the black, beetle-shaped exteriors.

"We are investing in new technology to protect against ever-evolving threats. These airships, when complete, will be the most advanced in the world, with electromagnetic pulse-resistant technology and the ability to sustain flight far longer than conventional aircraft."

Jordan almost smiled at that. He wondered if the engineers ever planned on a flight that would last over two and a half centuries.

The screen switched to a time-lapse video of a construction site. An extensive area was being excavated. Next came the concrete, but instead of going up, the workers were building their structure belowground.

"Cities like this one could someday house the human race in the event of an unprecedented natural disaster or global war."

The footage switched to images of vaults filled with seeds, and vast underground farms that put the one aboard the *Hive* to shame. Warehouses contained stockpiles of every supply imaginable, from computer parts to preserved rations. Next came the cryogenic chambers housing thousands of different species, including humans.

Few knew about the cryogenic silos or what ITC had been doing there. Jordan had kept it a secret ever since Captain Ash learned the truth about genetic engineering and shared it with him. Now that Ash was dead and the *Hive* was the only ship in the sky, he might well be the only person alive who knew the truth.

That would soon change. For his plan to succeed, he needed Rodger and the other divers to discover the truth for themselves.

The feed changed to a strange room that seemed to be underwater. Fish of all sizes swam past large windows. The narrator called it an "aquarium." What ITC had done was remarkable, but in the end, it hadn't been enough to save humanity. Humans had been driven from the surface into the great airships until, one by one, those fell from the sky.

"We have gone to great lengths to ensure the future of the human race," the narrator said. "That future is bright, and we hope you will join us there."

Jordan shut off the feed. The video ended on a happy note that now felt like a cruel joke. The future he lived in was anything but bright.

Only a few people on the *Hive* knew the rest of the story. The archives were vast, but bits and pieces of the big picture had been lost to time. Some of the files were corrupted; others had been erased. Though the details were vague, it seemed that mutually assured destruction had worked as designed, and brought the world to an end. During the Third World War, the very ships built to protect the United States had ended up destroying the planet with powerful bombs that turned the surface into wastelands.

Jordan still wasn't sure who had caused the last war of humanity, but he knew that no corner of the earth had been spared from the perpetual darkness and the electrical storms that the bombs had created. North America. Europe. The Middle East. Asia. It was all gone.

With a snort, he turned away from his computer. This was exactly why he didn't share the radio transmissions from the surface with the general population. Those messages could cause a riot.

No, he had to keep his people focused on their daily survival. There were only 442 people left on the ship. Scientists said it took at least 150 healthy humans to carry on the species. There were more bodies than that aboard the *Hive*, but they weren't healthy by any stretch. Most had cancer at one stage or another. The radiation poisoning was slowly killing everyone.

He put his head in his hands. How much longer could he stave off the inevitable?

Jordan raised his head and scooted his chair closer to the monitor. Captain Ash had marked the Hilltop Bastion as one of the most promising places that could hold survivors. She had taken a deep interest in places like it in the final year of her life. In the end, it had also driven her mad and forced Jordan into some very difficult decisions for the safety of those aboard the *Hive*. He keyed in his credentials and unlocked her final logs, which painted a grim picture of the woman Captain Ash had become during the last years of her life.

* * * * *

The lower decks smelled worse than Michael remembered from his last visit. The shit cans weren't being composted but once a week, and showers were running only a fraction of the time because of the energy curtailment. That meant overfill and the threat of disease, not to mention the rancid smells.

Curious eyes followed Michael and Layla down the corridor, which was lined with pathetic dirt-filled troughs where the lower-deckers tried to grow a few extra carrots or spinach plants. The leaves were pale and shriveled, like the people who lived down here. It made Michael sad and angry to see the way they were treated.

"Hell Divers," hissed an old woman as they passed. Norma, an elderly gardener with a crooked spine, staggered after them, holding up hands caked with dirt. "Tell that captain we need the grow lights back on!"

Layla approached her, smiling gently. "We're doing our best. I'll pass your request on to Captain Jordan personally."

Her calm voice seemed to soothe the old woman, who shuffled away toward one of the troughs and went back to propping up a tomato plant. How many thousands of times in her life had she performed that task? Michael wondered. Perhaps that was the reason she was bent like one of the struggling, stunted plants.

"Good job," he said to Layla.

"We can't stay down here much longer. People are going to start asking us questions."

"We're almost there," Michael said. They hurried through the dark hallway into one of the least-visited rooms on the ship.

"Ugh!" Layla groaned. "Why are we at the library?"

"Do you remember when Captain Ash died?"

She looked at him strangely. "Of course. We were in our first year of engineering school and about to start our apprenticeships."

"The last time I saw her and Mark, I was fifteen years old. Except that I didn't know it would be the last time. I visited her in her private quarters. By then, the cancer had eaten her throat. She couldn't speak, but she could write. The instructions on the note she gave me with this envelope said to open it here."

Layla wrapped her arms around him. "I'm sorry, Michael. I know how much she meant to you."

"I was close with Mark, too. They were the closest thing I had to parents after mine died." He thought of them both every day, but sometimes it was just too painful. Mark had died of a heart attack two months after the cancer took Maria. They had loved each other fiercely for over thirty years. Michael hoped he would get a fraction of that time with Layla.

She kissed his cheek and stepped back. "I went through the same pain when I lost my parents. It never fully goes away."

"No, it doesn't."

He pulled the note out of his pocket and pushed the door open. They stepped into a small room furnished with three desks and lit by a single candle. The glow danced over shelves of ragged books with faded covers.

"May I help you?" an ancient voice croaked.

"Hi, Mr. Matthis," Michael said to the librarian. "Been a while."

Jason Matthis stood and squinted in the candlelight. "I'm sorry, but my vision is failing me and I don't recognize your voice."

Michael and Layla crossed the small space, stopping in front of Jason's desk. He smiled, flashing decayed teeth at them. The whites of his eyes reflected the lonely, flickering flame.

"It's me, Michael Everhart." He paused and then added, "Tin."

"Ah," Jason said. "And who is with you, Commander Tin?"

"Layla," she said.

"And what brings you two here?"

She looked to Michael. He cleared his throat. "Research."

"Then please let me know if I can assist you."

"Thank you," Michael replied. He led Layla over to the desk near the starboard bulkhead and took a seat. Before sitting down beside him, she fished a lighter from her pocket, lit the candle on the table, and pulled it close.

Holding her gaze, Michael used a fingernail to unseal the yellowed envelope. For five years, he had held on to this note, and for five years he had fought the daily temptation to open it.

Captain Ash had been the one to lift Michael up. She had taken him in after X didn't return from Hades. She had saved his life, and he loved her for it. But she had always kept things hidden from him. Now he was finally going to find out the secrets she was hiding.

Michael unfolded the letter and held it to the light, reading the text in a whisper. "*The New World Order*. Page ninety-four."

"That's it?" Layla asked.

"No," he replied. "That was just the beginning."

ELEVEN

Rodger followed Andrew through the rubble. He swept his rifle over the terrain, searching for contacts. Though he didn't look it, he was one of the best shots of all the Hell Divers. That didn't mean he enjoyed killing.

He gripped the wooden stock with one hand and raised the other to check the rad readings on his monitor. There was a joke somewhere in his mind, but he couldn't bring himself to crack it. Today, he was all business. No jokes, no farts, no laughs. This wasn't some green dive. His life and the lives of his fellow divers depended on him.

Magnolia's life depended on him.

"You think she's okay?" he asked.

Andrew turned slightly. His big shoulders cast a wide shadow on the path.

"Shit, Mags is tougher than you think." Andrew stood there a moment and then laughed. "You really dig her, don't you?"

Rodger felt his cheeks warm. Was it that obvious?

He kept walking, eyes on the sky. The gift he had been making for her wasn't finished, but he had brought it with him anyway. Tomorrow was never a guarantee, and a mostly finished present was better than nothing.

The sharp crack of thunder made Rodger flinch. A few hundred feet to the left, and the strike would have ended him. But the lightning arced into a pile of broken rock and concrete instead.

Thirty minutes had passed since Weaver's last transmission, and Rodger was growing anxious.

"We need to find that crate," Andrew said. "It's gotta be close."

Rodger nodded. According to the minimap on his wrist monitor, they were almost on top of the supply box that their shipboard team had dropped. The nav marker he had set blinked.

"After you, Mr. Pipe," he said, bowing.

Andrew shook his head, shouldered his assault rifle, and took point on a path lined on both sides by ten feet of debris. The nearby buildings had been reduced to rubble. In the distance, a hill rose above the destruction. On top of it stood an almost cubical concrete structure with a domed roof.

That was their target.

But first, they needed supplies.

Rodger raised the scope to his visor and zoomed in on the charred slope of the hill. In his mind's eye, he pictured the trees that had once shaded the dirt. He had seen pictures of trees in the archives, from spindly saplings to forests of giant ponderosas. Why couldn't he have been born three hundred years earlier? He would have built himself a nice little cabin away from everyone, a place on a lake with a good view of the mountains.

It was a pipe dream. In this devastated world, his greatest ambition was that someday he would see a real tree.

They skirted an immense crater. This wasn't from a bomb. Rodger could tell by the radiation readings. They were high, but not that high. The hole was probably once a man-made lake. A place where people picnicked. Now it was just poisoned dirt.

He took a second to scan the sky, searching again for Weaver and Magnolia. "Those rads are increasing," Andrew warned.

Rodger checked his wrist monitor. They were already in deadly territory. Without their suits, they would have been dead after a few hours. The numbers didn't inspire confidence of finding any survivors—at least, not aboveground.

The mountains of rubble continued after they passed the crater. Andrew stopped in the center of the road to look at the one on his left, then his right.

"Damn," he muttered. "I bet the crate landed on one of those."

Rodger followed Andrew's finger to the top of the four-story pile on the right. It wasn't the first time their supply crates had been dropped somewhere inconvenient. Sometimes, he thought the support crew did it on purpose.

"Better start climbing," Andrew said.

"Why me?" Rodger cradled his gun across his chest and glanced up the pile of concrete, glass, girders, and plastic.

"'Cause I hold rank. Stop wasting time and get your skinny ass up there."

"Whatever you say, Mr. Pipe, sir," Rodger said. He laughed and looked for a route up. Hunks of concrete sidewalk stuck out from the pile. They looked sturdy enough. He would use them as makeshift steps. He threw the strap of his rifle over his shoulder and climbed up the first two with ease. Then he jumped onto the loose rubble. The loose grains slid under his boots. He took another step, packing it down, but still it felt unstable. He grabbed a piece of rebar sticking out of the mess and used it for balance.

Glass crunched under his boots. There was a little bit of everything out here, like a giant scrap yard of shit from the Old World: plastic, sheet metal, concrete, brick, and even some preserved wood. He was always on the lookout for it. But rarely did he find anything he could use in his shop. Most of the time, he didn't have lift capacity in the crate to get any noncritical items back anyway.

He stopped halfway up the pile to check the sky again. The higher vantage point gave him a good view of the scrapers near the ocean. The flashing glow in his night-vision optics seemed weaker. Each green pulse illuminated the skyline, and by its light he saw a flurry of motion.

"I think I see them," Rodger said. He took another step and stopped to focus on the spot where he had seen movement. He shut off his optics, expecting to see the blue glow of battery packs, but there was only darkness.

"What the hell?" he whispered.

He bumped the optics back on. There to the east, just over the scrapers, something was moving just below the clouds. Rodger reached for his rifle and pushed the scope to his visor.

A transmission fired over the open channel as he zoomed in.

"Apollo One, this is Angel One. Do you copy?

"Roger, Angel One," Andrew replied.

"Have you found the crate yet?" Weaver asked.

"Negative. We're still looking."

Weaver's voice cracked, and not from static. "Find shelter immediately, Apollo One. I repeat, find shelter!"

Rodger bumped off his NVGs again and zoomed in on the dots he had mistaken for Weaver and Magnolia. He flinched as the red light of the towers backlit a sky full of winged creatures.

The otherworldly wail of Sirens sounded in the distance.

Rodger lost his footing, and his boots slid.

"No, no, no," he moaned. After regaining his balance, he pushed the scope back to his eye and saw just one sparkling blue dot.

His heart stuttered at the sight. Where was ...?

He zoomed in again on Magnolia and Weaver, sailing away from the beasts flapping after them. Now he knew why the commander had asked for the supply crate. They were going to need heavier weapons.

"Move your skinny buns, Rodger Dodger!" Andrew shouted. He looked up at Rodger from the street. "We need to find a place to hide."

"No, we have to help them!"

Rodger turned and loped down the hillside. The grit gave way under his boots, but he broke the slide with his heels. He leaped onto a hunk of concrete, then onto another. He jumped down onto the street and ran out his momentum. Halfway down the street, Andrew was already rounding the first corner of debris.

"Get back here!" Rodger shouted. "We have to help!"

Andrew yelled something in reply that was more profanity than anything else.

Rodger chambered a round in his hunting rifle and swung it up to the skyline.

"Don't worry, Mags, Rodger Dodger's got you."

He got the creatures in his scope. They were about a quarter-mile behind Magnolia and Weaver. It was a near-impossible shot from here, and Rodger knew better than to waste precious ammunition.

But Andrew must have had other plans. The crack of his gun sounded, and Rodger turned just as Andrew opened fire. He wasn't aiming at the sky.

Andrew shouldered his rifle and squeezed the trigger. The muzzle flashes silhouetted his broad shoulders as he fired at targets coming from the opposite direction.

Another round of swearing came over the channel. Andrew was calling for help, but Rodger needed to protect Magnolia and Weaver. Bringing the scope back up to his visor, he followed their progress. The chute was lowering them toward the city streets. Sirens, with their eerie high-pitched wails, were sailing in a V formation. And they were closing the gap.

"Rodger!" Andrew shouted. Through the incoherent streak of curse words that followed, Rodger heard a sentence that chilled him to the core.

"We're being flanked on all sides!"

* * * * *

The experience from eighty-nine dives kicked in as soon as Weaver heard the monsters' electronic discords. The alien shrieks echoed over the devastated city like an emergency siren on an airship. The sound of the alarms had paralyzed him as a child, but now it forced him to action.

"Hang on tight, Mags!" he shouted.

Sirens—at least a dozen, judging by the racket—were trailing him and Magnolia. The creatures were gaining on them, but Weaver didn't risk a glance to see just how much trouble they were in. He could already hear their leathery wings beating the air.

To the north, a road twisted like a river through a canyon of debris. Trash and blackened metal formed a skirt at the bottom of the heaps of destroyed buildings. The shells of old-world vehicles protruded out of the scrap yard.

At the end of the path was salvation. The Hilltop Bastion, now nothing more than a concrete bunker at the top of a dirt hill, enticed Weaver with its promise of safety.

About halfway there, standing on top of a mountain of rubble, was a lone figure. Weaver saw the muzzle flash, then heard the gunshot ring out half a second later. An enraged shriek followed as one of the beasts plummeted to the street below.

Farther north, behind the domes of rubble, came a flurry of gunshots. Weaver couldn't see who was who down there, but judging by the high rate of fire, it was Rodger. He never conserved the precious bullets.

Another flash from the crest of the eastward mound, and a second Siren spun down. The shrieks of rage rose into a cacophony that pricked up the hair on Weaver's neck. He turned his head to look at the beasts, but he couldn't see past Magnolia's helmet.

"How many are there? And how close?"

"Ten!" she yelled. "They're closing in!"

"Well, make yourself useful, princess," Weaver said.

"How? I don't have a gun!" she shouted into her mike.

Her voice hurt Weaver's ears almost as much as the screech of the monsters.

"Use my blaster. And don't hit the shroud lines!"

Weaver felt the gun being pulled from the holster on his thigh. Magnolia had clipped her locking carabiner to Weaver's armor, allowing her to let go of him with one arm and turn to fire. He pulled on his left toggle and steered the canopy toward the road curving between the mountains of destruction.

He heard the blast, and the recoil from the gun sent the canopy banking right. The blaster's barrel hit Weaver in the shoulder.

"Son of a..."

"I got one!" she yelled.

"Great. Now kill the other nine!"

Three rounds in rapid succession came from the pile of scree below. The flashes lit up the slope, and in their light Weaver saw skeletal figures scaling the sides toward the diver at the top.

"Pipe, you got contacts on your six!" Weaver shouted.

"They're everywhere!" Andrew replied. Gunfire sounded over the channel as he fired another burst. More Sirens crashed to the ground or rolled downhill. Piercing screeches, angry and desperate, filled the city.

Andrew did not relent. His muzzle flashes backlit the tower as the beasts scrambled upward, forsaking the easier prey in the sky to deal with the threat on the ground.

He's going to sacrifice himself to save us, Weaver realized.

A shot zipped toward Weaver, so close he could hear it rip through the air. In his peripheral vision, the round punched through the chest of a Siren swooping in with claws extended. It flapped backward into the sky, its wings buffeting the canopy with a gust of wind.

Weaver checked the ground as he fought with the toggles.

They were now a hundred feet from the road, passing over the twisted hull of a long vehicle with a strip of yellow paint still visible along the top. The sides were flayed open, and the jagged metal reached up like teeth at his boots.

He steered away from the vehicle and brought his knees up to clear the wreckage, then prepared to flare his chute.

"They're almost on us!" Magnolia shouted. She fired off another shotgun blast. The recoil knocked them off course. Now they were headed straight toward the swarming Sirens.

"God damn it!" Weaver yelled, jerking the left toggle.

The creatures were nearing the top of the hill. Andrew was putting up a fight, but it was only a matter of time before he ran out of ammo.

"Andrew, get the hell out of there!" Weaver ordered.

The man on the tower lowered his rifle slightly at the request. As Weaver sailed closer, he saw that it wasn't the thick frame of Andrew after all. The diver at the top was thin and scraggly.

"Rodger, watch out!" Weaver shouted as he realized his mistake.

Rodger turned just as a Siren crested the mound. The beast perched there as the others scrambled up to join it. Rodger stumbled, falling onto his back.

The crack of Magnolia's blaster sounded, masking Rodger's screams. A moment later, the gunfire to the north stopped.

The creatures had reached both Rodger and Andrew.

Weaver's heart thumped as he tried to form a strategy. They were still a good fifty feet off the ground, sailing through the canyon between walls of rubble. The Sirens were thirty feet or so behind them, flapping hard to catch up.

Behind the mountains of rubble, an unknown number of the beasts were attacking Andrew. Rodger was fighting for his life atop the hill. The *pop, pop* of his sidearm sounded, but Weaver could see only Rodger's helmet now as they continued to descend.

Twenty thousand feet above them, the future of the *Hive* depended on what happened next. In the sky, Jordan gave the orders that ultimately decided whether humanity lived or died, but down here the burden was on Weaver's shoulders. Sometimes it came down to the flip of a coin, but not today. Weaver knew exactly what he had to do.

"Hold on to me, Mags," he said. He steered the canopy toward a long panel of concrete that jutted from the side of the mound where Rodger was blasting away at the Sirens with his pistol.

Weaver waited for Magnolia to wrap her other arm around him. The smoking blaster dangled from her hand in front of his chest. As they sailed toward the ledge, he prepared to flare for the trickiest pinpoint landing of his life. It was only about twenty feet long and six feet wide. On the right was a wall of twisted metal that could easily rip their suits, and to the left was open air. If he missed the mark, they would either be skewered by rebar or fall fifteen feet to the road below.

"Oh, hell no!" Magnolia screamed when she realized what he was doing.

"Unclip from me!" Weaver shouted back. "You're going to drop on my three. One!"

"NO!"

They dipped lower, coming in at ten miles per hour.

"Two!"

"Weaver, no!"

Just before the ledge and six feet above it, he hauled both toggles down to his knees, flaring the chute and stopping its forward momentum.

"Three!"

Magnolia let go and dropped to the near end of the ledge, where she made a textbook parachute landing fall.

The sudden loss of Magnolia's weight made Weaver swing

farther forward than he planned, and he hit the concrete flat on his back, keeping his head up and slapping both arms down to absorb some of the shock. He had seen a rookie diver, after flaring too early, reach his hands back to break his fall, only to fracture his coccyx and break both wrists. This hurt like hell and rattled every bone, but he wasn't concussed and nothing seemed broken. He was at the edge of the slab, lower legs dangling off the end.

Ignoring the pain, he pushed to his feet, unslung his assault rifle, and looked for a target. Magnolia had rolled to a stop at his right, directly under a girder that ended in a jagged spike.

Weaver lined up shots on the incoming Sirens. Four of the creatures had been less than a hundred feet behind them. All but one pulled their wings in to their sides and dropped into a nosedive, their eyeless faces rocketing toward Weaver and Magnolia.

Crawling under the beam, Magnolia came up behind him and started plucking shotgun shells from his vest.

"Help Rodger!" he said.

"On it!"

She grabbed a protruding piece of rebar and pulled herself up, then swung to another hunk of concrete and started climbing.

Damn, she's fast.

Weaver continued to fire three-round bursts at the diving Sirens. The first two went wide, but he adjusted for windage and started hitting his targets, splitting open a shoulder of the creature on the left, blasting through the rib cage of the one flying point, and unhinging the monster on the right's elbow. They crashed into the rubble, squawking and shrieking.

The smallest of the three flopped onto the platform. As it thrashed on the ground, wings and arms flailing, Weaver stepped over and put a round through its temple.

Another beast dropped to the concrete on all fours. Snarling, it ran at him but collapsed, bleeding from its ruined shoulder. It pushed itself back up and scrambled unevenly forward on three limbs.

To conserve precious rounds, Weaver let the assault rifle hang from its sling and drew his sidearm. Thin lips opened across the beast's bulbous head, revealing a row of barbed teeth. He fired a bullet into the open mouth and turned to a third creature that was struggling to climb the wall of rubble. A shot to its spine sent it tumbling away.

The fourth Siren, still in flight, let out an angry screech and veered away, flapping back toward the scrapers. Weaver holstered his pistol and shoved a new magazine into the rifle as he looked for a way up the mound. Magnolia was already nearing the top. The slope below her was crawling with Sirens. At the top, Rodger was back on his feet, fending off the encroaching beasts, making each rifle shot count. Several corpses tumbled down the scree, leaving streaks of blood behind.

"I can't hold 'em!" Andrew yelled over the comms. "Where the hell are you guys?"

"Hold on! We're coming!" Weaver leaped off the platform and started climbing. Farther upslope, Magnolia fired at a Siren slinking up behind Rodger. The double-aught blast caught it in the side and sent it flopping and skidding down the hill. It caromed off a concrete boulder just above Weaver, and he ducked as the body cartwheeled over his head.

Magnolia fired again, and a creature twisted away with a gaping hole in its chest. Three more Sirens turned their eyeless faces her way as she fumbled to reload the blaster.

"Magnolia!" Rodger shouted. "Stay back!"

Weaver shouldered his rifle, paused his breath, and nailed a head shot. The beast crumpled at Rodger's side. Another leathery face tilted toward Weaver as he pulled the trigger, spattering Rodger's armor with a geyser of skull fragments and brain matter. Weaver's back foot slid in gravel, and the next shot came dangerously close to hitting Rodger.

More gunfire popped in the distance, followed by a loud crack. Andrew was firing both his sidearm and his blaster now. By the time they rescued Rodger, it might be too late for Andrew. This wasn't the first time Weaver had had to decide who lived or died, and he knew that it wouldn't be the last—maybe not even today.

Magnolia snapped the break shut and brought the blaster up as the final creature loped down to her. The blast took off a leg, and its broken body somersaulted toward Weaver. He fired, and it skidded down the slope and stopped almost at his boots, where it raised its head as if to plead for mercy.

Weaver stomped its skull on the concrete, then went for the monsters surrounding Rodger. There were five left, lunging and swiping at the diver. He dropped his empty pistol and smacked one in the mouth with his rifle butt.

Weaver took out two of them but couldn't get a clean shot on the others. The beast Rodger had hit was still on its feet, and howling in rage.

"Commander!" he shouted as the beast bowled him over, going in for the kill.

"Almost there!"

He walked an I-beam to its end and leaped onto the mound of rubble, his boots crunching over broken glass and brick shards. Not far ahead, Magnolia was scrambling to save Rodger. The young diver was beating back the creature that straddled him, but the gaping mouth was inching ever closer to his chest.

"Help!" he shouted.

Weaver planted his boots, squared his shoulders, and got the monster's face in his crosshairs. In the scope, he could see the thick spittle roped across the broken teeth.

The bullet punched a neat hole in the creature's smooth forehead. A blind cyclops gushing blood from its ruined socket. It went limp and collapsed onto Rodger.

Weaver was climbing again before the empty cartridge case hit the ground. He labored up the steep incline, the sound of his own breathing nearly drowning out Andrew's scream.

The gunshots from the north suddenly stopped.

"Hold on, Pipe! We're coming!"

At the top of the mound, Magnolia stabbed one of the beasts through the earhole. Yanking the blade free, she screamed to distract the final Siren, which whirled away from Rodger. Claws the size of her knife slashed through the air, but Magnolia jumped back.

Weaver rested the carbine against the sweet spot on his armor and fired a three-round burst into the Siren's ribs. Magnolia backed away, and it crashed to the ground, pouring blood onto her boots. It swiped at her one last time as she rushed over to Rodger, who was wiping gore from his visor.

"Get him up," Weaver said, searching frantically for Andrew. Now he saw why the gunfire had stopped. A small pack of the beasts had surrounded Andrew. The largest Siren Weaver had ever seen clamped its claws onto the diver's trapezius muscle and started dragging him, thrashing and screaming, down the road.

Weaver fired a shot that killed one of the beasts flanking Andrew. His next shot took out another, but he would never be able to kill them all.

He centered his crosshairs on Andrew's chest. Killing him now would be the merciful thing. It was what Weaver would want from his squad if he were in the same position. He lined up the shot, moved his finger to the trigger, and paused his breath on the exhalation ...

And couldn't do it.

Weaver lowered his rifle as the beasts pulled Andrew around the hill and out of sight.

Rodger was on his feet now, his arm wrapped around Magnolia's shoulder. She kept asking him if he was okay as she helped him walk down from the carnage on the hilltop. He was nodding slowly, but Weaver couldn't tell whether he was injured or just shocked to see Magnolia.

"Move your asses!" Weaver shouted. "We have to get to Pipe before they kill him."

As he started down the other side of the slope, following the trail of blood, he realized that the Sirens weren't taking Andrew to a lair in the city. They were taking him to the Hilltop Bastion.

It took them five minutes to get safely down off the rubble heap and reach the dirt hill. Weaver rounded it with his rifle out in front, ready to fire. But Andrew was already gone, with no sign of the monsters that had taken him.

Weaver lowered his rifle and glanced up. The Hilltop Bastion was like a three-layer cake, with earth on the outside and concrete and metal on the inside. Metal shutters covered the structure above—a lookout, he supposed.

At the bottom, a pair of massive steel doors pocked with rust sealed off the main entrance. Farther to the right, another door, about the size of a hatch on the *Hive*, stood open. The blood trail led through it.

Weaver turned back to Rodger and Magnolia.

"Looks like the mission has changed from a search and rescue for potential survivors to a search and rescue for Andrew," he said.

"How do you know there aren't survivors here?" Magnolia asked.

Weaver pointed at the open door. "I doubt humans have learned to cohabitate with Sirens over the years."

Rodger's eyes were wide behind his visor.

"Can you fight, Rodge?" Weaver asked.

"I think so," he whispered.

Weaver wasn't used to Rodger being quiet, and he checked to see that he wasn't in shock. Part of his duty as a commander was to make sure every diver was focused and not a liability to the rest of the team. Rodger's armor and layered suit were covered in gore.

The only clean part was his visor. He looked as though he had taken a bath in blood, but otherwise, he seemed fine. Just a little dazed.

Magnolia handed Weaver his blaster. "You can have this back. I found Pipe's rifle." She ejected the magazine to confirm that it was almost full. Slapping it back into its well, she said, "Let's go find him."

"I'll take point," Weaver said.

He walked up to the open door. Above it, a sign hung from one rivet. It was faded from countless years of exposure and pockmarked with bullet holes, but he could still make out the message: WELCOME TO ITC COMMUNAL 13. OFFERING SALVATION FOR THOSE WHO SEEK IT, AND SWIFT JUDGMENT FOR THOSE WHO DESERVE IT.

TWELVE

Michael held Captain Ash's note back up to the light, then flicked it in frustration. Was there some hidden message that he was missing? He and Layla had read page ninety-four of *The New World Order* a dozen times, but he still couldn't understand why they had been sent to find an ancient book about an extinct corporation.

Layla set the hardcover book back on the table and brushed off the yellowed page. She read over the text for several minutes in silence, which gave Michael time to think about everything that had happened over the past twenty-four hours. The quiet time wasn't exactly a good thing. His thoughts jumped from the storm and the rudders to Captain Ash, to Magnolia's fall, to the mission on the surface. Something was terribly wrong. He could feel it. Back in the launch bay, he had mused that the calm never lasted, but a chain of disasters like this hadn't happened since the day X died over a decade ago.

"What about this?" Layla asked. She pointed to a paragraph, and he leaned over to read.

> A growing number of scientists around the world continue to claim that the field of genetic engineering is key to the survival of our species. Others, however, argue that it will be our downfall. At the forefront are Industrial Tech Corporation and Raven Enterprises. Over the past

> five years, both companies have made breakthroughs in the field. Andy Robinson, the CEO of ITC, calls genetic engineering the most important part of his company's mission to safeguard humanity against the threats to our species, while critics call it a threat to humanity itself. Dr. Rod Emanuel claims that ITC's work, revealed in leaked documents earlier this year, "steps over a line mankind was never meant to cross."

Michael glanced up. "I didn't know that ITC was involved with genetic engineering. Did you?"

"Not at all," Layla said, fiddling nervously with the end of her braid. "What business did they have messing with that stuff, anyway?"

Michael read on but found nothing to answer their questions. Why would Captain Ash have wanted him to read this book? Maybe she really was crazy in the end.

The thought made Michael bow his head. He missed the captain terribly, but it seemed she wasn't herself when she died. He didn't want to remember her like that. He wanted to remember her as the strong, intelligent woman who had helped him become a man. But now he had to wonder. Had she hidden all this from him to protect him emotionally, or for another reason?

"Are you done?" Layla asked. Michael nodded, and she carefully picked up the book and walked over to Jason's desk.

"Sir, I'd like you to look up the checkout history on this title."

"Certainly, Miss Brower."

Michael joined her and whispered, "What are you doing?"

"Just wait," Layla said quietly.

Jason fired up his monitor and absently scratched his scalp. Like many of the older residents on the ship, he had lost most of his hair. All that remained on his wrinkled scalp were a few wispy strands.

"Ah, here we go," he said, peering at the screen. "Looks like … Hmm, that's odd."

"What's odd?" Layla said.

He put a finger on his chin as if in deep thought. "My records don't go back very far, Miss Brower, but it looks as if only two people checked this book out in the past three years—within two weeks of each other."

"Who?" Michael asked.

"Janet Gardner and Maria Ash."

"That can't be," Michael said. He stepped behind the desk to confirm that the old man was seeing right, but sure enough, Maria Ash had checked the book out three years ago.

"Something's wrong with your records," Michael said.

Jason frowned and shook his head. "No, Commander, my records are always accurate."

"Then how do you explain Captain Ash checking out a book two years after she died?"

Jason put his finger back on his chin. "Well, I … I'm not sure, but the rational explanation would be that someone used her credentials to check this book out under her name."

Layla thanked the old librarian with a polite nod. Then she stepped away from the desk and beckoned Michael to the center of the room.

"Who would use Captain Ash's credentials?" he whispered. "And why?"

"I don't know. Why does the name Janet Gardner ring a bell?"

It took Michael a second to remember. "I think she goes by Janga now. I heard she's a complete nut job."

"Janga, as in the woman Weaver kept sneaking off to see?" Frowning, Layla turned back to the circulation desk. "Jason, would you do us a favor?"

"Certainly, Miss Brower."

"If anyone ever asks, please don't tell them we were here today."

Jason took a moment to think on it and then smiled. "I will do this, but in return, I'd like you to bring me some fresh material for the library next time you dive."

Michael grinned back. The old man hadn't struck him as the bargaining type, but on the *Hive*, everyone wanted to make a deal.

"Sure thing, sir," Michael said.

Layla nudged him toward the door and whispered, "Let's go."

"What? Maybe we should look at the book again to see if we missed something."

She smiled, eyes shining. "We didn't miss anything. That was the clue, Tin. We have to go see Janga."

* * * * *

Sometimes, silence was more effective than swearing. Hands shaking with anger, Captain Leon Jordan grabbed a pen off his desk and bent it in half. Without uttering a word, he swiveled his chair to face Ensign Hunt.

Hunt took a step back. There was fear in his eyes, and something else that Jordan couldn't place. He didn't like making people fear him, but it was necessary. Fear was what kept order on the *Hive*.

And someone was threatening that order. Again.

"I'm sorry, sir," Hunt said. "It was an honest mistake. I thought Magnolia had discovered X's transmission in the archives, but it was Janet Gardner."

Jordan knew he should feel conflicted over having sent Magnolia to her death, but all he felt was rage—toward someone he should have dealt with a long time ago. She was back to meddling again, and that meddling had cost him a Hell Diver.

"Are you sure this time?" Jordan asked.

"Quite, sir. Only certain people on the ship can access the restricted archives. Members of the crew, a few ranking militia soldiers, and Hell Divers. The log-in was from a deceased diver."

"Who?"

"Xavier Rodriguez, sir."

Jordan carefully bent the pen back into shape and placed it back on his desk. Hunt looked at it, then back to Jordan, and continued explaining, the words tumbling out.

"At first I thought it was Magnolia, because Sergeant Jenkins reported one of his soldiers seeing her outside my hatch, eavesdropping. But after I tapped into the archives, I was able to determine where the hack came from: a terminal in communal living space three. The only one there who even understands how to access the system is Janga. Magnolia didn't know anything."

Jordan's fingers tightened on the edge of his desk. Hunt also had a roll to play in the death of Magnolia. His mistake couldn't be overlooked.

"Find Janet Gardner and lock her in the stockade," Jordan snapped.

Hunt nodded and began backing away.

"Hold on," Jordan said. He had allowed himself a breath to consider his decision. He couldn't afford to act on emotion. "Make it discreet, Ensign. Janga is old and frail. You need only one guard. Send Sergeant Jenkins, and tell him to keep this quiet. There are those who believe in her ridiculous prophecy. I can't afford an uprising over this."

"Understood, Captain. Um... you won't cut my rations, will you, sir? Mel and the kids need—"

"Dismissed."

The door to his office closed, and Jordan touched the monitor to continue reviewing Captain Ash's final logs. Placing the headphones over his ears, he listened to the scratchy voice of a long-dead woman.

> "There are two certainties in my life. The first is that the cancer will kill me. I don't have long now. The second and most frightening, however, is not my own death, but the death of my people—and, with them, the extinction of the human race. What I have learned has me questioning every belief I ever held."

Jordan skipped to the next log. He couldn't count the number of times he had listened to her ramblings. She had been crazy, and the mission he authorized to find the Hilltop Bastion was the only way to prove it to those who still believed in her dream.

> "I've spent my entire career searching for a place for the *Hive* to put down, a habitable spot that would allow our species to start over, to right the wrongs of our ancestors. I've scoured the archives for information on locations abroad that might have been spared from the horrors of World War Three, but every ITC ship that risked the journey across the ocean reported seeing the same destruction. In some cases, the radiation and electrical storms were even worse than in North America.
>
> "For several years, I kept in contact with Captain Sean Rolo of the *Victory*. He had made it across the Atlantic and was searching Africa, where he located a place called Mount Kilimanjaro that looked promising. No electrical storms, minimal radiation. Sometimes, they could even see the sun there. He made the decision to set the ship down, but shortly afterward, his transmissions stopped. That was over a decade ago. I never told anyone about it.
>
> "I believe that Captain Rolo intended to set down and start over. However, I also believe that the monsters

were already there. That's why I've decided to search for strongholds belowground that could house the population of the *Hive* and allow us to endure until it's safe to return to the surface.

"I've put together a list of bunkers that ITC built deep under the earth—places that could house and feed every member of the *Hive*, where we wouldn't have to fear electrical storms, monsters, famine, or the radiation that poisons our bodies. I've included the list at the end of this log for my second in command, Lieutenant Leon Jordan, to carry on this mission.

"Our future is no longer in the sky. Our future is underground."

Jordan could still remember the first time he read the log. It had seemed crazy then, and it seemed crazy now. Every single one of the locations in her list, including the Hilltop Bastion, was in a red zone. Their enemies had dropped bombs on the underground ITC facilities. Even if the bunkers had survived, the surface above them was a radioactive wasteland.

That was why none of the previous captains of the *Hive* had gone down there to start over belowground. It was suicide.

In her final years, Captain Ash had gone from single-minded determination to delusion. Jordan had not only decided to contravene her orders; he had decided to keep them a secret.

But he could keep them secret for only so long before curious people such as Janet Gardner started to ask questions. He could feel his control of the ship slipping away, like water dripping from a clenched fist.

A rap sounded on the hatchway. He hurriedly shut off his computer and straightened his uniform.

"Come in," he said.

Katrina walked in. She had that look again, the one that told him he would be sleeping on the floor tonight.

"Have you heard from the divers yet?" he asked.

Avoiding his gaze, she took a seat in front of his desk. He shut off his monitor and turned to face her.

"What?" Jordan asked, anxious. Whatever she had to say, it wasn't about the mission on the surface. She wiped her eyes and sniffed. Had she been crying? That wasn't like her, either. Katrina was a strong woman who rarely displayed emotion. It was one of the things he admired most about her. But he had seen her cry twice in one day now.

He got up and walked over to kneel in front of her. He put a hand on her calf and said quietly, "What's wrong?"

She put her hand on her stomach. "The baby. I think ..."

Jordan sprang up. "What? Is there something wrong? Are you not feeling well? Have you been to Dr. Free?"

Her sharp eyes met his. He couldn't read them.

"Katrina, what aren't you telling me?"

She glanced down at her stomach as tears streamed from her eyes.

"I'm not sure I want to have this child," she choked out. "I'm not sure I want to bring it into this doomed world."

* * * * *

Magnolia and Weaver followed the trail at a fast clip. Andrew had lost a lot of blood already, but he was strong—probably the strongest, toughest man on the *Hive*.

He was still alive; she could feel it. But he needed their help.

Flashbacks from the massacre of her team back in Hades surfaced in her mind. Those images had haunted her for a decade, and she was damned if she would let the creatures do the same to Andrew.

What a crazy-ass day, she mused as her flashlight beam swept over Weaver's back. His armored shoulders were covered in dust and the plant goo that she had accidentally smeared on him. She hoped the shit wasn't toxic, but down here, anything was possible.

He hugged the shadows, back hunched, scope at eye level, sweeping the darkness for contacts. Magnolia had never mastered the combat skills of divers such as Weaver, but she made up for it in speed and stealth.

"Hey, Mags," Rodger said. He was walking beside her with his rifle cradled, looking almost relaxed.

"What?" she snapped.

He leaned over, his arm brushing hers. "Most everyone up there pegged you for dead, but I knew you weren't. That's why I insisted on coming. I figured you needed my help."

She snorted. "I'm very much not dead. Not for lack of effort, though. Somebody up there must be feeling pretty disappointed right now."

"What? Why would anyone want you to die?"

Before she could explain, Weaver raised a fist as they neared the first junction. They all halted.

"Shut the hell up, you two," he said.

Magnolia thought about blaming the conversation on Rodger, but she kept silent. She still hadn't had the opportunity to tell Weaver about her sabotaged chute, and this wasn't the time for that conversation, either. She wasn't even sure she *should* tell Weaver. What if he had been in on it?

He saved your life back there. You can trust him.

She shook off the paranoia and swept her rifle over the hallway while Weaver raised his wrist computer. A screech sounded from deep inside the facility, echoing down the narrow passages, its source impossible to determine.

"This place is immense," Weaver said. He tapped his monitor.

"I don't even understand what I'm looking at. The tunnels look like a network of veins, but I can't find an access point for the actual facility."

He moved the monitor from side to side and cursed. "We're never going to find Pipe unless we split up."

Rodger nodded. "Good call, Commander. That will give me a chance to complete my other mission."

Weaver tilted his helmet ever so slightly. "What the fuck are you talking about?"

Rodger pulled something out of his vest and trained his flashlight on the square of plastic bearing the ITC logo.

"The only way Captain Jordan would agree to let me come look for Magnolia was if I did something for him on the surface. He wants me to find a cryogenics chamber. He gave me this card and said it would access the room."

"I got that," Weaver said. "But why? What the hell are you supposed to do there?"

Rodger shrugged. "He said to locate it and go inside, and that's it."

Weaver exchanged a glance with Magnolia. She didn't know a lot about cryogenics, only what she had discovered in the archives, but she knew enough to form a theory about the "survivors" they were looking for.

"Maybe the people who sought refuge here after the war froze themselves," she said. "Maybe they're still sleeping down here, waiting for the radiation to fade and the skies to clear."

Weaver let out a huff that crackled over the comm channel. "You're both crazy, you know that?"

Another nonhuman screech rang out, followed by a human scream that pierced Magnolia's heart. Weaver walked to the junction and looked left and right. He returned with a coin in his palm.

"Heads for right and tails for left," he said. "You call it, Magnolia."

She stared back incredulously. "Really? You flip a *coin* to make up your mind?"

"Superstition. Now, call it. We're running out of time."

Weaver flipped the coin, and Magnolia watched it spin upward in the air.

"Heads," she said.

He caught it in his palm. "Heads it is. You and Rodger take a right. I'll follow the trail left and keep searching for Pipe. Stay on the comms and report anything you find. But like I said, I doubt we'll find anyone down here, frozen or otherwise. Our best hope is to get Pipe out alive and maybe locate some fuel cells or other supplies."

"Aye, aye, Commander," Rodger said, throwing a lazy salute.

Magnolia wanted to insist on going with Weaver, but she wouldn't complain about getting stuck with Rodger on a wild-goose chase. Nope, she nodded like a good girl and patted Weaver on the back.

"Thanks again," she said. "You saved me. I won't forget that."

Weaver nodded slightly and brought his wrist monitor back up. "We rally outside in three hours, with or without Pipe. Understood?"

Magnolia and Rodger both nodded. She wondered what was going through Rodger's mind, but decided she didn't want to know. He'd been giving her a weird vibe lately, and she wasn't sure how to respond. Usually, when a guy was interested in her, he would buy her a mug of shine and then invite her back to his quarters for a little fun. Rodger was different, and she didn't know how to behave around him.

Get it together, she told herself. You're on a mission, not a date.

"Good." Weaver lowered his monitor and nestled the butt of his rifle against his shoulder. He strode toward the junction, then stopped just as he was about to round the corner. He looked back at Magnolia.

"You're welcome about saving your ass, princess, but I still ain't giving you two hundred credits when we get back to the ship. Now, move out!"

* * * * *

Michael had hated coming to the lower decks when he was younger. Back then, he and Layla hadn't understood why things were the way they were. They hadn't understood why people had to live like this, and Michael hadn't been able to grasp why a lower-decker such as Travis Eddie had resorted to brutal violence and attempted mutiny.

After the events on the farm a decade ago, Michael had forced himself to come down here with Layla a few times a week. Captain Ash had joined them on many occasions. It hadn't taken much time with these people for Michael to understand their plight. Travis hadn't been a bad man—just desperate for a better life. Michael didn't respect his tactics, but now he respected his sacrifice. Instead of meting out punishments after the failed coup, Captain Ash had agreed to provide extra rations and better health care to Travis' people. Things were still pretty bad, but they were better.

Today, Michael and Layla didn't have time to stop and share rations or play games with the children. He hurried after her, through the maze of packed aisles and shanty quarters. A few voices called out after them, but they didn't break stride until they entered the third communal living space. This was the worst area on the ship, the place where the undesirables lived. Some of these people had mutations from exposure to radiation, and some were petty criminals. Others were exiles from the upper decks or the other communal spaces. Scents of boiling cabbage and human feces drifted in the air.

Layla stopped at a stall with faded red curtains. The glow from a candle flickered in the gap.

“Hi,” said a voice.

Michael turned to see a little boy and girl across the aisle.

“Hey, Rex and Julie,” he said.

“Did you come to play with us?” Julie asked.

“Not today, but I will soon, I promise,” Michael replied.

Rex put his head on his sister’s shoulder and frowned, but he didn’t complain. These kids never complained, even though they had nothing. That was what had struck Michael the most when he started coming down here.

Across the narrow aisle, Layla knocked on the pole holding up the curtain rod. The red drapes parted, and a wizened face appeared, eyed their Hell Diver uniforms, and grumbled, “What do you want?”

“Hi, Janet,” Layla said.

“No one by that name here.” The old woman went to close the curtains, but Michael stepped up to Layla’s side and cleared his throat.

“Janga,” he said, “I’m Commander Michael Everhart. I was very close with Captain Maria Ash. I believe you served with her on the bridge?”

Janga gave him the once-over, then pulled the curtains shut.

“Hold on,” Layla said, pulling them back open. “We need to ask you some questions, and we don’t have much time.”

“Hell Divers and their questions,” Janga mumbled. She retreated into her tiny living space and sat on the edge of her bed.

“What do you mean by that?” Michael took a step into her quarters, which were furnished with bed, table, chair, and a shelf stocked with bottles full of herbs.

“What do I mean by *what*?” Janga said.

“Look, Janga,” Michael said, “we’re not here to bother you or harm you. But we need your help.”

He took another cautious step into her dwelling and held out the note from Captain Ash. Janga pushed her matted white locks back over her shoulders and leaned forward to read through cataract-clouded eyes.

"Captain Ash told me that if we ever received a legit transmission from the surface, we should look at page ninety-four of *The New World Order*." He paused to see if that resonated with her, but she remained silent.

"You know that book," Layla said, taking over. "You checked it out a few years back."

"So what if I did?" Janga said. She picked at a loose thread on the hem of her colorful floral-print dress. "What does any of this matter? Go away, children. I'm tired."

"It matters because someone checked it out a few weeks later under Captain Maria Ash's name," Michael said.

Janga shrugged. "I don't see your point."

"Captain Ash was dead by then."

That caught Janga's attention. She scrutinized him for a moment, then motioned him closer. She stood and peered right into his face, in the flickering glow of a single candle.

"You're the kid Maria used to talk about," Janga said after a moment. "I didn't realize it, because you aren't wearing that dumb little tin hat."

"It wasn't dumb," Layla said. "It was sweet."

Janga gestured for Michael to sit on the chair and patted the side of her bed for Layla.

"You'll have to forgive me," she said. "I don't usually get visitors from the upper decks, and when I do, they don't stay long. After all, it was the upper-deckers who exiled me here in the first place."

"I've heard the story," Michael said.

"Have you?" Janga said, giving him a crooked, mostly toothless smile. "Probably not the correct one."

"What do you mean?" Layla asked, scooting closer.

"Maria and I were great friends for a very long time, but I

broke her trust when I started searching the restricted archives for information about the war that destroyed the world. I discovered information about the surface and brought it to her attention, but she told me to keep it quiet. She said it would start a panic. We were supposed to keep certain things from the general population, for the greater good. But the truth was, I was already sharing facts that proved her dream of landing wasn't possible in our lifetime."

"What kind of facts?" Layla asked.

"Information that could have gotten me the noose. But like I said, Maria and I were friends. She exiled me down here instead of having me executed. And then she claimed everything I said was a lie, that I was crazy. It worked. The only people who believe me are the lower-deckers—them and one of your own."

Michael and Layla looked at each other.

"Weaver?" Michael said.

Janga shrugged again.

"What kind of information?" Layla repeated.

"About what's down there," Janga said. "Evidence of what ITC did. They took my credentials away when they exiled me, but I've got a few other tricks up my sleeve."

"So you didn't believe in Captain Ash's dream of finding a home on the surface?" Michael asked.

"I wanted to, kids, but I can honestly tell you that even Maria didn't believe it by the time she died."

"Why?" Michael said. "What did you find? Information about the bombs, or who started the war? The Sirens?" He started to reach out for her but stopped himself when she reared back.

"I'm sorry," he said. "I just want to understand."

Janga relaxed and sighed. "So did I."

"So I take it your prophecy didn't come from mystical visions," Layla said. "It's based on whatever you discovered in the archives."

Janga smirked. "You're a smart girl."

A whistling came from across the corridor. The noise caught the old woman's attention, and her smile folded into a frown.

"No," she whispered. "You have to leave before you're seen here with me."

The whistling got louder as others joined the din.

"What is that?" Michael asked.

Janga stood. "A warning. The militia is coming."

Layla and Michael both stood. He peeked through the curtains. Little Rex and Julie were whistling now, too.

Down the passage, at the entrance of the room, a militia guard had his club out. This wasn't some grunt, either. The muscular old man was Sergeant Jenkins, head of the militia.

Michael closed the drapes and said, "We'll stay here and wait till he's gone."

"That's going to be a problem," Janga said. "He's probably here for me." She grabbed a jar off the top shelf, unscrewed the lid, and pulled out a small piece of paper. "Here. Take this and go find a terminal. This will let you access the files I found. They will explain most everything. If you want to know more, come find me when they let me out of the stockade."

"They can't punish you," Layla said indignantly. "You haven't done anything wrong!"

Janga pressed the paper into Michael's hand, lifted the curtain on the other side of her bed, and shooed them toward the rusted bulkhead. "Go on, get out of here before you're caught."

Michael crawled over the bed after Layla, and they climbed out the other side. There was hardly enough room against the bulkhead for them to stand side by side. Janga nodded at them and said, "Good luck."

The whistling stopped abruptly, replaced by the heavy footfalls of Jenkins' boots. Michael and Layla began sidling along the bulkhead, their backs against the warm metal, but they halted when the boots stopped in front of Janga's stall.

"Janet Gardner," said the sergeant's gruff voice, "I'm here to place you under arrest."

The old woman chuckled and then coughed. "My name is Janga. People keep forgetting that."

THIRTEEN

Rodger was itching for the right moment to talk to Magnolia, but every time he tried, she raised a finger to her helmet to silence him. It was so quiet inside the tunnels that he could hear himself thinking. The echoey distant screeches were gone now, but Rodger knew that the creatures were still out there, on the prowl for fresh meat. He didn't like the idea of being on the menu.

He checked the mission clock as he followed Magnolia down the hallway. They had spent forty-five minutes searching the passages for a way into the main facility.

"Are we walking in circles?" he asked.

"No."

Magnolia swept her flashlight over the muddy footprints marking the floor. He followed a line of tracks onto the ceiling.

"Are those from Sirens?"

She nodded.

In all his dives up to now, Rodger had never seen one of the beasts. He had seen plenty of other creatures, from the rock monsters out west to the almost cute feathered lizards in the south, but the closest he had come to a Siren during other dives was hearing their high-pitched alien wails. He longed to see creatures from the Old World, like the ones he had studied in books.

"Hey, Mags, what do you think elephants were like?"

"*Shush*, Rodger," she hissed, whirling on him. "I told you to—"

"What's that?"

She followed his finger to a door at the end of the hallway, and her scowl turned into a grin.

"Hopefully, our way in," she said. "Come on, we've already wasted enough time."

He hurried after her but quickly fell behind. When he caught up, she was already kneeling at the edge of the partly open steel door. A video camera was mounted on the wall.

Magnolia shined her beam over the dented, rusted skin of the door. Long vertical scratches ran all the way to the bottom, as if someone had dragged a pitchfork across the surface. The door wasn't open after all—it was bent off its hinges.

"More Sirens?" he asked.

In Magnolia's light beam was a dent the size of a melon. It looked as if something massive had head-butted the door.

"I … I don't think so. I've never seen one with claws that could make scratches this deep."

She stood up, and Rodger's headlamp caught her face. He tried not to stare at her profile, but even with helmet and visor covering most of her features, she was pretty. She rolled her eyes when she caught him looking, and took a step toward the door.

"No," Rodger said, putting his hand gently on her shoulder. "I'll go first."

For once, Magnolia didn't argue.

He made sure he had a round chambered before shining his light into the passage. From his position, he couldn't see much but a flight of stairs on the other side of the unhinged door.

Flattening his body and ducking down, he slipped through the space between the door and the frame. As soon as he was through, he swept his beam down the stairway to a landing covered with metal shelves and crates. A sign hung on the wall there, but he couldn't make out the faded text.

As he turned and gestured for Magnolia, he saw that I beams had been welded in an X onto the other side of the door. Rodger moved his light over the broken barricade. The bolts that had secured the beams to the concrete were still there, but the metal had snapped from the force of whatever wrenched the door off its hinges. The steel was pocked with bullet holes. Raising his light, he slowly played it over walls bearing the scars of a firefight.

Not a fight. A battle.

Magnolia maneuvered through the opening and looked at the broken beams. "Shit, those were sheared right off!"

"Would take a lot of force to do that," Rodger said.

A raucous thud echoed below them, rattling the shelves on the landing. Both divers angled their guns down the stairs.

"What the hell was that?" he said under his breath.

"Not a Siren."

Rodger raised his wrist computer and brought up a map. The archives didn't have a complete layout of the facility, but if the fragments they had pieced together were correct, then the cryogenics lab—and whatever had made that noise—was directly beneath their feet.

Magnolia bent down and picked up a cartridge casing. "You know what this means, right? There were survivors here."

"But how long ago?" he said, following her down the stairs.

"No idea, but whatever broke through the door sure made quick work of this barricade."

As they crept down the stairs, Rodger paused to study the sign above the shelving. FLOOR 99. They rounded the next corner to find another flight of stairs covered in debris. A wall-mounted video camera was angled down over beams, desks, chairs, and shelves scattered across the passage as if a tornado had blown through. Dust floated around them in the glow of their lights. It felt as if they were entering a tomb.

Rodger kept picking his way cautiously down the steps, careful not to snag his suit. The radiation down here was minimal, but they still had the return trip to the *Hive* to worry about. If he tore his suit, by the time he reached the sick bay on the *Hive* he would have much bigger problems than abnormal bowel movements.

He glanced at the ceiling. Four miles above, his parents were waiting for him. They seemed impossibly far away. The thought gave him a twinge of dread, but he continued onward. Captain Jordan had entrusted him with a mission, and he wasn't going to screw it up. He patted the vest pocket containing Magnolia's gift and the ITC card.

There was a door on the next landing, as well as another sign.

"Floor ninety-eight?" he said. "That can't be right."

"If the signs are counting down, we've got a long way to go," Magnolia said. She brought her wrist monitor up. "And we have just over two hours to search this place and get topside."

"Searching ninety-eight floors will take days." He shifted his light to the door. An open space stretched as far as the beam would go. Magnolia stepped over a crate to look into the room. The warped and dented door lay on the floor, several feet in. The dust layer covering it suggested that nothing had been inside for some time. But that also meant the chance of finding any survivors was slim.

Their beams danced across the space, falling on lockers at the far end of the room. Space suits hung from hooks, and glass partitions were built against the wall. He recognized the chambers as clean rooms—something like the one they had in the *Hive*'s launch bay to decontaminate divers returning from the surface.

"Looks like some sort of staging area," Magnolia said. "You check the lockers. I'll see if I can get this computer online."

She hurried over to a hologram computer on a desk across the room. Rodger took his time crossing the space. It was about three times the size of the trading post where his parents had their stall. Carrying his rifle at port arms, he looked at the suits first. They were like those the Hell Divers wore, but with larger helmets and thicker padded layers.

He continued to the wall of lockers and used his glove to wipe off the inside of an open door. A faded picture of a man holding a baby was taped to the metal.

Rodger brushed off the dust and smiled. In the background of the photo was a dense green backdrop of trees. The man who had used this locker had once walked through a forest. A real forest, with real, living trees!

Rodger's smile evaporated as he realized what the photo meant. If this man had once seen a real forest, then this room hadn't been used in at least two centuries.

Magnolia waved him toward the wall-mounted monitor. Rodger put the picture back where he had found it, and trotted over to her.

She had brushed off the keyboard and was pecking at the sticky keys. A holographic image of the facility shot up over the desk. Rodger checked the entrance to the room with his rifle before turning back to the three-dimensional image of an underground silo beneath the hilltop. The first few layers were passages tucked under dirt and concrete—the same halls Magnolia and Rodger had been combing for the past hour. One of those hallways veered away from the silo and intersected with a staircase and elevator that went to the top of the bunker they had seen from outside. Another staircase went deep underground to a water treatment plant and a generator room.

"That's the route Weaver took to look for Pipe," Rodger said.

"Yup, and we're here." She pointed to the silo. "ITC Communal Thirteen. What became known as the Hilltop Bastion. Looks like there are ninety-nine floors after all."

She typed another command, and the hologram readjusted to show only the silo.

"Shit, the place has a swimming pool, tennis court, shooting range, luxury condos, seed bank, farm ..."

"And a cryogenics lab," Rodger said.

Magnolia pointed at a level a few floors below them and unslung her rifle. "Floor eighty-one. We better get moving."

"Wait," Rodger said. He bit the inside of his lip as a cool flood of adrenaline rushed through him. Before the jump, he had promised himself he would take the time to give Magnolia the present he had made for her—and to tell her how he really felt. But that was before he realized they were dropping into a facility full of monsters. Andrew was missing and likely dead, and they were almost twenty floors above their goal.

"What is it?" She looked at him quizzically. "Are you okay? You look, um, weird."

"Yeah, I'm good. It's just ... never mind. Let's get moving."

"I'm sorry," she said, unexpectedly putting a hand on his arm. For what?"

"For being such a bitch to you. I appreciate you coming down here to look for me. It means a lot."

"You're worth dying for a hundred times," Rodger said.

Magnolia's smile bloomed behind her visor, and Rodger thought he might have seen a hint of a blush.

She laughed and said, "Just a hundred times?"

"Okay, a million. But after that, you're on your own."

She tilted her head toward the exit. "Let's go before you have to prove it."

* * * * *

Jordan had been trying to reassure Katrina for the past hour that they were making the right decision, but she wasn't saying much. Her avoidance of eye contact told him that she was beyond angry. Something inside her had broken, and he didn't know how to fix it.

"Katrina," he whispered. "Please, look at me."

She glanced at him but then looked away.

Jordan's hands balled into fists. Why wouldn't she listen to him?

"It's no longer a question of whether you *want* to bring this child into this world, Katrina. We have a duty to the human race. We must do everything we can to ensure that this baby is healthy."

She placed her hand on her stomach and sighed. "I know, but frankly ..."

Jordan folded his arms across his chest. "Go on."

"After the electrical storm knocked out the rudders and we lost Magnolia, I started thinking about just how fragile things are. Things were good for a while, but it never lasts. We haven't heard anything from the team on the surface, either."

"I don't expect we will," he said.

Katrina's eyes shot up. "What do you mean by that?"

"The electrical storm is blocking their comms," Jordan said, catching himself.

"The clock is ticking. For them, for us—for everyone."

"The clock's been ticking for two hundred and sixty years, and we're still up here," he said.

"Unless Weaver finds something to save us down there, it's only a matter of time. Because we're nearing the end, Leon, and I know you know it."

She massaged her stomach and looked down as if she could see right through to their unborn child.

"We're one bad storm or a failed crop away from extinction," she said.

Jordan shook his head. "We've survived this long because men and women like me were able to make the hard decisions. Even when we're not popular—even when the people *hate* us and every sacrifice we are forced to make takes with it a piece of our own soul, we have a duty to these people. I thought you understood that."

Katrina finally looked at him for more than a few seconds. There was obvious contempt in her gaze.

Jordan considered telling her everything, but what good would it do? The only way to prove to her she was wrong was by sending Rodger to uncover the cryogenic chambers. He only hoped it didn't cost the ship too much in the process. Losing Weaver, Andrew, and Rodger on top of Magnolia was an expensive but ultimately necessary way to prove his point. Their only hope of survival was to stay the course.

"It pains me to see you look at me like that, but someone has to be the bad guy on the ship," he said. "I'm willing to shoulder that burden if it means the survival of my child."

"*Our* child," she corrected, sounding as though her thoughts were a million miles from him. Her hand moved ceaselessly, rubbing her belly in circles.

"Life will go on, Katrina," he said. "You just have to trust me. You're the only person I truly trust on this ship."

A knock sounded on the hatch.

"We'll continue this conversation later." He kissed her on the cheek and stood up. "It's open."

Sergeant Jenkins opened the hatch and stepped inside. "Captain, I've got Janet Gardner in custody."

Jordan could feel Katrina glaring at him, but he kept his eyes on Jenkins.

"Thank you, Sergeant. Bring her to the interrogation room. I'll deal with her myself."

As soon as Jenkins was gone, Katrina seemed to snap out of her daze. "You arrested Janga?"

"Yes," Jordan said. He walked to the hatch and grabbed the handle. "Just trust me. That's all I've ever asked from you."

Katrina straightened her back and threw up a stiff salute. Her eyes had gone cold and hard, and Jordan felt as though a door had been slammed in his face.

"I'm going to deal with something that Captain Ash should have dealt with years ago," he said. "In the meantime, you have the bridge, Lieutenant."

* * * * *

Weaver hated being alone, especially on the surface. The days he had spent trekking across Hades after watching his home crash had broken him. For months after he came aboard the *Hive*, he had slept each night with the lights on and the door open so he could listen to the voices of the passengers in the hallway.

For a man who hated silence and darkness, the Hilltop Bastion was a waking nightmare. The enclosed space was almost completely devoid of sound, as if he were walking in outer space. Sporadic high-pitched shrieks were the only break in the stillness—and the only thing worse than the silence.

Halfway down the next hall, he stopped and considered opening the comm up to Magnolia and Rodger, or even trying to reach Andrew, just to hear a human voice. But he resisted the urge, knowing that it would give away his position to anything hunting him.

The light from his battery unit and his helmet-mounted lamp spread over the passage. He moved out, keeping low and close to the wall. He had yet to see a single door, and the trail of blood had almost disappeared. Andrew's bleeding had slowed to just a few drops here and there. If he lost the trail, there was no way he would find the man in time to save him—assuming he could be saved at all.

Weaver halted to reconsider his plan. Andrew might already be dead. In fact, given what he knew of the Sirens, it was likely the case. He missed his wife and daughter just as much today as he had ten years ago, when he lost them in the wreck of *Ares*, but he wasn't in any hurry to join them.

A small, cowardly part of his soul worried that the darkness after death would be much worse than this, like being trapped underground for all eternity.

Think and focus, Rick. Think and focus.

The mission was screwed, no denying that. No one could have survived down here, and he didn't buy the fairy tale about cryogenic chambers housing any survivors. He pulled out his coin to flip it. Would anyone blame him if he abandoned the search for Andrew and cut their losses while he still could? Jordan would probably give him a goddamn medal.

But Weaver wasn't one to leave a man behind. Ever since X fell back to the surface of Hades, Weaver had made a promise to do everything he could to get all the divers home, no matter whose team they were on.

He put the coin away. Lifting his rifle, he continued into the darkness. The beam from his helmet illuminated a path that seemed to stretch on and on. He walked for several minutes until he saw what could be the outline of a door.

Weaver slowed as he approached, listening hard. The city was crawling with monsters, from the massive carnivorous plants to the Sirens, and he had a feeling even worse things lurked in this facility.

When he got to the door, he looked at his wrist monitor. His location was directly under the hill, but there were no details to show him what was on the other side.

He took a knee and brushed the dust off the ground. Tracks ran up and down the hallway, but the drops of blood stopped here.

Weaver stood and slung his rifle over his back. He drew his pistol and slowly pulled back the slide. The round clicked into the chamber. He winced at the noise and waited for a response.

The vacuum of silence remained undisturbed.

He grabbed the door handle. It felt loose. Bending down, he saw that it was already open. Claw marks covered the frame.

He was on the right track.

Okay, old man, let's see if you still got it.

He took a breath and slowly pulled the door open onto a stairwell landing. With his gun up, he stepped inside and angled the barrel up the flight above. Then he moved around the corner of the stairway and looked down. Up or down? This time, he was going to have to use the coin. He was reaching for it when the speaker in his helmet crackled.

"Angel One, this is Raptor Three. Do you copy? Over."

The sound of another human voice was reassuring and terrifying at the same time. He reminded himself that it would be difficult for the creatures to hear the voices from inside sealed helmets. Several seconds passed as he listened, but the monsters never came.

"Roger that, Raptor Three," he said quietly.

"Commander, have you found Andrew yet?"

"Negative, Raptor Three. I just found a door that leads to a staircase."

There was a short pause, followed by white noise.

"Angel One, if you are where I think you are, then down leads to a water treatment plant and a generator room. The backup power is still on over here. I found a hologram terminal and a map."

"What's above me?" Weaver asked.

"I think that's the lookout post we saw on our way in. Might be a command room; I don't know. Maybe a comms station."

"Good thinking. Have you found anything else?"

"So far, there's no evidence of survivors, but we did find something ..." Magnolia paused again. "Something big was here, sir. Hard to say when. Most everything is covered in dust, but someone did put up one hell of a fight to keep whatever it was out. We're heading deeper belowground to find the lab."

"Roger that, Raptor Three. Stay sharp. I'm going to keep looking for Apollo One. Good luck. Over."

"Good luck, sir. Over and out."

Weaver flicked his light up the stairs and found muddy tracks, but no blood trail. He went back to the landing to check the descending flight of stairs. Specks of red dotted the treads. He unslung his rifle and raised both guns into the darkness.

The beam from his helmet shifted across a stairwell as he made his way down into the black abyss. His cautious footfalls made little noise, but it was his battery pack that worried him most. The beasts couldn't see the light, but they were drawn to energy sources. One of the reasons the divers had such a hard time getting power cells for the ship was that Sirens tended to nest near the storage facilities.

The stairs led him deeper into the earth. With every step, he felt a growing sensation of being watched.

He turned and played his light over the walls.

Nothing.

The farther he descended, the stronger the sensation became. Something, or someone, was here with him. He could feel a presence.

Weaver reminded himself that he had enough firepower to kill a small army of Sirens. He passed three more landings before he finally saw a sign that read WATER TREATMENT PLANT.

Magnolia's map was right. He crossed the landing and was starting to walk around the corner when he felt the slightest draft of air rustle his right pant leg.

Weaver whirled and trained both guns back up the stairs. The gray walls and ceiling were clear. No Sirens prowling about.

He put his back against the wall and leaned left to peer around the corner. At the next landing, the double doors to the water treatment plant were wide open.

He moved back to the safety of the wall, trying to control his pounding heart, and the thought occurred to him that perhaps he was getting too old for this.

He licked the salty sweat off his mustache and holstered his pistol. Firing from the hip wasn't going to save anyone down here. Calculated shots were the way to go.

If Andrew was below, Weaver had to be stealthy. He pulled the sound suppressor from his cargo pocket and screwed it onto the end of his rifle. Next, he reached up and clicked off his headlamp. Darkness shrouded the stairwell. The blue light emitted by his battery pack gave him only a few feet of visibility, and even then he couldn't see much but shapes. He bumped on his night vision, but nothing happened.

Son of a bitch.

He tried a second and a third time.

A soft breeze hit his arm as he reached up for his helmet. His hand froze in midair. Was he imagining things, or was there a draft inside the passage? And if so, where was it coming from?

A snuffling came from his left. Then overhead. Another sniff came from the upper right corner of the stairwell.

Weaver closed his eyes and prepared to fight for his life. His heart was thumping like an air hammer. Could the monsters hear that?

He backed away, clicking on his headlamp in the process. Stealth didn't matter now. They knew where he was. The beam crossed over the cracked gray ceiling. A second pass didn't reveal any living thing.

Was he having auditory hallucinations?

Weaver was taking another step backward when the cracks in the ceiling suddenly shifted. His light captured a sinewy creature with gray skin skittering away. Falling onto his butt, he swung the rifle up by reflex. The thing, whatever it was, vanished around the corner.

For several moments, Weaver stayed on his backside, rifle shouldered and finger on the trigger. He had never encountered a creature with a camouflage response on any of his dives, but he had learned something about the monsters on the surface: where there was one, there were probably more.

He drew no comfort from having been right all along. Something had been watching him, and it was still here. He could feel it by the prickling hairs on the back of his neck.

He pushed himself up with one hand and held the rifle in the other. In quick movements, he scanned the walls, stairs, and ceiling.

Every crack in the concrete became a clawed limb in his mind, every broken hunk a mouth. He resisted the urge to unload his magazine in a wide arc.

His options were limited. He could run back up the stairs and abandon Andrew, or he could fight his way down to the water treatment plant.

In the end, there was only one choice.

X wasn't the only man Weaver had left behind during his long career as a Hell Diver. Over a decade ago, on a dive to Hades, he had abandoned one of his teammates. Jones had been dead, or at least close to it, from what Weaver had seen, but the decision had haunted him ever since. Andrew was probably past saving, but Weaver couldn't leave him down here if there was even a chance he still breathed.

Running back to the surface would make Weaver worse than a coward. He would betray the oath he had taken as a Hell Diver.

He made his way across the landing, stopping at the corner. Putting his back to the stair wall, he peeked around the side. The beam from his headlamp captured a skeletal gray figure the size of a six-year-old child, standing at the bottom of the stairs.

He ducked back around the stair wall and pressed his shoulders against the concrete, taking in a long breath. Risking another look, he shined his light on the floor beside the monster. The thing still didn't move. It stood on two peg legs, its webbed feet splayed for balance. Its bony back was turned to him.

Did it think it was hidden?

The beast was one of the most bizarre things he had ever seen, and he had seen his share of strange sights. It had three legs—two in back and one in front—and a torso that tapered to a narrow midsection, like an hourglass. Feathers sprouted from its round head, turning to shaggy fur on the rest of its body, but the oddest part of all was the stemlike growth on its forehead, which supported a single eyeball the size of an apple. The eye turned toward him, blinking in the light, then quickly swiveled away.

His first instinct was to shoot, but this thing didn't seem to be violent like the Sirens. A hard moment passed before he finally got up the nerve to step around the corner.

The creature remained frozen, almost blending in with the shadows. Past the beast, Weaver could see inside the water treatment plant. He tilted his headlamp for a better view, revealing a network of platforms and bridges over dozens of pools filled to the brim with liquid. The plant was many times larger than the one on the *Hive*.

As he played the light back and forth, something let out a scream. It was an unusual noise for a Siren, and Weaver wondered if there might be something even worse living in the plant. He cupped his hand over the light when he heard footsteps slapping toward him.

Weaver raised the rifle and pulled his hand away from the light just as the odd creature jumped to the ceiling above him. There it hung, tilting its feathery face at him. Beaklike jaws slowly opened and closed as if tasting the air.

The creature's eye focused on him for a fleeting moment before the stem curved back over its head to look at the treatment plant, and the same odd scream echoed through the room.

In a flash of gray, the beast darted up the stairwell.

The high-pitched shriek of a Siren rang out. It was then Weaver realized that the first scream hadn't been from a monster at all. It had been Andrew.

FOURTEEN

Michael stood in the shadows of the hallway as a crowd filed toward the trading post. At the head, Sergeant Jenkins led Janga toward the stockade. There was no telling what Captain Jordan had planned for her, but whatever it was, it couldn't be good.

Michael looked at the piece of paper Janga had given him. He hoped the log-in and passcode would answer all his questions.

"We need to find a terminal that can't easily be traced," he said.

Layla grabbed his arm. "I know just the place."

A frantic shout echoed down the hallway. "They've got Janga!"

The throng of passengers shifted away from the trading post and trailed after Jenkins and Janga.

"There's going to be trouble," Michael said. He jogged with Layla toward the corner and watched as Norma, grubby hands pressed against her bent back, shuffled after Janga.

"Where are you taking my friend?" she yelled.

Jenkins turned and swatted at Norma. "Get back to work."

"Commander Everhart, is that you?" a voice called. "What's going on?"

Michael looked back toward the trading post and saw Rodger's father. Cole Mintel had a clock in one hand and a rag in the other.

"The militia just arrested Janga," Michael said.

Cole wiped off the clock and shrugged. "Been a long time comin', if you ask me." His expression turned grim. "Have you heard anything about my boy? The divers have been down there for a couple hours now."

"I'm sorry, sir, but Layla and I haven't heard anything yet."

Cole nodded solemnly and walked backed to the trading post. By the time Michael looked back down the passage, Jenkins and Janga were gone. Norma hobbled toward them, tears running down her wrinkled face.

"They're going to kill her," Norma muttered as she passed Michael.

Layla frowned and turned to him. "You don't think they'd actually hurt her, do you?"

Michael shook his head. "The captain isn't a barbarian. Besides, too many people saw her being arrested. I'm sure she'll be fine."

Layla didn't seem convinced, but she led the way into the trading post and down a passage, past the entrance to the farm and the water treatment plant. Michael's heart was beating fast, and not from childhood memories of this place. He and Layla were close to finding out the truth at last.

They continued through the living quarters for upper-deckers and past several small shops, including the Wingman. Back in the day, if X went missing, the bar was where Michael would look first. Layla turned into the hallway where she had grown up. Michael could see the drawing of the sun on the hatch. At first, he thought she was heading there, but she stopped two hatches down and knocked.

"Don't worry," she said while they waited for a response. "Deborah's working right now, but she was a friend of my mom's. I'm sure she won't mind if we use her old terminal."

When no one answered, Layla opened the hatch and stepped inside.

"Over here," she said, crossing the cramped living space to a monitor on a small desk against a bulkhead.

Michael shut the hatch behind them with a click. "I don't like this. I know Jordan has someone monitoring log-ins. If this one's flagged, it won't take long for the militia to show up, which puts Deborah at risk."

Layla smirked. "You asked me if I trust you, Tin. Now I have to ask you the same thing. Do you?"

She sat down at the desk and held out her hand for the paper.

"You know I do."

He handed her the credentials, and she sat down at the monitor and placed the paper beside the keyboard on the desk.

"Good," she said as she typed, "because I'll make sure this shit ain't traced. Deborah taught me a few things over the years."

Michael pulled up a chair beside Layla as a list of files popped onto the screen.

"Some of these are Captain Ash's personal logs," Layla said, glancing up.

"They all look like they were saved at the end of her life."

"Yeah ... and these aren't all her recordings. Looks like a few of these videos were retrieved from the restricted archives."

Layla played with the bottom of her braid—a nervous habit that made her look more like the girl he remembered from their youth. "This is some heavy stuff. Treasonous stuff, Tin. We could get in a lot of—"

Michael put a hand on her knee and leaned over to her. "We've reached the bottom of the rabbit hole. You can leave if you want, but I'm finishing this."

Layla cracked a half smile and turned back to the monitor. "Well, okay then. I always wanted to get shot out of a launch tube without a chute."

She typed in several commands, and a moment later, a familiar voice came from the speakers—a voice that flooded Michael with memories both warm and painful. He had spent over five years living with Maria and her husband, Mark. Losing them both within two months of each other had been tough. Captain Ash had finally succumbed to cancer, and although it wasn't logged as Mark's cause of death, Michael believed he had died of a broken heart.

Layla had helped him get through the darkness back then, but the feeling of intense sadness returned at the sound of Captain Ash's scratchy voice. She spoke of the ship and her dream for its people. She told the story of Captain Sean Rolo of the airship *Victory*, and his discovery in Africa. She listed possible locations to scavenge in red zones that the *Hive* had never explored: bunkers, silos, and cities underground.

As they listened to the logs, the cracking in her voice grew progressively worse—the cancer spreading from her throat to her lungs. By the final recordings, the once-commanding voice of Captain Ash was barely more than a hoarse whisper.

"What's this?" Layla asked. She clicked on a video marked with the white ITC logo: a scraper with a star over the top.

A male narrator began telling them about the advent of the ITC airships, as well as of the underground cities Captain Ash had spoken of. This was new information to Michael, but it still didn't explain why the captain had sent him to read about genetic engineering in some ancient library book.

"ITC thought of everything, didn't they?" Layla said. "Shelters in the sky and underground? It was as if they knew what was coming."

"Captain Ash did say these airships were the ones that dropped the bombs that started the war," Michael said, motioning for her to go back to the previous screen. "What haven't we seen yet?"

"There are a few more videos here, and one last recording from Captain Ash."

"Play that first," Michael said.

She clicked the file and took Michael's hand. They sat there, hand in hand, listening to her final words. For several minutes, she spoke of the dream she'd had of a habitable place on the surface, a place to make a new home for humanity. Even though her voice was raspy, Michael picked up on the trace of sadness as she admitted that her dream would never come true. Her final words broke his already aching heart.

"Our future is no longer in the sky," said Captain Ash. "Our future is underground."

"Underground?" Layla said. "Like under the Hilltop Bastion?"

Michael massaged his temples. "I'm not sure."

"I don't understand. Why take us on this scavenger hunt just to tell us her dream changed from living on the surface to living underground in one of these communal shelters? Why not just tell you that from the beginning, in the note she gave you? And why wait until we got a radio transmission from the surface?"

"Maybe she feared that Captain Jordan wouldn't tell anyone the truth, and this was her contingency plan. He never did share her dream of finding a place to put down."

Layla paused to think. "But what about the stuff Janga found? I'm not seeing anything like that here."

Michael continued massaging his forehead, trying to think. Nothing was making sense.

"Every ITC facility is located in a red zone, including the one in Hades," Layla said.

"The same one that X helped blow up ten years ago?"

"That's my guess." Layla studied the screen and then pointed. "The Hilltop Bastion is on this list, along with twelve others. Looks like we've already searched the areas where communals eight, two, and ten are, right?"

Michael read over the locations. He never forgot a dive, especially one that resulted in a death. "We lost some good men and women on those missions."

"Yes, but look at the pattern, Tin. All these dives had two things in common."

He cocked an eyebrow. "What two things?"

"Sirens and ITC bunkers."

"You think there's a connection?"

"Maybe, but I think there's a third part of this puzzle that we're missing."

She turned back to the screen and looked through the other files.

Michael tensed as he heard footsteps approaching. If someone came in now, how could he and Layla possibly explain what they were doing? They would end up in the stockade with Janga. The footsteps passed, continuing down the corridor without slowing.

"Don't worry," Layla said, "I told you, we're safe ... Wait. What's this?"

She had highlighted a file labeled *XR*.

She clicked on it, and an error message popped up. "Says it's corrupted."

"Can you fix it?" Michael asked.

She shrugged one shoulder. "I can try."

Michael stood and paced behind her as she worked. He felt trapped in this tiny room. Worse, the questions wouldn't stop ping-ponging inside his skull. What hadn't Janga told them? And why had Captain Ash sent him on this posthumous wild-goose chase?

The computer speakers began to play a recording in a smooth baritone voice.

"To protect the human race, ITC is at the forefront of genetic engineering and modification," the man was saying.

"I think I got it," Layla said.

Michael walked back to the desk and sat. A warehouse packed with gray capsules appeared on the screen.

"Are those coffins?" she asked.

"No, they're cryogenic chambers."

Long cords stretched across the floor, and icy mist drifted through the room. The camera panned up, but where he expected a ceiling, there were towers with hundreds of the capsules. The feed showed a pair of scientists in space suits, working around an open capsule at the bottom of one of the silos.

A new image came on-screen, and this time the scientists were gone. Two young women stepped out of the chambers. One by one, more tubes opened, and a crowd of naked young adult humans gathered in the middle of the room.

"Holy shit," Michael said. "They grew *humans*?"

Layla couldn't speak.

"Do you remember what the governor of Hilltop Bastion said in her transmission?"

"Something about not being able to keep them back much longer, and to send support." His eyes flitted to meet Layla's as she said what he was thinking.

"Maybe the survivors at the Hilltop Bastion unfroze the cryogenic chambers too early, and somehow it backfired."

Michael considered the implications, shaking his head in awe. "If Jordan knows about all this, then why would he send Weaver, Rodger, and Andrew down there to check out one of the chambers? He has to know there are no survivors."

"Maybe he doesn't know everything."

Michael snorted. "Trust me, he knows a hell of a lot more than we do. So that raises the question: Why send the divers on a probable suicide mission in a red zone?"

"He never did buy Captain Ash's dream, did he?"

"No, they never did see eye to eye on that."

"You don't think he would do this on purpose, do you?" Layla asked. "To prove Captain Ash wrong. To prove that we have to live up here *forever*?"

"If that's true, then the monsters aren't just on the surface anymore. There's one at the helm of the *Hive*."

Michael got up, his mind racing.

"Where are we going?" Layla asked.

"To save our friends."

* * * * *

Hot breath fogged Magnolia's visor as she and Rodger entered a cavernous hallway leading to the cryogenics lab. The rust-coated doors loomed twenty feet high in the distance. They weren't moving very fast, Magnolia stopping every few feet to check their six. Their flashlight beams hit the open door. The landing and stairwell appeared free of any contacts, and they hadn't heard anything for the past half hour.

As they approached the doors, Rodger reached into his vest pocket and pulled out a small white card. This was the first room they had encountered that was completely sealed off. The personal quarters, cafeteria, and gymnasium they had passed on the way down had all been broken into. They had found evidence of another gun battle outside the gymnasium, but they didn't have time to stop and examine it. On the bright—or at least less gloomy—side, Rodger hadn't asked to search for wooden salvage, which meant he was spooked.

He stopped in front of the door and looked up. These rusted doors separated them from possible survivors suspended in deep sleep. It was hard for Magnolia to grasp that they could be so close to other humans. People she had never talked to, faces she had never seen. After spending her whole life on the airship with fewer than five hundred residents, she might finally meet a stranger.

But these people weren't like the ones she knew on the *Hive*. They had been frozen in the distant past, in a world wholly unlike the one she lived in. Would she even be able to relate to them? Have a conversation with them?

"I've got a bad feeling about this," Rodger whispered. "Maybe I should contact Weaver before we open this thing up."

"No, we're doing this now." She eyed the control panel and walked over to the sensors. She wiped away a thick layer of dust with her glove, then reached back for the card. Rodger's hand shook as he gave it to her.

"You okay?" she asked.

"I'm good. Just a bit on edge." He took a step back and readied his rifle.

Magnolia bent down to the control panel. She was nervous, too, but curiosity won out. In the past, that side of her nature had gotten her into trouble. Maybe they should wait—but what if they never had another chance to search this place?

"Doesn't look like this room's been accessed in ages," she said.

"Is that good or bad?"

Magnolia shrugged. "We're going to find out. Are you ready?"

Rodger gave a thumbs-up.

She waved the card over the sensors once, then twice. On the third try, the glass blinked green. She unslung her rifle and moved over to Rodger.

A hollow thud like a distant gunshot rang out above them. She cringed at the noise. Then came three more bangs as the locking mechanisms opened. A distant, guttural groan answered the sounds.

Both divers turned from the entrance to look down the hallway. The noise had come from the stairwell at the end of the hallway.

They had woken something.

The angry groan evolved into a series of grunts. The sounds rumbled up from the lower floors as if the whole facility's guts were rumbling. It was the same creature they had heard earlier, and Magnolia had just told it precisely where they were.

"Rodge, stay on point," she said. "I got our six."

They came together back-to-back, with Magnolia pointing her rifle at the landing and Rodger training his on the doors.

"Is that a Siren?" Rodger asked. "I've always wanted to see—"

The heavy doors opened, silencing him as the metal screeched across the concrete floor.

Magnolia took a step back as he moved. She didn't even turn to look inside the room, just kept her muzzle on the landing.

The grunts had changed to a screech that sounded like a dozen Sirens at once. The high-pitched din was followed by clattering from the stairwell. Snapping metal and the shriek of claws over concrete grated on her ears.

She swallowed and did her best to square her shoulders, preparing to fire at a split-second's notice. Sweat dripped down her forehead as she backpedaled after Rodger into the chamber.

"Where's the card?" he asked. "I need to close the doors!"

"Upper right vest pocket," she replied.

The clatter from the stairwell grew louder. The thing was climbing, scraping against the walls as it came. Whatever this beast was, it would be far and away the biggest living thing she had ever seen.

Rodger grabbed the card from Magnolia's pocket as she stepped into the room, keeping her muzzle trained on the landing, her finger on the trigger.

"Hurry up, Rodge!"

A faint orange light emerged in the stairwell. The bangs and thuds grew louder as the light brightened.

"Come on!" she shouted.

The doors groaned again. They were closing, but not fast enough. At the other end of the passage, the creature bounded up the last of the stairs and pounced on the landing so hard they felt the tremor. It rose to its full height: a staggering eight feet tall.

She zoomed in with her scope as the doors continued to shut

in front of her. The magnification revealed a muscular humanoid figure with a disproportionately small head. Her crosshairs flitted across glowing orange flesh and up to the thing's face. Two white irises with blue pupils stared back at her from a skinless skull.

"What the hell is that thing!" Rodger shouted. He was pushing the left door shut now, his boots slipping across the floor.

The creature bent down and let out a guttural growl from deep within its chest. It raised its muscular arms, revealing catlike paws that ended in three jagged claws.

Magnolia lined up her crosshairs and fired a burst into its chest. The bullets hit their target but only barely penetrated. She fired another shot at its small skull as it bent down to charge, revealing a back ridged with armored fins. The round chipped the bone and ricocheted off the walls.

"The fucker's got armor!" Magnolia shouted. She slung the rifle over her back and rushed to the other door. Putting her shoulder against the door and planting her boots, she pushed with all her strength. Her injured ankle flared with pain as she pressed against the heavy steel.

The beast charged down the hallway at alarming speed. The doors were only three-quarters closed, and it was coming in fast.

Magnolia could see they weren't going to get the doors shut in time.

She stepped back, unslung her rifle, and shouted, "Shoot it in the legs!"

He followed her lead, and together they open fired through the gap in the closing doors. Rounds lanced into the creature's tree-trunk legs, spattering blood over the concrete. Magnolia almost whooped in relief. Maybe they could kill this thing after all.

Despite the trauma to its legs, the monster kept barreling toward them, hunched down, screaming in rage. She could see the muscles constrict across its chest and arms, as it ran full tilt at them.

Magnolia and Rodger stumbled backward as it lowered its small head and spiky shoulders to crash through the opening.

The doors groaned, and the beast screamed back at them. Rodger joined the chorus with his own shouts, but Magnolia gave only the barest squeak as the massive armored shoulders slammed into the three-foot opening. The impact sent a rumble echoing through the vast space.

Magnolia looked up at the creature's face as it snapped at her with a maw full of yellow teeth. A crunch joined the din of the groaning doors trying to close. The beast was pinned in the middle. Another crunch sounded, and Magnolia realized it was the sound of bone breaking, not metal rending.

She took another step back, her rifle still leveled at the monster. It let out a terrible screech of pain, glared at her with piercing yellow eyes, and withdrew into the hallway. The doors shut with a loud boom, but Magnolia didn't dare lower her weapon yet.

On the other side, the beast slammed into the steel with such force that grit sifted down from the ceiling.

"I think I just pissed myself," Rodger said.

Magnolia flinched each time the beast hit the doors, roaring with every impact. Never in her life had she witnessed such towering rage from beast or human. It was as if the devil itself were trying to break in.

"Are you okay?" Rodger asked. He walked over and put a hand on her shoulder, making her flinch again.

Magnolia glanced at Rodger, intending to reassure him, but she gasped as she caught sight of the lab over his shoulder. They turned together to behold the immense space. She played her light over dozens of towers that stretched as far back as she could see, each of them covered with rows of capsules like kernels on giant ears of corn.

"This place has to be ten stories tall," she said in awe. Her beam illuminated the tower directly in front of them. The glass surfaces of the first two chambers were shattered like hatched eggs. She walked over to them and saw that most of the other capsules nearby were also broken and the occupants missing.

The light from Rodger's helmet danced over the walls. "There's got to be thousands of humans and animals in here."

She stepped up to the closest chamber. Reaching out, she carefully examined the glass. It wasn't shattered from the inside out after all. Something on the outside had broken its way in.

FIFTEEN

As he walked to the holding cell, Jordan felt something give way inside of him. He'd been struggling for years trying to keep a balance between making sacrifices to save the human race and being able to look himself in the mirror. Some days those lines blurred. Today was one of them.

He pulled at his sleeves, brushed off his uniform, and ducked under the lightbulb hanging overhead as he sat. Crossing one leg over the other, he studied the woman he should have disposed of a long time ago. She sat on the floor of the small isolation cell with her back to the bulkhead. Hair covered the right half of her face, and her eyes were downcast.

"Captain Ash lobbied hard to save your life. I really wish she were here to see you now." Jordan leaned down. "Maybe she would see how wrong she was about you."

Janga jerked her wrists, pulling on the chains that kept her bound. She flung her white hair to the side and stared at him with clouded eyes.

Jordan smiled with what felt a lot like satisfaction. He had her attention.

"You'll never be the captain she was," Janga said, spitting at him.

He backhanded her across the face so hard that the noise reverberated through the room. She let out a moan and fell to the floor.

Jordan pulled a handkerchief from his pocket and wiped the spittle from his face. He didn't particularly like interrogating people, and usually left it up to the militia, but he was going to enjoy this. Janga was poison, and he was finally going to cleanse the ship of her toxic prophecies.

"Look at me," he said.

Janga turned slowly, her rheumy eyes radiating disdain.

Jordan cracked another grin that was actually more of a grimace as he walked to the other side of the tiny room. "You're going to make this hard, aren't you?"

She watched him move, clicking her tongue in reply.

"I'll give you one chance to tell me everything you know before I bring out the ..." He made quotes in the air. "Tools."

"You think you're clever, don't you?" the old woman said. "You actually believe you can keep the *Hive* flying forever."

He folded his arms across his chest and raised his eyebrows. Despite his eagerness to be rid of her, he was curious to hear what she had to say.

"I've seen the restricted ITC files. I know what they did during the war, what they created. You've seen those files, too, but what you don't seem to realize is something that Captain Ash apparently never taught you." Janga scooted closer to him. "I guess that's the problem. You can't teach a narcissist to have an imagination."

Jordan clenched his jaw. "If I'm lacking imagination, why don't you inform me what I'm missing?"

She shook her head. "I don't teach fools what should be obvious."

Jordan went to hit the wall but decided it wasn't worth his energy. He forced his shoulders to relax, reached into his pocket, and pulled out a pistol cartridge. He dropped it on the floor in front of her. "You see that? I was going to put it into your skull myself, but I've decided not to waste it. No, I have other plans for you."

Janga hissed at him like the feral animal that he knew she was. He walked back to the wall.

"You know, it wasn't hard convincing most everyone that you're a washed-up old hag with more screws loose than the ship, but you just had to keep opening your mouth, didn't you? Had to keep fishing for information, had to keep digging."

Janga gave a hollow chuckle. "You really have no clue, do you? You have no idea that some of your crew actually came to *me* for advice. Even some of your precious Hell Divers."

"Who? Katib?" Jordan adjusted the cuff of his spotless white jacket. "She's been dealt with."

"Hell *Divers*, plural," she said.

The words hit Jordan in his gut. That couldn't be true. The divers all respected him. They would never go behind his back.

"You can't lie to me. I have eyes and ears all over the ship."

"Not enough of them, clearly. I spoke to three of your people just recently."

Jordan stepped away from the wall and bent down closer to her. "Names," he snarled.

Janga chuckled again. "I'd rather die than tell you."

"I can arrange that, but before I do, I'm going to make you beg for death." He walked over to the hatch and knocked twice.

"Tools, Sergeant," Jordan said when Jenkins opened the hatch.

Jenkins returned with a small bag and handed it through. After shutting the hatch, Jordan set the bag on the chair and unzipped it. He had never used the tools before and didn't particularly want to now, but he couldn't lose control of his ship. He had to know who had betrayed him.

"You're going to tell me exactly who came to visit you, or things are going to get very unpleasant."

She hesitated a moment, lips quivering, but when she spoke, her voice was resolute.

"When I'm gone, there won't be anyone left on this ship to give the people hope. That's why I made sure my prophecy will live on. They will know the truth about the surface and where we will find our new home, and they will hear about the man who will lead them there. And before you get any grandiose ideas in your head, no, you are *not* that man."

A knock sounded, and Jordan turned to see Jenkins open the hatch.

"Sir, the launch bay has been activated. Two tubes."

Jordan stood. "What? Under whose orders?"

"No one's orders, sir. It looks like Michael Everhart and Layla Brower are doing this on their own."

When Jordan whirled back to Janga, she was smiling. Her grin set him over the edge. He was done wasting time on her.

"You think it's funny, eh? We'll see how funny it is when I put you in a tube and shoot you back to the surface that you hold so dear."

* * * * *

Weaver made his way through the water treatment plant, searching for the missing diver. He kept one hand on his rifle and the other on his battery unit, prepared to pull it if the Sirens surrounded him.

Andrew's howls of pain had lapsed into silence, and the screeches of the monsters were sporadic now. They were inside the plant somewhere, but Weaver still couldn't see the creatures in the cavernous space.

He had never been in such a large room in his entire life. The beam from his light didn't even penetrate far enough through the inky darkness to reach the far wall.

He raked the light across the wide pools of water lining his path. A red sludge floated near the edges of the pool to his right. As he bent down to examine it, he heard the skittering of claws across the walls.

Standing up, he dug his fingers under the battery unit, ready to pry it free. The sound faded away. He walked a few more steps, stopped, and aimed his headlamp at the walls. As he took another step, the beam flickered, so he reached up to tap it gently. That did the trick, and a solid beam split the darkness all the way to the other side of the room.

Weaver halted at the sight of the first Siren. It emerged from the center of a bulb-like cocoon and tilted its conical, eyeless head. With two bony arms, it pulled itself past the thick bristles lining the lip of the nest, like some grotesque insect hunting for prey. The cocoon was one of dozens hanging from the ceiling.

Shadows fanned out across the wall below, and a long wail echoed through the space. Then, before Weaver could pull his battery unit, he glimpsed something else suspended among the nests.

He had found Andrew.

The diver's helmet had fallen onto his chest, and as Weaver examined the body with his light, his breath caught. The muscular arms and legs that had earned Andrew the nickname "Pipe" looked like strands of rawhide. The beasts were plucking his bones raw. A waterfall of congealed blood streaked down the wall, and smaller Sirens were lapping it up from the floor.

Several of the creatures tilted their heads in Weaver's direction, and a high screech echoed off the walls as the monsters homed in on him. He stumbled backward, eyes locked on what remained of Andrew.

"Pipe, I'm so sorry," he said softly.

A beast poked its head out of a nest above and squawked at the smaller Sirens. They chirped back and climbed up into the nest.

The sudden realization staggered him: those things were children.

With their offspring now protected, the rest of the pack skittered down the wall, led by the same hulking abomination

Weaver had seen outside. If these things had a leader, this was surely it. A pair of wings unfolded from the giant's back, and it took to the air just as its minions dropped to all fours and charged.

If Weaver didn't get moving, he was going to be their next meal. But first he had unfinished business with the huge beast that had taken Andrew.

Raising his rifle, Weaver took a shot that punched through a leathery wing. Concrete chips and dust rained down from the ceiling to the pool of water below.

The creature swooped away, and Weaver trained the muzzle on the small pack clambering across the platforms toward him. A three-round burst to the midsection sent one spinning into the water. It thrashed to stay afloat, but apparently, these skeletal beasts with no body fat didn't swim very well.

Weaver took down another as it climbed to the top of a walkway over the pools. The rounds took off one of its arms, and it plummeted screeching into the pool with the other monster. Both slipped beneath the surface, unable to stay afloat.

After firing off two quick bursts at a pair of Sirens galloping toward him, he swung the muzzle upward, looking for the winged devil. Blood painted the floor, and the other beasts slid in it, crashing into one another in a tangle of limbs and claws and leathery flesh.

Heavy wingbeats came from somewhere to the left, though his light revealed nothing but the derelict platforms and walls covered in nests. He checked the pack struggling over the wet floor—eight of them, and they were almost on him. He didn't have enough ammunition or time to kill them all, leaving him with two options: take his battery pack out and jump into one of the pools, or run for the exit and hope he got there first.

It was a tough call. He wasn't as fast as he used to be, and he couldn't swim. Drowning in ten feet of water wasn't the best way to die, but it beat getting torn to shreds.

Weaver raked the oncoming pack with a sweep of automatic fire. Some of the rounds went wide, but many found targets. The mortally wounded beasts flopped on the concrete by the pools, while the rest kept coming. When the magazine in his rifle was spent, he pulled his sidearm. The pop of small-arms fire did little to deter the others. Gunfire wasn't going to save him.

He squeezed off several more shots at the closest Sirens, thinning the pack further, then turned and sprinted for the exit doors. As he crossed the space, a guttural cry rose over the screeches of the pursuing monsters.

No, it couldn't be.

The sound came again, and this time he had no doubt. This was not the mindless wail of a Siren, but a human voice, crying out a single word that sounded like *hell*.

Weaver glanced over his shoulder and directed his headlamp at the wall, where Andrew was lifting what remained of his right arm. The jagged stump pointed toward Weaver, stopping him midstride.

Despite all odds, Pipe was still alive.

"Shoot me!" he screamed.

Weaver raised his rifle to do what he should have done outside, when he had the chance to end Andrew's suffering before it began. He lined up the crosshairs on his comrade's chest and pulled the trigger. The round punched through Andrew's armor, and his helmet slumped onto his chest.

Weaver didn't have time to mourn. He barely had time to brace himself as the flying behemoth slammed into him from the side. The impact lifted him off the ground. Arms windmilling, he flew backward, losing both guns.

In what seemed like slow motion, the Siren flapped up toward the ceiling, revealing a hideously muscular torso. Weaver fell backward, clenching his jaw in anticipation, but instead of hitting hard concrete, his back found a mattress of water.

He hit the pool with a splash. Bubbles rose overhead as he thrashed and kicked, the beam from his helmet cutting through the murky water as he sank. Above the surface, the winged beast flapped down and landed on the edge of the pool. Furling its wings, it perched and waited. Several smaller dark shapes joined it.

Weaver rolled to his side, kicking and pulling at the water, but this was literally the first time he had ever tried to swim. It didn't help that he was weighed down by the dense plates of armor. He took in a long, slow breath, knowing that his helmet had only a half hour of filtered air. His life support system had shut off the air filter the moment it submerged.

His frantic efforts to swim to the other side of the pool got him nowhere. Then his boots hit the bottom. He righted himself and directed his helmet light toward the surface. The beasts prowled above, waiting for him to surface.

If he wanted to live, he would have to find a way to climb out the far side of the pool and dash for the exit. But without his rifle and pistol, he wasn't going to last long out there. The blaster at his hip was waterlogged, and he doubted the homemade shells would fire. Unless he could find his other guns, he would have to fend the beasts off with his blade.

The odds seemed insurmountable, but that had never stopped him before.

He drew in a breath and turned slowly, searching the pool for a way out. Lifting his right leg, he took a step forward. It was slow going, but at least he could walk. On the third step, his boot hit something that rolled across the floor. He angled his lamp down at a pile of slime-covered sticks resting on the bottom. He stepped over them but soon crunched onto another pile.

Weaver angled his light down and saw that they weren't sticks at all.

They were bones. *Human* bones.

Long bones, rib cages, and skulls had been dumped into the pool and were covered in the same red sludge he had seen earlier.

Weaver halted at the sight. He had finally discovered the remains of the people from ITC Communal 13—and, in the process, a way out of the pool. It felt wrong to climb over the dead, but he wasn't yet ready to join them.

* * * * *

Michael secured his battery pack in the chest slot of his armor. Ty, the Hell Divers' longtime launch technician, was not happy about prepping the tubes without orders.

"You have to trust me, Ty," Michael said. "A lot of lives depend on us. Layla and I have no choice but to dive."

"But Captain Jordan—"

"Fuck Captain Jordan," Layla spat. "He's going to get us all killed, starting with the team he just sent to the surface."

Ty's uncertain gaze hardened. He plucked the herb stick out of his mouth and threw it on the ground.

"I never did like him," he said. "Now, get your asses in the launch tubes before the militia breaks down the doors."

Michael put on his helmet and nodded at Layla as she climbed into her tube. She wore a vest stuffed with as much ammunition and supplies as she could carry.

Both divers looked as if they were preparing to go to war. If his hunch was right, they were going to need every bullet.

"Open up!" shouted a guard.

Michael pulled his blaster and pointed at Ty's head as the guard looked through the windows into the launch bay.

Ty held up his hands. "Uh, Michael, what the hell are you doing?"

"Just play along," Michael said. "If Jordan finds out you helped us, there's no telling what he'll do."

Another guard slammed into the door.

"There's a piece of paper in my pocket, with coordinates," Michael said. "When we send our SOS, you have to make sure the ship is there."

"But how? Captain Jordan has control over the ship."

"Samson can override the navigation systems. I don't have time to explain everything, but Jordan's been lying to us all along. We have to stop him, but first I have to help the other divers. We'll need them. Now, take the paper."

Ty hesitated. "I've got your back, Commander," he said at last. "Just like I had your father's back, and X's, and every other diver who goes out there."

That was good enough for Michael. He wanted to pat Ty on the shoulder, but instead he kept the blaster leveled at his forehead while climbing inside his tube. He reached up with his other hand to pull the lid down. Layla's tube shut with a loud click that was followed by a thud on the launch bay doors.

Glass shattered as one of the militia guards smashed the window with his rifle butt. He reached through, fumbling for the lock below.

Ty glanced over and continued punching in commands at the monitor that controlled Michael's tube. The green launch button on the pedestal lit up.

"Screw the launch protocols," Michael said. "You hit that button as soon as I give you the go-ahead."

Ty nodded. "You go get our friends back." He patted the top of the tube and ran over to Layla's tube.

Michael looked at the glass floor. His entire body was warm with the prickle of adrenaline. There was no going back now. This was treason. Even if they made it back, he and Layla might be facing a long stint in the stockade.

The comm link from the speakers in his helmet clicked on. "Commander Everhart, this is Captain Jordan, do you copy?"

Michael ignored the transmission and opened a line to Layla instead. He kept his gun pointed at Ty as he prepared her tube for launch.

"Are you ready?"

"When you are, Tin."

As soon as the countdown on his HUD flickered, Michael holstered his blaster. There was no turning back now.

"Fifteen seconds," Ty said.

Michael snugged the rifle strap over his back and made sure his blaster was secure. Then he checked the pistol holstered on his boot. He buttoned the strap that had snapped open. A quick glance at his HUD revealed that all systems were online.

Two beacons blinked on his minimap, one for each of them. Seeing the lights made him realize this was the right thing to do. He was going down there with his person. Together. That's how they did things.

"Handle your present with confidence," Michael whispered. "Face your future without fear." He had found that quote in a fortune cookie over a decade ago. Never had that it felt more significant than right now.

"Commander Everhart, I'm not going to tell you again," Jordan said. "Stop this launch, or I will have you both thrown in the stockade without rations!"

There was only one thing left for Michael to say. He bumped his comm pad to open a private channel to Captain Jordan and yelled, "We dive so humanity survives!"

He felt the floor beneath his feet fall away.

SIXTEEN

Rodger had finally stopped flinching each time the beast pounded on the doors. A few minutes ago, he had pissed himself from fright. Fortunately, it hadn't overfilled the bag in his suit.

He took a drink of water from the tube in his helmet and swished it around his mouth. The taste of beer still lingered. He wasn't proud of his worst habit.

Another thud rattled the warehouse of cryogenic chambers, and he jerked his gun back toward the doors. The monster seemed to be growing tired now. The impacts were sporadic, and Rodger could hear the thing wheezing and snorting.

Warehouse. Yeah, that's what he would call this place, he mused, looking out at the hundreds of capsules. Magnolia was checking the chambers around the base of the first tower.

"These are all compromised," she said quietly. "Something got to them before they were opened."

Rodger kept his voice low. "What an awful way to wake up."

Magnolia drew her knife as she approached the next capsule. She waved him over, and he ran to catch up. What he saw inside made him shiver. The interior bed was shredded and covered in small flakes of charcoal.

Rodger reached inside and picked up a piece. It turned to dust between his fingers and wafted to the floor.

"Whatever happened here, happened a long time ago," he said. "These remains are mummified."

"Keep searching," Magnolia said. "Maybe one of these capsules is intact. You take that tower; I'll take this one."

"Copy that, Mags. Want to bet on who finds the most horrible thing?" he said, trying to conceal his fear with bravado. It didn't work.

With a shiver, he directed his beam at the crushed glass below the next silo. He really didn't like splitting up, but Captain Jordan had given him a mission, and although Rodger wasn't sure exactly what he was looking for, he wasn't about to back down now.

He played the light on the ceiling, where a crane ran on a steel track overhead. The claws were clamped shut. He shifted the beam to the next tower. The glass surface of the chamber at the bottom was shattered, and a skirt of glass shards surrounded the base. His boots crunched over the debris as he circled and checked the tubes farther up. Each chamber was destroyed, the occupant missing. He angled his light inside to reveal a padded bed covered in brown stains. He held the beam there for a moment.

"Over here," Magnolia said, waving at him across the room. She stood at the base of another tower, but she was looking around the corner.

Rodger jogged over to her, trying to ignore the sounds of the creature still slamming itself against the door. He hoped it would either get bored or give itself a concussion soon.

"Everything I've found so far has been destroyed," Magnolia said. "But maybe if we can get those fired up, we can figure out what the hell happened here."

She centered her light on a raised platform in the middle of the room. A dozen computer monitors circled a central station. Perhaps they could operate the giant crane from there.

They crossed the dark room, their lights dancing over the towers. Everywhere Rodger looked, he found destroyed capsules.

"You stand guard," Magnolia said. "I'm going to see if I can get these working."

She jumped onto the platform and pulled the chair away from the rotunda desk. After a final scan of the room, Rodger climbed the two stairs and joined her.

"How about *you* stand guard?" he said. I'm the engineer here, and I think I already know how this warehouse operates." He raised his eyes to the crane on the track above them.

Magnolia shrugged and then stepped out of the way. He grabbed the back of the cracked leather chair and pulled it away from the desk. The cushion was surprisingly soft, and the computer equipment looked fairly well preserved. It was as if this room had somehow been frozen in time.

He brushed the dust off a keyboard and hit the power key. The button stuck, and the screen remained blank. For the next few minutes, he tried turning on the other computers, but none would activate.

"Well, we know there's power," he said, mostly to himself. "My guess is, the system is protected.

Footfalls tapped on the platform as he worked—Magnolia, pacing behind him. He pulled his minicomputer from his pocket and patched it to the ITC machine.

The screen of his device flickered on, and he typed several commands on the small keypad. He connected to the mainframe, but just as he had suspected, the system was firewall protected.

"It's gone," Magnolia whispered.

"What?"

He couldn't see it, but he was pretty sure Magnolia rolled her eyes behind her visor.

"The giant glowing monster that was trying to kill us," she said.

Rodger listened, but there was only silence. He had been so focused on starting the computers, he didn't notice that the beast had stopped ramming the door.

"Great," he said, glancing back down.

"How are you coming along?"

Rodger just shrugged. He didn't like to talk when he worked, and right now he needed to focus. Nothing he was trying seemed to work. The security wall protecting access to the operations system was more complex than anything he had ever seen. Someone had really wanted to keep unauthorized people from accessing it, which, in a way, explained the broken glass capsules. Whatever had destroyed the chambers had found the easiest way around hacking the system.

"Rodge, you sure you don't want me to try?"

"Nope." Then he tried the last thing he could think of: finding a back door to get through the firewall. A few lines of code and a very low belch later, a white glow suddenly filled the circle of monitors. He smiled, but not because he was into the system. Magnolia looked glorious in the light, like an angel.

"You did it!" She slapped her hands together softly, then looked over her shoulder, back the way they had come, but the door was out of sight.

He set his minicomputer on the desk and scooted the chair closer to the ITC computer while Magnolia hovered behind him. She brought a gloved hand to her helmet, as if trying to chew her fingernails.

"Let's see what we can find," Rodger said, clicking the ITC logo.

"Welcome," said a smooth voice behind them.

Both Rodger and Magnolia whirled around to see the ghost of a middle-aged man with dark skin, standing on the floor ten feet from the rotunda. The translucent apparition took a step forward and clasped his hands behind his back.

Not a ghost. A hologram.

Rodger stood and smiled at the odd-looking man with a neat beard and short-cropped hair.

The man smiled back at Rodger with a perfect set of teeth. He was wearing a suit and creaseless pants. Rodger had never seen anyone in such nice, new clothes.

"My name is Timothy Pepper, and I'm the manager of this facility."

Magnolia and Rodger exchanged a look.

"I'm Magnolia," she said, "and this is Rodger."

"Very pleased to meet you, Magnolia and Rodger," Timothy replied. He unclasped his hands and spread his arms out as if he was about to give praise. "You have accessed the cryogenic chambers of ITC Communal Thirteen."

He pointed at the towers framing the rotunda on both sides. "There are one thousand and twenty capsules containing various species here, all of them slated to be opened in ..." Timothy raised his wrist to check an elaborate watch and continued, "Two hundred forty years, two months, five days, twelve hours, forty-five minutes, thirteen seconds."

Rodger nudged Magnolia. "This guy has no idea."

Timothy cocked a bushy brow at Rodger.

"How long has it been since the system was accessed?" Magnolia asked.

The hologram checked his watch a second time. "One hundred three years, two months, fifteen days, fourteen hours, fifteen—"

"Yeah, we get it," Magnolia said, cutting him off. "Timothy, something's happened to your facility, and we're trying to figure out what."

"I'm sorry, but my system has been damaged and I have been dormant since *error: time stamp not found.*" The hologram flickered, and Timothy said, "Please stand by while I access my archives."

A second later, the apparition vanished, and a loud clicking sounded overhead. Magnolia and Rodger both raised their weapons as banks of lights on the towers switched on, filling the entire room with a bright glow that forced Rodger to shield his visor with his arm.

"Something is wrong," said a voice. "Something terrible has happened."

Rodger's eyes slowly adjusted to the light, and he pulled his arm down to see Timothy standing in front of the computer to his left.

"Shit, man!" Rodger said, jerking away. "Don't scare me like that."

"My apologies, Rodger."

"What happened here?" Magnolia asked again. "And did any of the capsules survive?"

"Ten capsules are still functioning in loading bay nineteen," Timothy replied. "I will retrieve unit nine hundred eighty-seven shortly."

The claws on the crane clanked open, and the unit screeched across the rusted track. It moved around a corner, out of sight.

"So you going to tell us what happened?" Magnolia asked.

"The system was damaged in the attack one hundred and three years, two months—"

Rodger grabbed his rifle when he saw a flash of movement dart between towers. He jerked the muzzle up at a Siren skittering toward the bottom chamber of the nearest tower, but Magnolia reached out and put a hand on the barrel.

"Just a hologram, Rodge."

The beast straddled the capsule and clawed at the lid, nails shrieking over the glass. In a fit of rage, it smashed its head into the pane again and again. Another holographic Siren joined the first, jumping onto the chamber. Together, they smashed through the glass and pried it open with their claws.

It was then that Rodger realized they were watching footage of what happened over a century ago.

The beasts pulled a bald, naked young man from the capsule

and dragged him to the floor. Another flurry of Sirens rushed into the room, circling the fallen man as he reached for his head, dazed. He blinked at the encroaching beasts and scrambled away, screaming. A moment later, the creatures attacked, tearing the helpless man apart. They yanked an arm from its socket and fought over it as a geyser of blood sprayed their pale bodies crimson.

"My God. It was the Sirens," Magnolia said. "How could this have happened?"

They were just holograms, but Rodger had a hard time watching the poor soul being ripped to pieces. Hundreds of Sirens spilled into the room and climbed the towers like ants. They broke through the capsules and dragged humans and animals away.

Timothy's smooth voice spoke again. "Stand by."

The grotesque scene vanished, replaced by the holograms of several humans wearing clothes like Timothy's but in worse repair. A woman led a group of emaciated people through the room. She stopped at a tower, putting her hands on her hips and looking up. Just by her movements, she reminded Rodger of Captain Maria Ash: strong, proud, and in charge. The other people circled around her.

"I've been in contact with the governors of all the other communal shelters, including those in other countries, and we have agreed to awaken 5 percent of the human population and 20 percent of the animal population. With resources so low, we will use the extra manpower to keep the Hilltop Bastion running. The animals will become part of our livestock. We will slaughter several right away and breed the rest."

"Governor, I would strongly advise against that," said another voice. It sounded just like Timothy. He turned toward the rotunda, and Rodger saw that it was indeed a younger version of the hologram, but without the beard.

"That must be Governor Rhonda Meredith," Magnolia said.

"Timothy, when was this? And just give me the years, please."

"Two hundred two years ago," came the reply over the speakers.

The holograms continued talking, and Rodger jumped down off the platform and joined Magnolia to listen.

"I understand your concerns, but we have no choice," Meredith said. "Unless anyone else can give me a good reason not to do this, I want it done. Now."

Yup, she definitely reminded him of Captain Ash.

The younger version of Timothy clasped his hands behind his back and said, "There could be severe consequences for waking them up nearly four hundred years early."

"Noted," Meredith said. She nodded at the man holding the tablet, and he nodded back.

The holograms vanished, replaced by a scene in some sort of command room. Governor Meredith was sitting at a table with civilians and soldiers. Timothy was there again, seated directly across from the governor.

"We can't control them," Meredith said. "Something is wrong. They aren't *normal.* They're killing people for scraps of food."

"Basic predatory instinct," Timothy said. "The scientists who designed the chambers and created this place are all dead now, but I understood enough from their notes to tell you that these hybrids are not like you and me. They underwent genetic modifications to help them survive in hostile conditions."

"They are monsters," Meredith began to say.

"They weren't supposed to be woken for five hundred years," Timothy said. "You've opened Pandora's box."

"We all have," Meredith said coldly. "The other governors are all reporting the same problems. We just lost contact with the communal in Hades."

Magnolia's eyes widened behind her visor as she looked at Rodger. "Hades," she said. "That's where ..."

"I had my suspicions that they would be different," Timothy continued, "but not like this. I'm sorry, but there's only one thing to do: a complete cleanse."

The holograms faded away and were quickly replaced by a scene inside a stairwell. A makeshift barricade of chairs and desks blocked the passage. Soldiers fired their weapons as they escorted Governor Meredith down the stairs. It was obvious to Rodger that the cleanse had failed, but watching it unfold was still horrifying, especially knowing he had just walked down the same stairwell.

The governor held a radio to her lips. "We're low on food and ammunition. We can't keep them back much longer. Please, *please* send support to the following coordinates..."

The scene vanished, and Timothy's hologram reappeared. "That was an abridged version of what occurred here. As I stated, my system was damaged, but I was able to access these memories."

"Mags, do you remember that message from Governor Meredith we heard on the *Hive*? They were trying to keep the things they unleashed from killing everyone."

Magnolia took a step backward and motioned for Rodger to join her.

"What are you?" she said to the hologram.

Timothy tilted his head quizzically. "I am Timothy Pepper, the manager of this facility."

"No, you're a computer hologram wearing someone else's face. Who was Timothy Pepper?"

"Was he one of them?" Rodger asked. "One of the survivors of the war?"

The AI nodded. "Timothy Pepper was the last survivor. I took his form after he was killed by the hybrid humans. I watched as they left the Hilltop Bastion and returned to the surface, where they evolved into the creatures you call 'Sirens.'"

"No way," Magnolia said. "I don't believe it."

"His hope was that someday he would meet another survivor," Timothy said. "Now it appears I have—two of them, in fact."

He smiled, but Rodger didn't feel like smiling back. He felt sick to his stomach. Why had Captain Jordan ordered him to come here?

Then something clicked in his mind.

"That son of a bitch," Rodger whispered, turning to Magnolia. "He sent us down here to prove we can't ever return to the surface."

"What? Who?"

"Captain Jordan. He ordered us to risk our lives just to prove a point."

Magnolia scowled. "I told you someone was trying to murder me. I guess now we know who."

"I'm going to kill him myself," Rodger said.

A metallic cracking and squealing sounded above, and both divers raised their weapons at the crane moving down the tracks. In its grips, it carried a chamber, which it slowly lowered. Magnolia hurried over as the claws gently set it down on the floor.

"I warn you, this will not—" Timothy began to say, when a cry of shock cut him off. Magnolia stepped back, bumping into Rodger as he approached.

Rodger moved around her to get a look at the capsule. Inside was the shriveled form of what had once been a person. The leathery skin over its bony chest moved slowly up and down.

"It's still alive," Magnolia said. "What the hell is it?"

Timothy approached and glanced down, blinking as if he didn't recognize it at first. "Artificial evolution. The system—most of it, I should say—is connected to surface sensors that monitor radiation, temperature, and so on. They didn't start like this, but over the years, almost every hybrid developed mutations. Many of the animals underwent the same changes."

"I don't buy it," Rodger said. "Evolution—artificial or any

other kind—takes a lot of generations just to make one tiny change in the genome. So maybe fifteen human generations since those shit-for-brains at ITC started playing God—or playing Darwin, I should say."

"So it would seem," said Timothy, "if evolution did indeed occur at an even pace."

Magnolia gave the hologram a streetwise glare. "What's he talking about, Rodge?"

"If I may," Timothy continued. Apparently noting his audience's impatience, he added, "I'll stick to just the main points, I promise."

The two divers exchanged a look, and Rodger gave a grudging nod. "Enlighten us, then. You've got five minutes."

The hologram cleared its throat and spoke in a more professorial tone: "Way back in the late twentieth century, a theory known as *punctuated equilibrium* was proposed, to account for unexplained gaps in the fossil record. The radical new theory suggested that the plodding pace of evolution is occasionally 'punctuated' by rapid flurries of change, giving rise to new species in only an eyeblink of geological time. Hence the absence of fossils to account for their development.

"Hold up there," Magnolia drawled. "How 'bout a translation for those of us who speak English?"

"Bear with me, please," Timothy said. "It will all make sense very soon. The theory was controversial, to say the least, and after a while, even the founders lost faith in it."

"That's all fascinating, I'm sure," Rodger said, nodding toward the ghastly creature in the capsule. So how does that get us from humans to *that* monstrosity in just a couple of centuries?"

The Timothy hologram gave a tolerant smile. "Well, it turns out that those daring scientists were barking up the right tree after all: punctuated equilibrium does indeed happen—they just never found its triggering mechanism. But ITC's scientists did find it—in some humble marine invertebrates known as bryozoans, which underwent a burst of evolutionary change back during the age of the dinosaurs, thus proving out the theory."

"I hate to break up this thrilling lecture," Rodger said with a theatrical sigh, "but we've got a mission to complete."

"*Sh-h-h-h!*" Magnolia hissed. "This could be important." She turned to the hologram. "Please don't mind him. You were saying?"

Timothy picked up without missing a beat. "So ITC studied the bryozoans' genome and found the genetic switch in their DNA that made this rapid evolutionary burst possible. Then they went way outside the box, using one of the millions of rapidly evolving viruses in a single cupful of polluted seawater."

This is where it gets interesting," Timothy said. "By splicing a specific strand of the viral RNA with the particular bryozoan DNA sequence, ITC's scientists gave their modified humans the capacity to evolve rapidly—that is, mutate—to adapt to a hostile environment. But to the geneticists' astonishment, the spliced-in bryozoan DNA and viral genetic material did something they could never have expected: it allowed the modified humans and domesticated animals to mutate *within a single lifetime*. Until then, mutations occurred only through sexual reproduction. But all of a sudden, genetic change that should take thousands of generations could occur within a single living creature as it slept in cryo-suspension."

"The scientists were playing god," Rodger said, thunderstruck.

"Indeed," Timothy said. "Their genetically modified organisms—people as well as hogs, chickens, and other useful vertebrates—could respond immediately to environmental changes by evolving and mutating within their cryo capsules. Of course, the ITC scientists hedged their bets by leaving a small control group of human and canine capsules largely isolated from the sensors relaying the atmospheric data."

"Yeah," Magnolia said. "What could possibly go wrong?"

She raised her rifle at the glass and had flicked the safety off when a frantic voice came over the comm.

"Magnolia, Rodger!" *Gasp.* "Do you copy?"

It was Weaver, and he sounded as though he was having a hard time breathing.

"Copy that, Weaver," Rodger said. "Where are you?"

"I'm trying to get to the command room at the top of the facility." Static crackled over the channel as Weaver struggled to get enough air. "Pipe's gone. I've got to find a radio to send an SOS to the *Hive*. Meet me at the command room."

Magnolia looked at Timothy. "How do we get out of this place? We can't go out the front door."

He pointed to the top of the towers. "The Sirens accessed this room through the utility tunnels."

Rodger thanked him with a nod as they turned to climb the towers. Timothy was just an AI, but his personality was that of a man, a real survivor from the Old World. Something about leaving him behind, all alone, felt wrong.

SEVENTEEN

"You're never getting—"

The electromagnetic storm silenced Captain Jordan before he could finish his sentence, but Michael could fill it in: they weren't ever getting back on the ship again.

But Michael had more immediate concerns. He had to reach the surface in one piece, then find the Hilltop Bastion and the other divers before it was too late.

He torpedoed through the black clouds, eyes flitting between Layla and his HUD.

They were at three thousand feet. The light-blue residue of a lightning streak lingered across his vision. To the east, a hundred feet above him, the light of Layla's battery unit glimmered. He could hardly see her through the ice crystals that had formed around the edges of his visor, but he saw every inch of the electrical arc that flared across her flight path.

The bolt seized the air from Michael's lungs. He resisted the urge to blink, terrified that in the millisecond his eyes were shut, his best friend and lover might tumble away into the darkness.

"Layla!" he yelled.

The maddening reply of static came over the channel. Ignoring the risk of crosswinds throwing him out of his dive, he tilted his helmet up to watch her. She was still plunging fast, which made her difficult to track. And like that, she was gone, vanished in the cloud cover.

"No," Michael whimpered, staring at the spot where he had last seen her. "Layla, you can't..."

He stared at the darkness, his heart aching. If something had happened to her, it was his fault.

"Layla!" he shouted. "Layla, can you hear me?"

He closed his eyes for a full second before snapping them back open to search again. His heart was hammering so violently, it seemed enough to throw him off course.

A few beats later, a faint glow emerged to the east. In the wake of blue, he saw the outline of a free-falling body, still positioned in a nosedive—something Layla couldn't do if she were hurt or unconscious.

Michael exhaled and tilted his visor back toward the fort of black clouds. They weren't out of this yet.

The wind howled around him, tugging and lashing from every direction. The numbers on his HUD were going haywire, flickering between two thousand and three thousand feet. He reached for a flare but thought better of it and brought his arm back to his side.

The sky was still a colossal static generator, and the quickest way through was by splitting it at a terminal velocity. Even without his instruments, he knew that he was moving at around 180 miles an hour.

Michael tried to calculate his exact speed and altitude based on the last reading. If he was correct, they were close to the edge of the storm. He searched the muddy clouds for the surface. There was no seeing through the black, however, and he risked another sidelong glance to check on Layla.

Thunder cracked and lightning rippled across the sky to the east—another immense storm brewing. The red zone wasn't far now, and the Hilltop Bastion was right in the center of it.

Michael pulled his arms out from his body and fought his way into a stable position. Wind rippled his suit and whistled over his armor as he spread his arms and legs. Looking skyward, he saw Layla doing the same thing.

The numbers on his HUD came back online, and the comm channel clicked on.

Michael bumped his chin pad. “Layla, are you okay?”

“I’ll be fine,” she said, but he could hear the lie.

“How bad?”

“It’s nothing, Tin.”

He could hear the pain in her voice. She was injured, perhaps badly.

“Just hang on,” he said.

He forced his gaze away from Layla. The blackness had transformed into a brown and gray wasteland backlit by arcs of lightning. Most of the city had been leveled, but a cluster of gutted scrapers stood at the edge of a small valley. Farther east, about a mile from the devastation, the land seemed to be moving, undulating. He bumped on his night-vision optics and gasped.

“Tin, is that the ocean?” Layla said over the comms.

She sounded better, more like her energetic self, but Michael was still worried.

“I think so,” he said. He wasn’t exactly sure how the ocean was supposed to look in real life, but he knew that it was as gray and dead as everything else in the world below.

He brought his wrist monitor up and tapped the screen with his finger. “We’re pretty far off course,” he said. “The Hilltop Bastion is two miles west. Pull your chute and follow me.” He reached up and pulled his rip cord. The chute fired, and he felt the familiar sensation of being yanked into the sky by a giant hand. He grabbed the toggles and scanned the city rising up to meet him. Sailing west, he set a course to the Hilltop Bastion.

There was no sight of the winged Sirens, and he couldn’t hear their otherworldly wailing from the streets below. But they were out there somewhere, watching and waiting for the right opportunity to strike. But the monsters weren’t the only things on the surface tonight. His friends were down there, too.

He just hoped he wasn't too late to save them.

Michael kept his voice low as he bumped his comm to open a channel to the other divers.

"Apollo One, Angel One, Raptor Two, Raptor Three, does anyone copy?" Michael said.

Only thunder answered him.

"This is Commander Everhart, heading west over Charleston toward the Hilltop Bastion. Does anyone copy?"

"Do you see that?" Layla said.

Michael scanned the city again before replying.

"What am I looking for, exactly?"

"To the east, those scrapers."

He blinked off his night-vision goggles. Where there should have been only the dead brown and gray of the surface, Michael saw a faint orange glow. One of the buildings near the shoreline was flashing like a beacon.

"What the hell is that?" he whispered. It would be naive to think there weren't other strange creatures down here, but Michael had never seen anything like this on another dive. Whatever it was, it didn't matter. They were too far away to check it out.

He bumped his optics back on. "Apollo One, do you—"

Weaver's rough, uneasy voice broke over the channel. "Michael, is that you?"

"Yes! I'm here with Layla. Where the hell are you?"

"I'm underwater and trying to get to ..." Weaver's words were strangled, as if he couldn't get enough air. "I'm trying to get to the lookout. What the hell are you doing here?"

"Underwater?" Michael asked.

"We came to save your ass," Layla cut in.

Weaver gave a bitter laugh. "You're too late. This place is crawling with Sirens and—"

A crosswind rocked Michael, breaking up the transmission. He worked his toggles and fought his way back into position.

"Come again, Weaver," Michael said. "Didn't catch your last."

"Magnolia and Rodger are on their way. I think. I haven't heard from them for a while. This place, this *tomb*—it's crawling with monsters. Like nothing I've ever seen before."

Michael almost swallowed his mouth guard. He knew it! Magnolia was still among the living, but if she and Rodger had gone radio silent, it meant they were in trouble.

"Where's Pipe?" Layla asked before Michael could.

The silence was enough to confirm that Andrew wouldn't be making the trip home this time.

Weaver drew a long breath, exhaled, and said, "I'm going to try to reach the command center and send an SOS to the *Hive*. Look for the windows at the top of the bunker."

"No, wait," Michael said.

Several seconds of static rushed over the channel.

"Weaver? Do you copy?"

"Must have run into trouble," Layla said.

"I guess so. Stay close to me."

Michael cursed himself for not explaining more in their brief conversation, but there had been no time. The wasteland below was rising fast to meet them.

He readied to flare his chute as he searched for their target. To the west, a canyon of debris piles led to a dirt hill topped by a squat concrete structure with small windows. That had to be where Weaver was headed.

"Good luck," Michael said even though the other diver couldn't hear him.

* * * * *

The corpse of a Siren floated on the surface directly above Weaver. The eyeless face seemed to stare down at him, its wide mouth open in a macabre grin full of bits of its last meal. Andrew's flesh, likely enough.

Weaver looked away. He was standing on the pile of human bones, holding his knife and trying to conserve his air. He was running low, way past the allotted thirty minutes, but the corpse and the monsters prowling the poolside weren't helping him manage his intake.

He could see their distorted, bony figures through the murky water. They knew he was down here. His conversations with Magnolia and then Michael had sent the beasts into a frenzy, and he had been forced to shut down the channel. Getting out of here wasn't going to be easy, but a plan was forming. All he needed now was the courage to do what came next. He was down both of his main weapons and he couldn't risk trying to find them. He also didn't trust his wet blaster, and his knife wasn't going to do much against the monsters.

Instead, he scooped up a jagged femur in one hand and groped for a skull with the other. Each was slick with the same reddish slime that lined the edges of the pool. He didn't know what it was, but from what he could see, even the Sirens weren't drinking it.

Weaver steadied himself on the bone pile and looked back up at the surface. The door was about three hundred feet away. He took a mental picture as two Sirens skittered by. A third stopped to examine the water, dipping a talon beneath the surface and sending a ripple overhead before moving on.

He waited several minutes before taking another step up on the bone pile. The rush of his heart sounded in his ears. Eighty-nine dives had put him in some rough spots, but this was maybe the worst.

Drown or be torn to shreds? Neither option had much to recommend it.

Come on, you old bastard. You can do this.

With the femur and skull in his hands, he sucked in a long breath. Exhaled. Sucked in another. Exhaled.

One ... two ...

A flash of motion came from the left. A Siren was leaning down toward the water. Weaver lunged, spearing the beast in the face with the sharp end of the femur. It sliced through flesh and hit the skull with a crack that Weaver could hear under the water.

The creature darted away shrieking.

This was Weaver's only chance.

He shut off his headlamp and climbed up on the bone pile, tripping and sliding, pushing himself up through the bubbly red sludge. As soon as his torso was above the water, he tossed the skull into the air, then stumbled up the last steps onto the floor. He slipped again but righted himself, prying out the battery unit with his free hand just as he spotted a pair of Sirens making a run for him. Clenching his jaw, he raised his weapon and waited for the beasts to strike.

The skull bounced off the far wall and clattered onto the floor. Then came the sound of running footfalls changing direction. Shrieks rang out all around him. It seemed the distraction had worked, but he remained frozen, clutching the femur and his battery pack. He held his breath and stared into darkness so deep, he couldn't even see shapes. Somewhere behind him, wings beat the air. His muscles tensed as he waited to be yanked upward, but the only thing to hit him was a draft of air. The creature sailed overhead toward the skull, its screech morphing into the electronic sound that Weaver hated most.

He fought the urge to bring his hands to his helmet. The horrid wail transported him back to his childhood, when he would hide under his bunk and hold his ears to block out the emergency siren warning of disaster aboard *Ares*.

The wailing, the darkness, and the thought of Andrew's corpse hanging from the wall was all too much. He couldn't wait in here an instant longer. He pivoted toward the exit—at least, he thought the exit was this way. With each step, he half expected to splash into another pool of water.

Holding the bone and his other hand out in front lest he crash into something, he ran on his toes to keep the sound of his boots low. The water-slick soles of his boots made it tricky. Along with being wet, they had collected some of the red gunk from the pool. Each step made a wet squelch that drew the attention of the beasts behind him.

He flinched as something clanked on the ground in front of him. It was the same sound the skull had made. Could that be possible? Had the beasts thrown it back at him?

Weaver ran harder. Never mind the noise. Wailing and the skittering of claws over concrete followed him. He had to be near the exit now.

Another sound joined the racket—the whoosh of wings.

Run, old man! Run!

The wingbeats grew louder, reminding him of the turbofans on the *Hive*. A strong wind nearly knocked him to the floor as the creature sailed overhead. Weaver couldn't hold out any longer. He jammed the battery unit back in his chest socket and bumped on his night vision.

Nothing. His HUD wouldn't activate, either. The water must have short-circuited his electronics.

Weaver reached up and turned on his headlamp. The beam captured a sinewy figure crouching in the open doorway not ten feet away. A piece of meat hung from its beak. Not just meat—a tattered swatch of a Hell Diver uniform.

The scavenger reached up with its single webbed hand to shield its huge eyeball from Weaver's beam. It let out a squawk that attracted the attention of the winged Siren. But instead of turning to grab Weaver, it changed course and snatched up the smaller creature in its talons.

Weaver plucked his battery unit out a second later and lay flat on the floor as the Siren returned to its nest. A flurry of wails sounded as the rest of the pack retreated.

For several moments, he worked on calming his heart. He wasn't sure what had just happened, but whatever the strange little beast was, it had likely saved him from a terrible death.

As the Sirens plastered the creature up next to Andrew on the wall and began plucking off limbs, Weaver made a run for the staircase to the operations center. He wasn't sure what had prompted Jordan to send Michael and Layla down here, but he was happy they had come. Getting out of this place was going to be harder than getting in.

* * * * *

"Commander Everhart and Raptor Diver Brower have jumped ship," Jordan announced from the top level of the bridge. "This is a betrayal of the worst kind, and it will not be tolerated!"

Below, every officer on the bridge avoided his enraged glare. Even the apprentices stationed in navigation took a sudden interest in their boots.

Jordan stepped up to the railing, flanked by Sergeant Jenkins. The sergeant had been instrumental in quelling a riot five years ago, and in taking back the farm a decade earlier, but that didn't make him invaluable. Jenkins hadn't said anything when Jordan was plucking out Janga's fingernails for information, but his eyes had showed his disapproval. The old soldier's leadership style had served the *Hive* well for decades, but if he wouldn't follow Jordan's orders, plenty of younger soldiers would happily take his place.

Jordan grabbed the railing and looked out over the tiered floors of the bridge. One officer didn't shy away from his eyes. Katrina, gripping the spokes of the oaken wheel, looked right at him.

He could find no hint of affection left in her eyes. Over the past twenty-four hours, the last of her love had drained away.

But he would get it back; he was confident. She would learn to trust him again. She would learn to *love* him again. Confidence and patience were key. He couldn't afford to trip up now. The divers on the surface would all be dead soon. If they somehow made it back with supplies, he would figure out what to do with them later.

For now, he had to cleanse the ship before someone else betrayed him.

"Sir, I have a sitrep," Ensign Hunt announced, stepping away from his station.

No matter how many extra rations Jordan allowed, the young ensign was still rail thin—and soon he was going to get even skinnier. For he had joined the ranks of people Jordan didn't trust.

"We're coasting through clear skies ten miles due east of the storm over Charleston, sir," Hunt said. "Still no word from the surface."

Jordan replied with a nod, then stepped away from the railing and walked down the stairs. He replayed the launch in his mind again and again as he walked. The militia guards had confirmed Ty's story: Michael had held a gun to his head. But Jordan still wasn't sure he believed the technician. He did have an easy way to test his loyalty, however. The *Hive* was about to lose five divers—six, if you counted Magnolia—and Ty knew a lot about diving. He would be a good replacement.

"Captain," Katrina said. She eyed the blood on his hands with disgust.

"At ease, Lieutenant," he said.

"A woman," she sneered. "An old woman."

"An old woman who put every life on this ship in jeopardy, and don't forget that, Lieutenant. We can't be soft just because someone is old."

"She sold herbs, Captain, and everyone knew she was crazy."

"Not everyone, sadly. She convinced Commander Everhart to jump ship."

Jordan looked at the wall-mounted monitor. On it was a map of the area surrounding the Hilltop Bastion. He still wasn't sure what Janga had told the divers before her arrest. Despite his best efforts, she had revealed little in their "interview" after Michael and Layla jumped.

But now he realized that Janga had actually done him a favor. Even if she had revealed secrets such as the SOS from X, those secrets would now die with the divers on the surface. The cost was high; their valuable experience would be hard to replace. Fortunately, there were always lower-deckers who would jump at the chance to risk their lives if it meant eating well.

"Launch bay is ready, Captain," Sergeant Jenkins said.

"I'll be right there," Jordan said.

Katrina reached out for his arm. "Please don't do this, Leon."

Jordan hesitated. She pulled on his sleeve—an act of desperation and disobedience that annoyed him. Her lack of professionalism on the bridge was testing his patience. He was starting to wonder whether he could still trust her.

"You can be merciful," she said.

He pulled his bloody cuff away and frowned. "That's where you're wrong, Katrina. There is no room for mercy in the sky."

EIGHTEEN

Magnolia was going to kill Jordan when she got back to the ship. Trying to murder her was one thing, but getting Andrew killed and risking the lives of the other divers to prove a point? That was psychotic. She wasn't sure how she would kill him, only that it would be up close and involve her hands.

First, though, she had to find a way out of the Hilltop Bastion and back to the ship. So far, they weren't making much headway. She crawled ahead of Rodger through the utility tunnel. He seemed to be enjoying the view, judging by the beam from his light. It danced across the tunnel but conveniently seemed to center on her backside most of the time. A free view of her ass was the least she could give him for coming down here to find her.

Her light picked up another pile of feces ahead. The sight almost made her gag even though she couldn't smell it. Bones and a single feather protruded from the pile. The Sirens had been inside the passages, and while these remains weren't fresh, the number of piles was alarming. She began to wonder whether the creatures lived in the ducts.

The thought made her check the knife sheathed at her thigh. She continued crawling, doing her best to keep her rifle from banging against the metal. Rodger was having a hell of a time behind her. She couldn't see him, but she could hear the ruckus he was making. Whatever was sticking out of his vest pocket kept catching on the strap of his rifle.

"Stow your shit," she hissed.

Magnolia continued wriggling through the narrow passage, her elbows scraping on the metal walls, and her helmet grazing the ceiling. She squirmed faster, like the soldiers she had seen ducking under barbed wire in the films from the archives. Her HUD clock showed they had been moving for thirty minutes, but with Andrew dead, the mission clock didn't mean much anymore. Their mission had changed from rescue and salvage to survival.

The light on her helmet showed another junction ahead. She pushed on until she was about five feet away, then pulled in her knees and turned to look at Rodger. He was scrunched like an animal in a crate. His beam hit her in the visor, and she ducked, shielding her face with her arm.

Rodger moved it away and then scooted up so they were visor to visor. His eyes searched hers in the half-light of her low beam, and for the first time in years she felt a flicker of something other than disdain for the opposite sex.

"Didn't Timothy say to take a left here?" she asked quietly.

"A left, then right, then left, then another left." He nodded confidently. As she turned away, he covered his vest pocket.

"What the hell do you have—"

The sound of claws scratching metal cut her off.

"Move!" Rodger said. Crouched on his knees, he brought his rifle muzzle up as she pivoted back toward the junction. Her light captured a Siren moving on all fours toward them, spiky back hunched and scraping against the sheet metal. A rope of saliva swung like a pendulum from its wide mouth.

A deafening crack filled Magnolia's helmet, and the flash dazzled her eyes. Another shot followed, and she scrunched down to give Rodger more room. Agonized screeches bounced off the walls. She blinked away the stars and saw the beast flopping around, crashing off the metal ductwork.

"Hold your fire!" Magnolia barked.

As soon as Rodger lowered his rifle, she was crawling toward the monster. It was making too much noise; the racket would draw every Siren in the area to their position. She centered her light on the beast as it thrashed, smearing its blood all over the sheet metal. With a side-armed motion, she threw the blade down the tunnel. It sank halfway to the hilt in the side of the creature's head. A moment later, it went limp, and Magnolia was moving on her elbows and knees toward it. She stopped a few feet away to make sure it was dead before grabbing the hilt of her knife. She tugged, and the blade came free, releasing a stream of gore onto the floor. It was hard to believe this had ever been human.

Magnolia went to push the corpse out of the way when the beast suddenly slashed at her. Something stung her right shoulder as she brought her elbow pad down on the creature's skull. There was a screech followed by a *thunk, thunk, thunk*. Fueled by adrenaline, she slammed her pad down over and over. Soon the creature's skull was like the shattered shell of a boiled egg, and her armored elbow was covered in blood.

"You can stop now," Rodger said. "It's dead, okay?"

A guttural roar seemed to answer him. The noise came from somewhere below them, but Magnolia didn't need to see through the duct to know the source. The glowing beast from the cryogenics lab was out there, hunting them.

She looked down at her arm. The beast had gotten her good. Her light captured a pair of deep, bloody gashes. The claws had shredded her layered suit, and blood seeped out of the tears.

"Magnolia?" Rodger said again.

She applied pressure with her left hand and said, "I'll be fine."

The wound burned, but it was the radiation, not blood loss, that concerned her. Here inside the facility, the rads were minimal. She could survive for a while down here, but before she went topside—if she ever got out—she would need to patch the tears in her suit.

One thing at a time, Mags.

She pushed the pain and thoughts for the future out of her mind, and they moved quickly down the passage for several minutes. Her light ran over walls covered in scratch marks, and before long they came upon another pile of feces. This one was fresh, and she instinctively held her breath as she crawled over the top.

Halfway to the next junction, she came across an area with three vents on the right side of the wall. The metal grate of the center vent had been pried off.

She kept her rifle cradled as she squirmed toward the opening, waiting for a Siren to pop out into the passage. Every few feet, she stopped to listen, but the ringing from the gunshots made hearing difficult. Beyond the high-pitched whine was a faint humming that reminded her of the nuclear power plant on the *Hive*.

Timothy had mentioned that they would cross over the engineering room on their way through the utility tunnel. If that was where they were now, then they weren't far from a passage that served as a back door to the control room.

She didn't stop as she passed the first two vents, but approaching the third, she slowed. Her light captured the opening but barely penetrated the space beyond.

"Lights off," she ordered.

Both beams flickered off, and darkness filled the tunnel, leaving only the faint blue glow from their battery units to guide them. Pain shot up her right arm as she heaved the gun up toward the opening.

She squirmed a few feet on her elbows and knees and slid over the vent cover. The ringing in her ears had finally faded away. She couldn't hear the monsters, only the reassuring hum of machines. Curiosity prompted her to bump her light back on. If this was the engineering room, it could contain valuable fuel cells for the *Hive*. Perhaps she could use them as a ticket back onto the ship. She would deliver them to Jordan right before she plucked the eyes from his skull and fed them to him.

Shifting her helmet toward the opening, she raked the beam back and forth. Below was a room so big, the beam didn't reach the other side.

"What do you see?" Rodger asked.

Magnolia angled the light downward, capturing the outline of several tarp-covered mounds. Beyond these, she could see shelves stacked with what could be supplies.

"Hand me one of your flares," she said.

Reaching back with her uninjured arm, she felt one of Rodger's sticks in her palm. She pulled off the top and hit the flare's tip against the striker surface. The flame burst out, and she dropped it into the room. Two heartbeats later, the flare clanked to the floor.

The red flare lit up a room larger than the lab they had just left, revealing a fleet of vehicles. Trucks, cars, jeeps, and even a motorcycle were parked below. Unlike the rusted hulks she had seen on the surface, these vehicles had intact windows and unblemished paint, although their tires were flat.

Curiosity once again getting the best of her, she reached back for another flare.

"Weaver's waiting on us," Rodger protested.

"This'll only take a second."

He scooted up closer and tried to see past her, but Magnolia just moved her fingers, signaling for the flare.

"Fine," he huffed.

She grabbed it, struck the surface, and flung it out as far as she could. This time, the red glow bloomed over something that took her breath away.

"Come on, Mags. Tell me what you see."

She waited just to be sure, but the familiar beetle shape sitting on raised platforms across the room wasn't a figment of her imagination.

"Hey, Rodge, do you remember Timothy saying anything about an airship down here?"

She moved aside to let him see.

"Holy shit," he murmured. "Is that really a ship?"

Magnolia smirked. "Think you can figure out how to fly it?"

* * * * *

Sweat rolled down Weaver's forehead even as his armor shed the water from the treatment plant. He couldn't see much without his night vision, and the quiet darkness was starting to unnerve him.

The optics weren't all that had malfunctioned after his swim. His battery charge had dropped from 70 to 20 percent, and the glow from the dying unit penetrated only a few feet around him. If the heart of his suit gave out, his worst fear would come to pass and he would die in this tomb, blind and deaf.

But Weaver refused to die alone, in the darkness underground. He had lived his whole life in the sky, and he couldn't bear the thought of spending his last moments trapped down here. He wouldn't go out like Andrew, especially at the hands of the Sirens.

Blaster in one hand and broken femur in the other, he continued up the steps. He had discarded the wet shells, and though the ones on the outside of his vest were just as wet, he had found a couple of homemade buckshot rounds, which he kept in a pouch. The two shells weren't going to save him if he encountered the Sirens again, but the ammunition made him feel a little less helpless.

A rattling around the next corner signaled a new threat approaching. He set the thighbone down and placed his palm over his headlamp before switching it on. He took his hand away for an instant before covering the lamp again. In the single moment of light, he glimpsed something unexpected in the stairwell above.

Tubes webbed across the walls at the next landing. He pulled the cup of his hand away from the headlamp and ran the light over them. Pores dotted the rubbery black skin, and every few feet, a halo of spiky growths surrounded bulbous black openings like lashes protecting an eyeball. The walls that the tubes ran across were not equidistant here. They appeared bent inward, and Weaver quickly saw why. The tubes fed into wider holes in the concrete, leaving gaps that exposed the earth. Feathers and white grit had piled on the floor.

This wasn't another nesting area of the Sirens—it was the home of the cyclopean camouflaged beasts he had encountered outside the treatment plant. The tubes appeared to be some sort of passage or burrow to move from the facility through the earth, and perhaps back to the surface. The openings appeared to be doors of some sort.

Vultures, he mused. These mutants looked something like the carrion birds from the archives. But the camouflage made them even better scavengers.

Not good.

Weaver was sandwiched between the nesting grounds of a new type of mutant, and the home of the Sirens ten floors below. This place, unlike the other ITC facilities he had raided on past dives, seemed to be home to a variety of monsters.

As he picked the femur back up, he considered the barrier in the stairwell. For some reason, the Sirens didn't seem to venture up this way, which meant these emaciated vultures must be more dangerous than they looked.

Holding his weapons loosely in his gloved hands, he continued up the landing. There was only one logical way out of this monster-infested facility, and that was up. He would take his chances with the one-eyed, one-armed scavengers over the eyeless beasts below.

On three, you're going to stop this lollygagging around and run like a man.

He bolted up the stairs on the count of two. The ceiling and walls had shifted as if an earthquake had hit the stairwell. Wide cracks spiderwebbed across the concrete. Navigating around the barbed spikes that lined the holes, Weaver brushed up against one of them, and the lash-like growths scraped his armor. But they weren't hard like teeth after all; they reminded him more of stems from the glowing bushes he had encountered on other dives.

He leaped over a tube crossing the stairs and ducked under another hanging from the ceiling as he approached the next landing. All the while, he heard a low, insistent hissing sound, like air escaping from a ruptured pressure suit.

Weaver kept running, but the sound seemed to surround him from all sides. Motion flickered from an opening in a tube above him, and the spiky eyelashes fluttered. All at once, eyeballs on stems popped out like periscopes to peer at him. A vulture pulled itself out of the tube overhead and plopped onto the landing.

Weaver swung the femur. The bone connected, and splattered the eye with a loud pop. Milky fluid peppered his armor as he ran past the beast. It crashed into the wall, clawing at its ruined eye.

He rounded the corner and halted before running up the steps. The rubbery surfaces of the burrows bulged as vultures crawled through them. Spiky lashes opened like the mouths of Venus flytraps, disgorging a dozen of the feathery beasts into the passage. And those were just the ones he could see with his lamp. Others, fully camouflaged, skittered across the walls.

This must be why the Sirens didn't venture up here, he thought grimly.

The gray creatures snapped their hooked beaks at him as he ran. Those that ventured too close on the right, he batted away with the femur; those to his left, he smacked with the barrel of the blaster.

He fought for every step, swinging, stabbing, and bulldozing his way through the small army of mutant creatures. But it wasn't the beasts he could see that were the problem. How many more were hiding in the shadows?

The tubes around him continued to bulge with reinforcements. He considered firing his blaster, but the two shots were too valuable to squander on beasts the size of a dog. Their curved beaks and claws were sharp, but they weren't as strong or as fast as the alpha-predator Sirens.

He batted three of them out of the way and rounded another corner, followed by the squawking din. Creatures he couldn't see grabbed at him with their single arms and pecked at his armor with their beaks. A sharp pain stabbed his right shoulder. Claws slashed his ankle, drawing a cry of pain as he dropped to one knee. He swung both weapons in a wide arc, sending several of the creatures crashing into the wall.

Something moved above him, and only then did he realize how badly he had underestimated the little monsters. If there were enough of them, they didn't need to be strong or fast to take him down and pick his bones clean.

By the time he looked up, the beast was already on him. It landed on his booster with such force that he hit the stairs with a grunt. The hiss that followed wasn't from the vultures; it was from the escaping helium. Worse, a crack now rickracked across his broken visor, letting in the toxic air.

Through the cracked visor, he could just make out a door at the top of the stairs. He was almost to the operations room. The rusted door was at the landing not ten steps above him, but with his suit and visor compromised, he wouldn't survive long even if he made it there.

In a fit of rage, Weaver bucked the vulture off him. He stabbed another beast through the chest with the ragged end of the thighbone and swung the barrel of his blaster into a pair on his left. Then, lowering his helmet, he bolted up the last stairs, spearing through the remaining vultures as they snapped and pecked at him with their beaks.

Summoning what strength remained in him, he pushed away the pain and fear. He barreled through a vulture that came darting down the stairs, swatting it with the thighbone. Claws slashed at his legs, and a beak sank through his boot as he crushed the thing. Gritting his teeth in pain, he shrugged off another creature that had landed on his back.

Weaver could smell them now: a mixture of gamy meat, body odor, and filthy feathers. His battery unit continued to drop, and each breath filled his lungs with toxic air, but through it all, he held on to hope that he could still escape.

He kept his gaze on the door ahead and smacked another vulture to the floor below with his blaster. The tubular burrows ended at the upper landing, but they continued to bulge with more of the creatures. Weaver stabbed the jagged end of the femur through the rubbery skin on the final step, impaling a vulture he couldn't see. He pulled the bone free and stabbed another before it could emerge. Then he squeezed the trigger of his blaster. Fire flashed from the muzzle, and buckshot punched through the control panel beside the door.

Past the ringing in his ears came the shrieks of the frightened vultures. He jumped onto the landing and turned to see the beasts flocking down the stairs, squawking in their ghastly language. Hell, if he had known it would scare them off so easily, he would have fired earlier.

Injured and exhausted, Weaver stumbled over to the door. He shined his light through the crack and listened for hostiles, but all he heard were the squawks of those still retreating down the stairs. Placing both palms against the door, he pushed it open, fully expecting to find it overrun with monsters.

The station was deserted. Desks covered in dusty computer equipment furnished the small room. He took a step inside and dragged the nearest desk over to block the door. Metal screeched across the floor as he added two more tables to the barricade.

He scanned the room, playing the light across the steel shutters on the far wall. He found the radio station on a desk in the center, then looked for the backup power. A control panel was mounted on the wall to his right.

Weaver flipped the breakers, and the overhead lights blazed to life. His eyes closed at the sudden brilliance, but opened again at the sound of a voice.

"Hello and welcome."

Blinking in the brightness to locate the source of the voice, he banged into a desk.

"Do not be alarmed," the voice said. "I am Timothy Pepper, the manager of ITC Communal Thirteen. How may I assist you?"

Weaver eyed the hologram skeptically. He had heard of AIs, but this was the first he had ever met. According to the archives, the cost of the technology had made them unaffordable over 260 years ago. Others, like the one on the *Hive*, had malfunctioned not long into service. Captain Ash had told stories of those days, but Weaver didn't know the details. He wasn't even sure his old airship, *Ares*, ever had an AI.

All Weaver knew was that he didn't trust the image standing in front of him. Hell, he barely trusted *humans.*

"Sir, you are injured," Timothy said. "May I provide medical assistance?"

"I don't have time for that. I need to use your radio."

Timothy clasped his hands behind his back. "Certainly. I can assist you with that."

Weaver limped over, leaving a streak of blood on the tile floor. His leg and foot were in bad shape, and his visor was useless. Although he knew it was only his imagination, he swore he could already feel the radiation eating away at him.

"I need you to transmit an SOS over this channel," Weaver said. The piece of paper he pulled from his vest was wet, the numbers streaky. "Think you can read these?"

Timothy checked the paper and then gestured for him to take a seat at the radio desk. The speakers crackled and coughed after years of sitting idle as Timothy scanned through the channels. As he worked, Weaver tried to reach Magnolia and Rodger on the channel.

"Do you copy, over?" he said.

Static crackled over the channel. They were still radio silent.

"The other divers are on their way to this facility," Timothy said, without taking his focus off the radio.

"How do you know that?"

"Because I provided them a map to get here," Timothy replied.

Weaver relaxed a bit. If Magnolia and Rodger trusted Timothy, maybe he could, too. He held up his hand at the sound of another voice. This one was coming from the speakers on the radio.

"Wait, go back," Weaver said. "What is that?"

"One moment," Timothy said.

Static filled the room. Then a voice. Not Rodger or Magnolia, but an oddly familiar voice that Weaver hadn't heard in years.

"If anyone's out there, this is Commander Xavier Rodriguez. I'm leaving Hades and heading east toward the coast."

* * * * *

Jordan strolled into the launch bay for the first time in months. He usually sent Katrina to supervise these things, but this was one launch he didn't want to miss. He nodded at Sergeant Jenkins, and the militia guards closed the double doors. One of the windows was missing, the glass shattered by a militia soldier trying to stop Michael and Layla. The valuable glass wouldn't be replaced anytime soon.

Outside, people jostled for a look through the small windows.

That was fine. Jordan wouldn't stop them from watching; it would be good for them. An execution from time to time reminded the citizens of the *Hive* just who was in charge.

He crossed the room with his hands folded as if in prayer. It seemed fitting, really, since he was about to cleanse the ship of a false prophet.

Janga stood inside drop tube 13, with only her head visible beneath the domed lid. A single tear rolled down her bruised face. She wiped it away with bloodied fingers when Jordan began walking toward her.

He stopped at the red line surrounding her tube and let his hands drop to his side. He tried to appear nonthreatening, as if he were about to have a conversation with an old friend. Ty stood a few feet away, arms folded across his chest, jaw clenched. Jordan could see he wasn't happy about his new position as a Hell Diver, but so far, his only protest was the frown on his face.

"Leave us," Jordan said to the former engineer.

Ty glanced at Janga once more and walked over to the operations room. The hatch shut with a loud click that echoed through the vaulted space.

Jordan stepped over the red line and smiled at the old woman. "Part of me was hoping it wouldn't come to this," he said. "Part of me was hoping you would keep your mouth shut belowdecks and stay out of the archives. But you gave me no choice."

A snort of disgust came from inside the tube. Janga looked up at him with a stubborn gaze that reminded him of Captain Ash. Both women had believed they were doing what was best for humanity.

Both had been wrong.

Janga knitted her brow, squinting. "You know what's down there, Jordan. You know why Maria's dream of finding a home on the surface can never be in our lifetime. But you also know you can't keep the *Hive* flying forever."

Jordan looked over his shoulder to make sure the guards weren't paying attention. Both men were facing the doors, backs turned. He took another step toward the launch tube and leaned down toward the plastic surface so his face was just above Janga's.

"Before Captain Ash died, she told me in detail what happened to those facilities, and I put the other pieces together by reading the restricted archives. Why do you think I've stayed clear of those red zones for so long?"

"Because you're a coward."

"I'm a realist," Jordan said.

She met his eyes again. "Your lack of imagination prevents you from seeing past your fear. We all will die up here unless you follow the path Maria laid out."

"You're the only one dying today."

Jordan retreated outside the red barrier and shouted for Ty to prep the launch tube. He kept his eyes on Janga. There was sadness there, and pain, but he saw no sign of fear. That didn't sit right with him. He had beaten her, so why was the old woman looking at him as though she had just won?

She pulled a chain from her robe and kissed the smooth surface of a black stone pendant. "Your time will come, Leon Jordan," she said. "The man from the surface *will* lead these people home—but you won't be among them."

A voice crackled in his earpiece as he prepared to launch her into hell.

"Captain, do you copy? Over."

Jordan pulled his hand away from the green button and flipped the minicomm to his lips. "This better be important, Hunt."

"Yes, sir. I just received an SOS from Weaver. He's requesting that we move back into position to evacuate the divers."

"Have they found any power cells?"

"Negative, sir, but they did rescue Magnolia."

Jordan ran a finger under the collar of his uniform. Magnolia was a tough woman to kill. Good thing he had a contingency plan.

"Weaver said he and the other divers will be ready for evac in less than an hour."

"Who knows about this?"

Hunt hesitated for a moment. "Just me, sir."

"Let's keep it that way," Jordan replied. "I'll be on the bridge in a few minutes."

Jordan glanced down at Janga once more and shook his head. He would have liked to stay, but he had more pressing issues to deal with.

He pressed the launch button and strode away without a backward glance.

NINETEEN

Michael frowned. He had heard something on the wind. It must have been a Siren, though it did sound a bit strange for one of the beasts. In a way, almost human ...

The noise unsettled him, and he squeezed Layla's hand as they hunkered down in the shell of a bus near the Hilltop Bastion. The distracting beep of an incoming message jolted his attention to his HUD. Finally, the channel was back online. They weren't alone after all.

Weaver's voice came over the line. He sounded shaky and short of breath.

"Michael? Magnolia? Does anyone copy? Over."

Michael kept his voice low on the reply. "Copy that, Weaver. This is Michael. Layla and I are a quarter mile due east of the target. Where's Magnolia and Rodger?"

"I don't know. They're still off comms." Weaver coughed, the sound rattling deep in his chest.

"You hurt?" Michael asked. "You sound awful."

There was a short pause. "Do you see the beacon for the supply crate?"

"Yeah, we passed it on the trek in."

"Good. I lost my rifle and pistol. I'm also going to need a new helmet, a suit repair kit, and a booster. Grab that shit and then get your asses up here. I'll try to get the windows open."

Michael peeked around the corner of the bus where he and Layla were sheltering, to look up at the Hilltop Bastion. The concrete bunker rose toward a sky glimmering with lightning.

They were so close, but there was no telling how badly Weaver was hurt. Michael reminded himself that the reason they came down here in the first place was to save the other divers. If that meant backtracking into hostile territory to find the crate, then so be it.

"Michael, do you copy?" Weaver said.

"Copy that. We have hostiles out here. Have to sneak past them to get to the crate."

"Before you go, there's something you need to hear." White noise surged over the channel, and then he heard Weaver addressing someone. "Timothy, can you turn that up?"

Before Michael could ask who the hell Timothy was, a message began playing in the background. Michael recognized the rough voice instantly.

"If anyone's out there"—*crackle*—"this is Commander Xavier Rodriguez." *Crackle.* "I'm leaving Hades and heading east toward the coast."

Michael felt his heart catch. "No," he whispered. "No, it can't be."

"Was that X?" Layla asked quietly. "How is that possible?"

"Weaver, I ... I don't understand," Michael said.

"Sorry, kid, but I thought you should hear it just in case something happens to me before you get here. I don't know if he's still alive, but X survived that dive ten years ago."

"We're coming, Weaver. Just hang on."

Michael considered telling Layla to wait here, but she would never follow that order—and to tell the truth, he didn't want to go out there without her for backup.

"Stay low and hold your fire until I tell you," he said, pushing away thoughts of X. There would be time for questions later. Right now, he had a mission to complete.

Michael bolted away from the bus and ran for the wall of debris across the road. Bringing the scope to his visor, he glassed the area for contacts. The shadows he had seen earlier were gone.

At his nod, they moved out, hugging the piles of broken asphalt and concrete. Fallen girders covered the path ahead. Farther down the road, one of their chutes flapped over the concrete, the motion attracting a flurry of shadows. A single Siren skittered into view, tilting its head and swiping at the billowing canopy.

Michael made a hand signal, and they recrossed the road to a mound of rubble. A building, toppled from a long-ago blast, was just a pile of rusting metal, shattered glass, broken mortar, and rotted wood. He couldn't see the supply crate yet, but according to his minimap, it had landed just above them.

Lightning bloomed across the sky, revealing the treacherous path to the top. Shards of glass and ragged ends of metal jutted out between upended foundation slabs and clumps of brick. It was a minefield of hazards.

"Slow and steady," Michael said quietly.

After a final scan of the road, he led the way across in a low crouch, stepping over the smaller debris skirting the bottom of the toppled building. He slung his rifle over his back and grabbed a flange of channel iron to pull himself up onto a masonry ledge. Layla swung up behind him. From the ledge, they clambered up the incline, boots finding purchase in the shifting scree.

To his left, a gray steel door jutted out of the pile like the fin of a shark. They crouched beside it to listen. Gusting wind stirred up grit on the street below. The cries of hunting Sirens rang down the corridors of the demolished city.

"I hear them out there," Layla whispered.

"Me, too. Let's hold here for a few minutes."

As they waited, Michael's cluttered mind shifted back to the message from X. He didn't understand how it was possible. While

Captain Ash was alive, Michael had pestered her to send a rescue mission for X just in case he had somehow survived. She had assured him that she was monitoring all transmissions from the surface. Michael had trusted Maria, but now he couldn't help but wonder whether she, too, had lied.

Layla reached over and put her hand on his forearm. "I love you, Tin. Everything's going to be okay."

She always could tell when he was upset, even wearing a visor and a bulky armored suit.

"I have to find him," he said. "Ten years alone on the surface."

She shook her head. "I'm sorry, but I don't see how he could still be alive."

"If anyone could survive out here, it's X."

Michael stood up and peered over the edgewise door. Unslinging his rifle, he scanned the road below. The eyeless mutants had vanished, the only movement the flicker of the parachute in the distance.

Lightning flashed overhead, and the thunder crack rattled his armor. They were almost to the top of the pile, closer to the storm and more exposed to the elements. They made the final push carefully, Michael selecting each step and looking back every few feet to check Layla's progress. He squeezed between a pair of beams protruding like horns from the mound. They crunched over loose concrete and sand encrusted with shiny black glass formed by the blast that had leveled most of the city. At the very top, looking strangely whole and symmetrical amid such bent and broken surroundings, was the supply crate.

"There it is," he said. "Stay here while I check it out."

She raised a hand to protest, but Michael was already moving. Keeping low, he crept up the slope. He dug boots in, dislodging a piece of concrete. It slid down and over the side of the metal overhang below. The chunk tumbled the rest of the way down the pile, clanking and clattering all the way to the street.

"*Shit*," Michael whispered as a high wail answered the sound.

Layla looked up from her position, frozen in place while Michael unslung his rifle. In the green hue of his night-vision optics, he searched the street. The wind seemed to carry the screeches to them from all sides.

He angled the muzzle down at the street, where the bases of the fallen structures lay in shadow. In the residue of lightning flashes, the shadows seemed to stretch outward and recede like the surf on a beach.

Another wail joined the first, then another. Michael swept the gun back and forth, searching for a target, but the beasts remained hidden.

Over the wind and screeches came another sound: the whoosh of what could have been turbofans on the *Hive*. Michael felt a moment of confusion, followed by a spike of adrenaline as he realized his mistake.

Before he could warn Layla, a beast flapped around the side of the tower and grabbed at her.

"Layla!" Michael shouted.

He aimed his rifle at the abomination's right wing and squeezed off three shots, cutting through the wing. Despite the injuries, the beast continued to climb.

"Help!" Layla screamed.

Michael aimed at the other wing, firing three gaping holes into the leathery hide. That did the trick, and the creature spun down into the rubble, where he delivered the kill shot to the head.

Layla slid nearly ten feet down the incline, letting out a yelp of pain as her boots hit the ground.

"To me!" he shouted.

She pushed herself up and limped toward him as he fired on another Siren swooping in from the cloud cover. A round cut through its body and it flapped away, shrieking in its otherworldly voice.

Michael turned toward the heart of the city, holding the scope just shy of his visor. In the small circular view, he saw a swarm of what looked like bats flapping away from the girders. He slowly moved his crosshairs across the city, watching in horror as streams of the monsters lifted off and rose from the husks of gutted scrapers. The first two had been just a recon party. Now the main force was on the way.

Layla squeezed between the pair of beams and scrambled up to Michael. He reached out and grabbed her hand. Although they needed to move, he couldn't help but hug her tight.

"I thought I had lost you!" He pulled away to look her up and down. "Are you hurt?"

"I hurt my ankle and I'm going to have a bad burn from the dive, but I'll live," she said, trying to smile through the pain. "Good shooting."

Michael looked over her shoulder to the hilltop in the distance. They were nearly half a mile away now, not counting the time it would take to pick their way back down to the street and then climb the hill to the bastion. By the time they reached the street, the monsters would be on them. If they were to survive the next fifteen minutes, they couldn't make a single mistake.

Movement near the bus where they had sheltered revealed another threat. The Sirens weren't just in the air—another pack was darting across the street. Loping on all four limbs, they skittered toward the tower of debris.

"We're being surrounded," Michael said, pointing. "Hold back that bunch."

Layla scanned the sky and then the ground, where she picked out a target. Her first shot cut through a finned back, severing the spine. The Siren flopped like a landed fish. The others fanned out around the dying creature and charged forward, undeterred. She wouldn't be able to keep the creatures off their position for long.

He punched his four-digit code into the panel on the supply crate. It beeped and flashed red as Layla fired off another three shots. Steadying his shaky fingers, he entered his code a second time. The lid popped open, and he began stuffing supplies into his pack. Inside went a helmet, pistol, and three boosters. Then he grabbed a parachute.

The screeching armada of monsters reminded him that they were running out of time. Layla continued firing on the beasts below. They had reached the hill of rubble and were already scrambling up the side.

"Put this on," he said, handing her the backpack. He swung his rifle up and fired several shots while she slung the straps over her armor. In the sky, the beasts had formed a V beneath the floor of the storm clouds. In the lead was a meaty creature with a spiked and ridged back that reminded Michael of something prehistoric.

He bumped his comm pad. "Weaver, how are you coming with those windows?"

Back to back, Michael and Layla fired at the monsters closing in around them. He squeezed off several bursts at the formation, but without tracers it was nearly impossible to hit anything at this range.

"Windows are all jammed and too heavy to raise manually," Weaver reported. "But I'm working on it."

"We have to get out of here," Layla said.

"Grab on!" Michael shouted.

As soon as she wrapped her arms around his waist, he reached back and punched his booster. The canister fired, launching a balloon into the sky. Next, he punched her booster. The two balloons yanked them off their feet. He grabbed his toggles and directed them toward the Hilltop Bastion. Below, the creatures had summited the hill and were batting at the sky with their claws. Several others hunched down to spread their wings, preparing to leap. By the time they took to the sky, Michael and Layla were already two hundred feet above them and drifting west with the wind at their back.

Layla gave a snort of laughter. "You're crazy, you know that?"

"I learned it from X. Now, clip your locking biner to my armor."

"I hope he taught you how to multitask, because those things are gaining on us!"

Michael didn't even try to glance over his shoulder. "You have to be my eyes, Layla."

She tightened her grip around him and turned. "Three Sirens about five hundred feet to the east. The larger formation is another thousand feet behind them."

Michael kept his gaze on his HUD, watching their altitude. To make this work, he must time it perfectly. Every decision, every movement, had to be precise.

At four hundred feet, the wind picked up, and he used his toggles to position them directly in the air current, giving them more speed.

The screeches grew louder as they rose higher in the sky. More lighting arced through the clouds. Michael squinted at the bunker. They were coming in fast, but fast enough?

"Whatever you plan on doing, you better do it soon!" Layla shouted.

Michael worked the toggles as they ascended higher. Even aided by the wind, they weren't going to outrun their pursuers. The Sirens were closing in. He could hear their wings slapping at the air. At eight hundred feet, he let go of the left toggle and grabbed his blade.

"What are you doing?" Layla shouted.

"Going with plan B. Hold on!"

"What do you think I'm doing now?" she said, but she squeezed him so hard his armor pressed in on his rib cage.

He grabbed the toggle again, blade in hand, and watched the number on his HUD tick upward. The wailing was so loud now, it sounded like standing beneath a klaxon on the *Hive*.

Michael's heart was fluttering, but he remained calm, remembering the fortune he had handed X all those years ago: *Handle your present with confidence. Face your future without fear.*

At 850 feet, he cut through the lines attached to their balloons. Layla screamed, and Michael didn't have the breath to reassure her. He watched the towers rising up to meet his boots as the Sirens screeched in confusion directly overhead. He didn't need to look up to see they were seconds from being snatched away by those talons and torn apart in midair.

So far, his timing was spot-on, but they still had the landing ahead of them.

Michael waited five beats before pulling the ripcord on the new chute. The lines snapped taut and yanked them up, and for the moment before the wind caught them again, the chute seemed to pull them toward the monsters above. Now they were sailing straight toward the bunker. A single white light, like a beacon in the night, shone from the side of the concrete structure.

"Give us some covering fire, Weaver!" Michael shouted. "And if you haven't already gotten a window open, break one quick!"

"It's open, but I told you I don't have a rifle!"

Michael cursed. In the chaos, he had forgotten that detail. They weren't going to get any help in the final stretch. Worse, they were descending too quickly. If they continued to drop, they wouldn't make the window. The only way this would work was if he held them steady and sailed right through the opening.

This would require a perfect flare.

He bumped his chin pad.

"We're coming in hot, Weaver. Clear us a path. As soon as we land, you need to close the window behind us!"

Michael brought his knees up as they soared over the spilled entrails of buildings. His boots were just feet away from a bent girder rising up in their path. He toggled again to adjust their trajectory one final time.

Inside the bunker, he could see a room furnished with desks and computer equipment. Lots of corners and hard surfaces to run into. There was no way around it—this was going to hurt. It was a good thing Layla couldn't see the approach, but she could still see the monsters.

"They're almost on us!" she shouted. "Michael, hurry!"

"Pull up your legs!"

At the last second, he flared his chute and they sailed inside the room, both of them bringing their boots up just in time to avoid injury. Michael hit the ground hard and tried to run out the momentum. He made it two steps before her weight pulled him down. They crashed in a heap, rolling and tumbling across the floor until they fetched up against a desk. The impact knocked the air out of his lungs.

"Layla," he gasped. "Are you ...?"

Weaver darted forward, hauled in the tail of Michael's canopy, and slammed the window. Thick metal shutters clattered over it. Seconds later, the monsters slammed into the hatches. Claws slid down the metal outside.

"Jesus Christ!" Weaver shouted.

Head pounding and stars drifting before his vision, Michael closed his eyes. When he opened them a moment later, he saw a pair of bloody boots hurrying away from the windows.

Michael pushed at the ground and looked at Layla, sitting beside him with one hand on her helmet.

"Nice job, Commander," she said, flashing a weak smile.

He helped her to her feet. When they turned, they saw Weaver standing next to a hologram of a man in an immaculate suit. The contrast couldn't have been sharper with Weaver, who looked as though he had been dragged through hell and back. The man was covered in blood and dirt, and his visor was cracked.

"I got your gear," Michael said, tossing him the bag.

"Thanks," Weaver grunted. He jerked a thumb at the ghostly image beside him. "This is Timothy. He runs this madhouse."

"Welcome to ITC Communal Thirteen," the hologram said.

A gunshot sounded from somewhere inside the facility.

"That must be Magnolia," Weaver said. He ran over to the desks that had been hastily pushed against the door. "Help me with these!"

Michael joined him, and together they pulled the desks away. Two more shots went off, and a squawk sounded from the passage beyond the door.

"Get ready; they're going to have company," Weaver said.

Michael unslung his rifle and raised it at the battered metal door. Weaver grabbed the handle and yanked it open. The light from their helmets shone over a landing. Weird tubes as thick as Michael's waist crawled over the walls and stairs below. Sprawled in the middle was the body of a mutant creature unlike anything Michael had ever seen. Blood pooled around the carcass.

"What the hell is *that*?" Layla said.

"Vultures," Weaver said. "If you see any more, shoot 'em! Sirens aren't the only things that want to eat us."

Light beams danced up the stairwell. Michael still couldn't see the other divers, but he could hear them.

"Weaver!" Magnolia shouted. "Get that door open!"

Michael squared his shoulders and readied his rifle at the landing. Another gunshot reverberated off the walls. The squawks that followed were different from the screeching of the Sirens, but that was small comfort.

He moved his finger to the rifle trigger as two figures bounded around the corner. It was Magnolia and Rodger, and they were running for their lives. They raced past him without stopping.

Movement flickered over the stairs below as Michael backpedaled after them, but he had trouble focusing on the creature, which seemed to blend in with the shadows. At last, he caught the gray, feathery thing in his crosshairs. He squeezed the trigger, and nothing—the magazine was dry, the action open on an empty chamber.

A single eyeball on a stalk roved toward him. The creature cried out, and suddenly, the passage was alive with the beasts Weaver had called vultures. But where had they come from?

Staggering back toward the doorway, Michael lost his footing and fell on his butt. Hands grabbed him under the armpits and pulled him into the room.

He reached for his pistol as the other divers dragged him to safety. A dozen of the little beasts bounded up the stairs, a dozen single eyeballs peering at him.

Rodger and Magnolia slammed the door and helped Layla push the desks back into position. The hands under Michael's arms relaxed their grip, and Weaver limped over to help reinforce the barrier.

Dazed, Michael stood as the vultures clawed at the door. All around them, the Sirens were still slamming against the metal hatches covering the windows. The divers were surrounded, but at least they were together.

Magnolia and Rodger were both bent over, hands on their knees, panting. Weaver was resting his back against the barricade of desks. His lungs were crackling with each breath—a bad sign that he had breathed in something toxic. After a moment, Weaver crossed his arms and looked at each diver in turn.

"First, get Magnolia's wounds disinfected and dressed, and get that suit closed and sealed. Meanwhile, somebody's going to tell me what the hell is going on."

"It's a long story," Michael began as Layla fished a medical kit and a suit repair kit out of the backpack.

Magnolia cut him off. "Jordan tried to kill me. Now he's sent the rest of you down here to prove some psychotic point about the ship not being able to return to the surface. Ever."

"Point received," Weaver said. He unfolded his arms, and for the first time, Michael saw the extent of his injuries. Multiple tears in his layered suit revealed blood gashes where the beasts had torn his flesh. But it was the cracked visor that concerned Michael the most.

"You're here now," Weaver said, looking at Layla and Michael. "Any ideas on what we should do? I've already sent an SOS to the *Hive*, but if Jordan's gone bat shit, then I have a feeling it won't matter. We didn't find any fuel cells or anything else to barter our way back onto the ship with."

Michael felt deflated. He had come down here to help his friends, but he had no idea how they were going to get out of this room. All his clever plans had only managed to get them trapped in Hilltop Bastion's command center. Layla gripped Michael's hand as they listened to the macabre chorus of hungry beasts.

"Jordan's going to leave us down here, isn't he?" Rodger said, shaking his head. The normally cheerful engineer-turned-diver looked on the verge of tears. "I'm never going to see my parents again."

"Yeah, you are, Rodge," Magnolia said. "You just gotta figure out how to fly that ship."

"What ship?" Michael, Layla, and Weaver all said at the same time.

"An airship," Rodger said. "Not as big as the *Hive*, but a ship nonetheless." He stood up a little straighter. "We found it on the way here."

"There's an underground hangar not far from here," Magnolia said.

"Can you fly it?" Weaver asked.

Rodger shook his head. "I ... I'm not sure."

"You, Michael?" Weaver asked. "Layla?"

"I haven't had that sort of training," Layla said.

Michael shook his head. "Me neither."

"I can operate the aircraft," answered another voice. "I can also provide, from memory, schematic diagrams for its every bolt, rivet, and wire; run diagnostics; and direct all repairs for any conceivable malfunction or damage, down to a likelihood of ten to the negative ninth power."

Every helmet turned to the hologram. The AI known as Timothy smiled. "There is nothing else for me here. It is time for me to leave ITC Communal Thirteen."

TWENTY

"Everyone but DaVita and Hunt, out!" Jordan shouted from the top of the bridge. Sergeant Jenkins stepped up beside him, glowering at the crew.

The dozen officers and support staff quickly cleared the room, leaving Katrina at the wheel and Hunt at his station. They both watched Jordan walk down the stairway to the lower level.

He passed navigation, communication, and all the other stations where officers had served proudly for hundreds of years. They had all had the same mission: to keep the *Hive* in the sky. That was the mission he had taken an oath to uphold. Not to set down on the surface, not to hide underground. To stay here where they had survived for 260 years, far above the decaying wasteland of the Old World.

Jordan had thought of all the ways he might convince Katrina that he had no choice but to leave the divers down there, but he hadn't yet found a scenario where she wouldn't end up hating him even more than she did right now. In the end, he opted for the truth—or a portion of it, at least.

"The Hell Divers have decided to betray the *Hive*," he said. "I uncovered the plot while interrogating Janga. Commanders Weaver and Everhart and Raptor Diver Brower were all seen conspiring with her belowdecks. Magnolia Katib is also suspected of having classified information. At this point, I have to assume that the Hell Divers have all been compromised."

Katrina's eyes were full of fire. "Conspiring about what exactly?"

"They were planning a coup," Jordan said. His gaze shifted from Katrina to Hunt, and his eyes widened ever so slightly.

"That is correct," Hunt said. He swallowed and then added, "Commander Everhart and Diver Brower launched themselves to the surface after talking with Janga—"

"So they abandoned ship?" Katrina said, cutting Hunt off. "Why would they do that if they were planning a coup?" She folded her arms, revealing the tattoos on her forearms. "Why dive to the surface first?"

"To get reinforcements," Jordan said.

"No way," Katrina said. "This is insane. I've known Tin and Layla since they were kids. They're good people. They would never betray the *Hive*."

"Really?" Jordan interjected. He pushed his mike to his lips. "Sergeant Jenkins, bring in Ty."

The doors to the bridge whispered open, and two of Jenkins' men pushed the technician inside. He staggered to the top of the bridge, holding up a hand to protect his bruised and swollen eyes from the bright LEDs. The militia guards had done a number on the traitor.

"Ty!" Katrina cried out. "Oh, no. What happened to you?"

She ran for the stairs, but Jordan held out a hand to stop her. He needed her by his side now more than ever. Convincing her the other divers were trying to overthrow him was the only way to make that happen.

"I was told Michael held a gun to Ty's head," Jordan said, "but it appears that was just smoke and mirrors. This traitor was part of the coup all along." He held up a crumpled slip of paper. "These coordinates were found in Ty's pocket after Michael and Layla dove to the surface. It didn't take much persuasion to get him to reveal the truth."

Ty looked at the ground.

"Tell Lieutenant DaVita what Michael said to you," Jordan urged.

Split lips trembling, Ty choked out a reply. "He told me to tell Samson to override the navigation systems. He wanted us to pick them up so he and the other divers could board and take over."

Jordan spread his arms. "You see? Now do you believe me, Katrina?"

She shook her head again and let out a sigh. "I knew something would happen eventually, but not like this."

Jordan motioned for the guards to take Ty away. Nodding all the while, he let her do the talking. He could tell he was making headway with her. Patience was the key to winning back her respect and trust—and, eventually, her heart.

"You're not the first captain to face challengers, you know. I'm sure we all remember the failed mutiny on the farm. But the question is, what will you do now? You can't just leave them down there. We have to find a solution to this. A *peaceful* solution, Leon."

Jordan blinked in surprise. "You would have me welcome the divers who want to kill me back onto my ship?"

"The *Hive* needs them," Katrina said. "And it's not *your* ship."

"Hell Divers come and go, but the *Hive* remains in the sky."

"We can't leave them," Katrina said. "I *won't* leave them. I was a Hell Diver, too, or have you forgotten?"

Jordan held back a sharp remark. He had one more card up his sleeve.

"I didn't want to do this, but there's something you need to hear, Katrina." Jordan nodded at Hunt. "Play Weaver's transmission."

"The one about Commander Rodriguez?" Hunt asked.

"*What!*" Katrina said, turning to Hunt. "What about X, Ensign?"

Jordan glared at Hunt from behind Katrina's back. A glare that promised punishment. The ensign's slip had just cost him the upper hand. God, why couldn't he trust anyone to be competent? Why couldn't *anyone* just do as they were told?

"What Ensign Hunt meant to say was the message about ITC Communal Thirteen," Jordan said. "And what they found down there."

Realizing his mistake, Hunt turned to go back to his station, but Katrina grabbed his arm.

"I asked you a question. What was the message about X?"

Hunt looked over at Jordan. Neither said a word. Monitors beeped and the ventilation system hummed. It was a moment of calm before the tempest that Jordan knew was about to break.

Katrina shattered the silence with an angry shout. "Leon, you are going to tell me what the hell is going on. And you're going to do it right now!"

Jordan could see the hatred in her eyes. He knew then that he had lost her. There was no lie he could tell now that she would believe. His skull pounded from the pain of the realization.

"Go ahead, Ensign, play it all," Jordan said. He slowly massaged his temples to relieve the tension headache. "Start with the earliest transmission."

"Sir?"

"That's an order!"

Hunt sat at his station and tapped his touch screen. The voice of a dead man filled the bridge. Jordan watched Katrina's reaction as X reported his position and status over the past ten years. There were dozens of messages as X trekked across the wastelands nearly four miles below.

Jordan expected Katrina to shout again, or maybe even cry, but to his surprise, she remained calm and grimly silent.

"Now play that transmission from Weaver," Jordan said. Hunt hurried to comply, not daring to meet the captain's eyes.

"Command, this is Angel One requesting evacuation," Weaver's voice said. "The facility is compromised. Apollo One is dead, and there is no sign of survivors here. Rodger and Magnolia might still be alive, so please send help as soon as possible."

Katrina curled one hand protectively over her belly. "We have to send down another team and help them," she said, her voice rising to a maddened shout. "We can't leave them down there like you left X. I won't do it!"

Jordan shook his head incredulously. "Were you not listening? The divers want to kill me, and there is nothing on the surface for them—or us—but death. Now, I'm the goddamn father of the child growing in your womb, Katrina, and I will not have you harming it by getting hysterical over a handful of traitors. You will calm down, or I'll—"

"You'll *what*?" she snarled. "You don't get to tell me what to do ever again. I can't believe I ever loved such a coward."

The words stabbed Jordan's fast-beating heart, but his pain quickly turned to anger. Blinded by rage, he turned to Sergeant Jenkins. The old soldier looked back at him uncertainly.

"Sergeant," Jordan said. He paused, but there was no turning back. He could no longer trust Katrina and there was no gaining back her trust. "Sergeant, escort Lieutenant DaVita to her quarters and post a guard."

"Yes sir," Jenkins said. Katrina glared poison at Jordan as the soldier grabbed her upper arm and started half-dragging her from the bridge. She swore at Jenkins and jerked her arm away.

Jordan let out a sigh through his nostrils and released the tension in his jaw. The anger began to subside as he drew in a new breath. He chose to view this as a fresh beginning.

"Ensign, plot a new course to the closest green zone," Jordan said. "We're leaving."

* * * * *

Magnolia led the divers through the utility tunnel. Every movement hurt her shoulder, but she was too full of questions to pay much attention to the pain.

"Why would Jordan keep the fact X is still alive a secret?" she whispered.

"Katrina." Michael's one-word reply told the whole story.

Magnolia shook her head. She should have figured that out. Of course Jordan wouldn't want to rescue X. Katrina had loved the diver once, and anything that threatened the thin-skinned captain was dealt with swiftly—fatally, if necessary.

"I'm going to enjoy plucking his eyeballs out," she muttered.

"Nope," Weaver said. "Jordan's mine."

"Quiet, or you may not get the chance," Michael snapped.

Magnolia continued squirming through the narrow passage. Weaver was right behind her, then Layla, Michael, and finally Rodger. She stopped at the next junction and tried to remember Timothy's directions. The AI couldn't travel places where there was no power, but she sure wished they had him along now.

"Right," Rodger said over the comms. "Take a right."

It was the first time he had spoken since they left the operations room. Jordan's betrayal had hit him hard. Rodger loved his parents more than anything, and he was nearly frantic to get back to the ship. Magnolia couldn't help wondering what it would be like to have someone waiting for her back up in the sky. She had been alone for a long time.

"Hold on," Magnolia whispered. She wiped vulture blood off the edge of her visor so she could see around the next corner. The birdlike mutants had put up a decent fight, but the five divers had killed so many of them that she doubted the survivors would be coming out of their burrows for a while. Those things were seriously weird. Next time she had the chance, she would ask Timothy what in God's name the ITC scientists had been thinking when they mashed up the DNA of so many different species. What had the vultures even evolved *from*?

A distant screech reverberated through the tunnels, reminding her that the surface creatures' ancestry didn't matter—they were all monsters now.

"That's a Siren," Weaver whispered.

Magnolia maneuvered onto her stomach and crawled around the corner. She stopped to raise her rifle, searching for a target, but the beam from her helmet showed a clear passage. As soon as she was moving again, the sound of claws on metal raised the hair on the nape of her neck. She wiggled forward using her elbows. The faster she crawled, the worse her shoulder hurt, but fear was rapidly eclipsing the pain.

Another screech rang out ahead. Or was it behind them? She stopped at the next junction and listened.

"I thought you knew where we were going," Weaver growled.

"Keep going," Rodger said. "Then take the next left!"

Magnolia followed his instructions—and came face-to-face with a Siren at the next junction. An impossibly wide grin opened across its leathery face, revealing the tips of barbed teeth. It gnashed them together, flattened its dorsal spikes as it clambered toward her.

"Come on," Weaver said, bumping into her from behind. "What's the holdup?"

She choked out a cry and fired a burst.

A yelp came from behind her even as she pumped more rounds into the monster.

"Help me!" Rodger screamed. "Somebody!"

More gunfire broke out, filling the duct with deafening noise. The creature in front of her dragged its body forward on a broken limb, blood spurting from holes in its torso. She fired two shots into its head, and it finally collapsed, providing a view of the other end of the passage, and the open window over the hangar.

"Almost there!" Magnolia shouted.

She scooted around to look over her shoulder. Helmet beams were dancing wildly over the passage, capturing a flurry of motion. At the end of the line, Michael was gripping Rodger's hand. She could just see the claws wrapped around Rodger's left boot.

"Somebody shoot it!" Michael yelled.

Layla moved her pistol back and forth, trying to get a clear shot, as a second beast emerged and grabbed Rodger's other leg.

"Shit!" he screamed.

Magnolia lost sight of him in the chaos. By the time she got her light back on their position, Rodger was gone and Michael was crawling off into the darkness. Layla grabbed Michael around the waist and hauled him back.

"Rodger!" Michael shouted.

Screeching voices answered him, and Michael pushed himself to his knees, blocking Magnolia's view.

"Rodger's gone!" Layla cried. "We have to get out of here."

Feeling sick, Magnolia turned back to the hangar. The passage was clear of hostiles, and she squirmed up to the fallen Siren. This time, she stopped to make sure it was dead before crawling over it.

At the opening, she pulled a rope from her cargo pocket. It was actually a collection of lengths from the other divers, knotted together. She fastened one end to the spidery-looking contraption Rodger had rigged up back in the control room. The stake was designed to be placed in dirt, but he had said it would work in just about any material. She jammed it into the metal and deployed the claws that secured it to the wall. After testing it with a yank, she picked up the coil of rope and tossed it through the window. Next, she pulled two extra flares she had snagged from Michael. She struck the ends and tossed them into the room below. By the time she was finished, Weaver, Layla, and Michael had caught up.

"We can't leave him," Michael kept saying. "He's not dead."

Rodger's distant shouts confirmed it. Magnolia flinched at each one, tears streaming down her cheeks.

"If we go after him, we all die," Layla said. "I'm sorry, Tin."

"We can't do anything for him up here," Weaver said. He checked the slack on the rope and pulled it taut. "I'll go first."

"No," Magnolia said. "I got this."

She grabbed the rope and wriggled through the opening, scanning the cavernous hangar for hostiles. The glow from the flares revealed nothing but the beetle back of their ride out of here. After running the rope under her left thigh, across her body, and over the right shoulder, she jumped out and slid down the thirty feet to the bottom.

As soon as her feet hit the deck, she was sweeping the area with her rifle. She had landed along the western wall, and the airship was in the center of the room.

Weaver came down next, then Layla, and finally Michael. They fanned out, weapons covering every fire zone.

"Looks clear," Weaver said quietly.

"I don't see anything," Layla said.

The divers all turned to the airship, their headlamps sweeping over the hull. Michael flashed an advance signal toward the ship.

"I'll go turn on the backup power," Weaver said. "You get to the ship." He turned to run but hesitated. "Can I borrow someone's rifle?"

Michael handed Weaver his carbine and two extra magazines.

"Thanks," Weaver said. "See you in a few."

Magnolia ran after Layla and Michael toward the ship. Before they reached it, the lights came on. Several of the LEDs flickered, and a few panels remained dark, but there was ample light to cover the room.

Magnolia got her first good look at their new ride, resting on platforms ten feet high. The turbofans and rudders were still covered in plastic. The thing had never seen the sky.

Timothy flickered into existence, nearly scaring the crap out of her. "Welcome to the latest, lightest, fastest member of ITC's lighter-than-air flee—"

"Save it," Magnolia said.

"Where's the door?" Michael asked.

Timothy pointed at the underbelly of the ship. The gray skin cracked open, and a metal gangplank extended.

"You kids fire that thing up," Weaver said over the comms. "I'll be right back."

Magnolia whirled about to see Weaver opening a door on the far side of the room.

"Where are you going?" Michael shouted after him.

"To get Rodger. Everyone else stay here. That's an order!"

TWENTY-ONE

Weaver bumped off his comm channel as he half-limped, half-ran down the passage. His body was running on fumes. He had lost a fair amount of blood and breathed in more toxic shit than he wanted to think about. Michael had come through with the new helmet, but Weaver had to wonder whether it was already too late. His lungs burned as he held back a cough.

Loping toward the water treatment plant, he found his thoughts turning to his wife and daughters. Something about the darkness brought the painful memories to the front of his thoughts, but he quickly shook them away.

Right now his mission was to do what he hadn't been able to do for X and Pipe. He was going to save Rodger. But first, he had to find that scrawny engineer. Timothy had given him directions to the treatment plant where the Sirens nested two floors below.

If he could beat them there, he might have a chance.

He moved as fast as his wounded legs would carry him. The sight of a door at the end of the concrete tunnel pushed him even harder.

Ten feet away, he slowed and raised his carbine. No movement, but he had learned to scope the shadows for those tricky little vultures. He cautiously reached out and opened the door. This was a different route from the one he had taken earlier. According to Timothy, it was the back door to the treatment plant.

Weaver loped up the stairs beyond the door, leaning on the rail for support. At the next landing, he shouldered his rifle. Seeing no sign of tubes or openings in the walls, he continued up the next flight. At the top, he stopped to catch his breath outside a door marked, sure enough, WATER TREATMENT PLANT.

He pulled the coin from his pocket, but instead of flipping it, he just rubbed the surface for good luck and tucked it away. He was as ready as he would ever be. Clicking off his night-vision optics, he turned the door handle and stepped inside.

The sound of monsters hit his ears: crunching and squawking and the flapping of those hideous wings. Crouching low, he moved toward the first of the pools.

Rodger's anguished shout stopped him in mid stride.

"Please, please, I'll do anything! I'll build you better nests!"

Weaver almost laughed at that. He couldn't see how badly Rodger was hurt, but somehow, his sense of humor was still intact.

Pressing the scope to his visor, Weaver spotted two of the beasts, dragging Rodger toward a gaggle of their young. The little ghouls darted back and forth, some of them circling and jumping excitedly at the prospect of a fresh meal.

Weaver swallowed hard and counted the targets. On his first sweep, he saw fifteen adult hostiles, plus the adolescents. He didn't know whether a distraction would work again, but it was his only gambit.

This time, he didn't wait for the "right" moment. The only moment he had was now. He grabbed a flare, struck the end, and tossed it as far as he could. It plopped into a pool, and the light flickered out.

Cursing, he grabbed another, this time tossing it at a wall. All but three of the beasts guarding Rodger darted away toward the heat and noise.

Weaver was already moving. He ducked under a bridge bisecting two of the pools and peered at the flurry of motion under the wall.

Rodger was flailing, trying to take on the remaining Sirens with his bare hands.

Keep still, you idiot.

Weaver stopped at a hundred yards out and picked his targets. The screeching across the room broke his concentration, and the first shot pinged off a wall. This, however, provided another distraction. The sentries around Rodger fanned out. Weaver's next shot was true, dropping one of them with a round through the throat. He swung the rifle to a second target and shot it through the chest.

Rodger kicked the other beast away.

"I told you ugly fucks my friends would come for me!" he shouted.

"Run, Rodge!" Weaver shouted. "This way!"

The shrieks of the monsters answered, but Weaver kept his gun on Rodger's position. He squeezed off a shot as an adolescent Siren sprang at Rodger. The round ricocheted off the floor, scaring the beast off, and Rodger limped away, gripping his side.

"Weaver, izzat you?" Rodger shouted. "Where are you?"

"Over here," Weaver shouted. He turned on his headlamp and laid down more suppressing fire.

Rodger stumbled and fell, groaning. Weaver lowered his rifle and hurried over, squeezing off shots every few steps. The beasts were already closing in again as the flare petered out. When he got to Rodger, he bent down and grabbed him under the arm.

"On your feet, diver," Weaver said. He gave Rodger the pistol Michael had retrieved from the supply crate.

A quick scan of the room told Weaver there was only one option.

"We make our stand here," he said.

Rodger managed a nod and raised the gun.

Standing side by side, they fired at the beasts crossing the room. Their helmet beams captured pallid, leathery skin as the mutant creatures darted back and forth to avoid the barrage of bullets. High above the melee, Weaver spotted the hulking monster that had nearly killed him earlier.

"Kill that big son of a bitch!" he shouted.

Weaver fired a burst that punched into the ceiling, then squeezed off another shot that hit a wing bone. The creature corkscrewed, and Weaver trained the crosshairs on its midsection to deal the finishing shot. He squeezed the trigger and ... nothing. The action was half closed on a jammed round.

"*Shit*," Weaver muttered. He pulled back the action to clear the round as the Siren sailed toward them, talons reaching.

"Shoot it, Rodger!" Weaver said.

Rodger fired, and the Siren veered off course, shrieking angrily. Weaver worked to free the round, but it was jammed diagonally against the bore. Across the plant, the winged giant was wheeling to make another pass at them. Below, a dozen beasts were running across the floor and climbing over the platforms.

Rodger's gun went silent, and he pulled the blade from Weaver's sheath. "I'm out!" he yelled.

The jammed round finally popped out of the carbine, and Weaver took down two more of the approaching pack with body shots and maimed a third before training the gun back on the creature in the air.

Ejecting the spent magazine, he dropped to one knee, slapped in the fresh magazine, and fired off a burst. All three shots hit the ceiling. He had to lead the beast more.

He squeezed the trigger again, hitting a wing, but the rounds weren't enough to bring this one down. And this time there was no escaping.

More Sirens were charging toward them. In seconds, their claws and teeth would tear both Weaver and Rodger into confetti.

"Get down!" a voice shouted.

Weaver turned to see three figures race into the room. Muzzle flashes dazzled his eyes. He bumped off the optics and hit the deck.

Rounds cut through the humid air, punching through mutant flesh and bone. In seconds, the remaining monsters were retreating. Weaver could even hear the beast in the air flapping madly for the exit.

"Rodger!" Magnolia shouted. She ran over and embraced him, her helmet clacking against his.

"Oh, sorry," she said when he yelped. "Oh, shit, are you hurt?"

"It's okay. I'm happy to see you, too, Mags."

"Thanks for the save," Weaver said, "but we don't have time for a reunion. We need to beat it before those things go get some friends."

Michael hesitated even as the others moved, and Weaver quickly saw why. The beam of his headlamp had captured the remains of the diver they had been too late to save. Weaver put a hand on the young commander's shoulder and said a silent goodbye to Andrew before they turned and ran for the stairs.

* * * * *

Michael was more than ready to leave the Hilltop Bastion behind. Maybe there was a facility somewhere deep underground that wasn't inhabited by monsters—a place that could safely house the people of the *Hive* for generations until the surface was habitable again. But ITC Communal 13 was not that place.

"Man, you guys should've heard Rodger," Weaver was saying. "He offered to build those things a better nest!"

Magnolia let out a cross between a laugh and a snort.

"Doesn't surprise me," Layla said. "He once offered to build me a better boyfriend."

Michael grinned, but it didn't last. They were still alive, but with no real plan for what came next.

Handle your present with confidence. Face your future without fear.

The divers hurried down the passage, gear clanking and lights cutting through the darkness.

"You said Jordan put Janga in the stockade?" Weaver asked Layla.

She nodded solemnly. "He had her arrested earlier. I just hope he didn't hurt her."

"I guess her gift of prophecy wasn't real after all, or she would have seen it coming. She said a man from the surface would lead us to the promised land. A place that's under water, or something. I can't believe I actually bought into—"

"That's it," Michael said, interrupting Weaver. "She was talking about X, don't you see? We have to go find him."

"What do you mean, kid?"

"Janga knew about X all along. She hid that information inside some crazy prophecy, both to protect it and to get people to pass it on. She knew that if he could survive down here, then maybe he could show us how to survive, too."

"Shit, he's got a point," Magnolia said.

Weaver shook his head. "Have I ever told you you're all nuts?"

"It's a job requirement," Rodger said.

"Fair enough," Weaver said. He stopped just outside the hangar door and lowered his rifle. "We'll finish this conversation later."

Weaver grabbed the door handle, and as he opened it, an orange glow flooded the hallway.

"Watch out!" Magnolia shouted a moment too late.

On the other side of the door stood a giant skinless beast out of a fever dream. Swollen muscles flashed orange across a body as wide as the doorframe. Looming a good two feet over Weaver, it tilted its nightmarish face down at him, snuffling and opening a bony jaw rimmed with yellow teeth the size of sheath knives.

Weaver staggered backward as the other divers screamed a warning. But before he could bring up his rifle, the creature reached out an enormous, black-taloned hand and clamped it around the commander's helmet. He dropped his gun and grabbed the beast's wrists as it plucked him off the ground, feet kicking.

Michael moved to the side and fired a shot into the monster's chest. It let out a frenzied roar and squeezed its hands together. Every muscle flashed and flexed as it pushed in on Weaver's helmet.

There was no scream or cry—just the crack of metal, glass, and bone as the diver's helmet caved in like a tin can in a vice.

It all happened so fast that the world seemed to grind to an agonizing halt as Weaver's limp body collapsed to the floor in a heap. Michael could hear Magnolia's screams, and he could see the rounds cutting through the monster's flesh, but the bullets weren't from his rifle. He seemed unable to move.

Layla fired her carbine, and Magnolia was emptying her magazine into the beast. Shell casings fell into the puddle of Weaver's blood that spread across the floor.

The abomination slapped Magnolia's gun away and picked her up by the throat with one paw. Michael finally snapped out of his trance and reached for his blaster.

Rodger had the same idea. He pulled Weaver's blaster from his holster and pushed it to the bony head of the monster.

The buckshot slammed into the creature's skull, cracking through bone and into brain. It dropped Magnolia and stumbled back into the wall, a wedge of its head missing. Letting out a final grunt, the beast crashed to the floor with a thud that shook the corridor.

Rodger hurried over to Magnolia as she scooted away on her butt.

"Weaver," she choked. "Where ...?"

"He's gone," Michael said. He grabbed Layla's hand, and Rodger helped Magnolia to her feet. They ran past the monster, and all looked down as they walked through the blood surrounding Weaver's crushed helmet. There was nothing they could do for him now but honor his memory.

As soon as they were inside the room, Timothy's hologram appeared.

"Why didn't you warn us?" Magnolia shouted.

"I am sorry, but I had transferred my program to the ship. When I detected the gunshots, I—"

"Just get us the hell out of here!" Michael shouted.

They ran up the metal platform into the ship. This craft was perhaps a third smaller than the *Hive*, but the most striking difference was that everything here was new. Dusty plastic covered the upholstery, and nothing was patched or dinged.

Timothy sealed the door behind them.

"Is there anything on board that we need to be aware of?" Layla asked. "Any monsters you've forgotten to mention?"

"There are only four life forms present," Timothy said. "Follow this light strip to the bridge. I will join you there."

They ran down a long hallway that ended at a circular steel door. Timothy was already waiting there. He raised a hand as the doors parted, revealing a bridge fitted with more advanced computer technology and control panels than Michael had ever seen. The operations room was furnished with metal stations and a single steering wheel. Control panels were already flashing, and a mounted monitor taking up an entire wall came online with the view above them.

Heart pounding, he staggered inside. Blood sang in his ears, and a wave of vertigo passed over him.

Michael blinked and drew in a long breath as he followed the other divers onto the bridge. A distant thud rang out, and the ship trembled.

“Stand by for launch,” Timothy said. “The air is safe and clear of toxins, by the way. Feel free to take off your helmets and settle into your seats.”

He sat at a station and watched the monitor as the other divers stripped off their gear. The doors above them opened slowly. Lightning zigzagged across the storm clouds over the Hilltop Bastion. The floor rattled, and the bulkheads groaned.

Michael removed his helmet and inhaled his first breath of unfiltered air outside the *Hive*.

“Engines online,” Timothy said. “Now activating the turbofans. Please fasten your harnesses.”

“Hold on, Timothy,” Rodger said. He looked at Magnolia, his eyes bright with unshed tears. “Weaver gave his life to save mine, so I’m not going to waste any more time.” The ship vibrated as Timothy activated the turbofans, and they rose off the platforms.

Rodger steadied himself and reached into his vest. He pulled out a small wood figurine and handed it to Magnolia.

“I made this for you,” he said. “I’ve been waiting for the right moment to tell you how I feel, but now ... well, if you don’t already know, there’s no point in saying it.”

“It’s an elephant,” she said. “You remembered!”

She held it in her palm and began to sob.

“I’m sorry,” she said, wiping away the tears with her sleeve. “It’s just, I’ve never had anyone be so nice to me.”

Rodger put a hand on her arm. “It’s okay. Everything is going to be okay now. You can trust me. Trust is the only thing that’s going to keep us alive.”

“He’s right,” Michael said. He grabbed Layla’s hand as the ship slowly rose out of the hangar. The frame creaked and groaned like a beast coming out of hibernation.

“Please fasten your harnesses,” Timothy said again. “This could be a bit rough.”

The divers all strapped in to watch the ship rise out of the Hilltop Bastion. On-screen, the ruined city stretched around them, a gray and brown halo of devastation.

As soon as they were hovering over the ITC facility, Timothy turned from the screen to look at Michael. The other divers all looked at him as well. With Weaver gone, Michael now held rank.

"What heading should I set, Commander Everhart?" Timothy asked.

There was no hesitation in Michael's reply. "To the last known coordinates for Commander Xavier Rodriguez."

Timothy nodded, and the ship slowly rotated to change course, giving them a view of the ocean to the east, and the red lighthouse they all had seen on the dive.

"Guess I won't be dipping my feet in the ocean anytime soon," Magnolia said.

"I wouldn't be so sure about that," Timothy said. "It appears the last known location of Commander Rodriguez is in southern Florida."

"Florida," Layla said. "I think I've heard of that place in the archives. There was a magical kingdom there once, according to the old stories."

Michael felt a smile coming on, but he didn't let it. Instead, he gripped her hand tighter. They had lost Weaver and Pipe, and Jordan had forsaken them, but they were going to find X. If he was still alive, he was their best hope of saving the human race.

Magnolia put the elephant on her lap and waved at Timothy. "Hey, I forgot to ask you something. What's this ship called?"

"*Deliverance*," Michael said. "We're calling her *Deliverance*."

Before you go ...

Check out Nicholas Sansbury Smith's thrilling new postapocalyptic series, **Trackers**. Now available in audio/e-book/paperback. Don't forget to sign up for his spam-free monthly newsletter for special offers and info on his latest releases.

Join Nicholas on social media:
Facebook: Nicholas Sansbury Smith
Twitter: @GreatWaveInk
Website: www.NicholasSansbury.com

COMING SUMMER 2018

HELL DIVERS III

DELIVERANCE

Nicholas Sansbury Smith's *USA Today* bestselling trilogy began with his acclaimed novel *Hell Divers*, an Audible Editors Best Audiobooks of 2016 Top Pick and a finalist for the 2016 Foreword INDIES Award for Best Science Fiction Book of the Year. Now the high-stakes adventure continues in *Hell Divers III: Deliverance.* Will the Hell Divers find a new home, or is humanity doomed forever?